My Famous Brain

My Famous Brain

A Novel

Diane Wald

SHE WRITES PRESS

Published 2021
Printed in the United States of America
Print ISBN: 978-1-64742-205-9
E-ISBN: 978-1-64742-206-6
Library of Congress Control Number: 2021908385

For information, address:
She Writes Press
1569 Solano Ave #546
Berkeley, CA 94707

Interior design by Tabitha Lahr

She Writes Press is a division of SparkPoint Studio, LLC.

In memory of Garth Pitman:
wisest of colleagues,
sweetest of friends.

"There are so many little dyings that it doesn't matter which of them is death."
—Kenneth Patchen

CONTENTS

1. Cunning and Theatrics

I called Eliza's mother, whom I had never met, about a year and a half after Eliza and I had parted. I don't know what I expected from that call, except that it fell into the general scheme of "tidying up one's affairs," one of the tasks I had assigned myself before moving from New Jersey to Massachusetts. It was almost noon, and I wasn't dressed yet. I was gravely ill. No one, I think, among my modest circle of acquaintances—except of course for Eliza, and later, Don Rath—quite realized the extent to which my condition had deteriorated, nor did they understand that my exodus from Norman State University in Clifton, New Jersey, where I had been teaching in the psychology department, was, for me, a final and mercilessly passed sentence.

I had managed pretty well, through cunning and theatrics, to conceal my illness. After a series of frightening episodes, including a concussive headlong fall off what I had perceived as a very shallow step, a brief period of semi-blindness, and a bout of memory loss, I was eventually diagnosed with a brain tumor. It was benign, but growing, and it was positioned

1

in what was then determined to be an inoperable location. Benign is a funny word, because eventually it would kill me. Truly frightening was the morning I woke up, opened my eyes, and saw all the world as wobbly and dim. Fortunately, this effect passed in a few weeks, but the "insult," as my oph- thalmologist called it, had done quite a bit of damage to my vision. Quarter-inch-thick spectacles were prescribed for me, but they were really little more than a prop. I wore the glasses because I thought they made me look distinguished and bookish, but they didn't help a whole lot. My vision was deemed "uncorrectable." I could read pretty well if I held the page fairly close to my face, and I could do most things without assistance. I was functional, but paranoid and feeling immensely vulnerable. That vulnerability pretty much ruled my existence. Fearful that something would happen to reveal my situation, I had become a virtual prisoner in my office at NSU, venturing out only to teach my classes, visit the lavatory, and make my way to and from the parking lot. I still had a few private patients, but they would come to see me in my office after my teaching hours, so that worked out fine.

You will wonder about the parking lot: it's true that I continued to drive. The fact that I did not have a fatal accident— or murder someone else—is an amazing one. And one that only increases my belief that there must be someone—something— guiding our fates. Each weekday morning and evening I would fold myself into my aging Cadillac with both trepidation and resignation, knowing full well that the worst might easily occur and fearing only that my life might be spared over that of some innocent who had blundered into my darkened path. I knew the route more than by heart; the only stop I ever made was at a small gas station near my apartment where the proprietor, Benny, treated me like royalty. (He was also the one who kept my automotive relic in top repair.) I was able to distinguish traffic lights and police car lights, and I traveled only in the daytime, to increase my chances of survival. In the winter, I had to abandon my afternoon schedule of classes, which I could hardly afford to do: they would have kept me out after dark.

At any rate, there I was in my office prison that sweet-smelling May morning, when I decided to call Eliza's home. I knew the chances of Eliza being at her mother's house were slim, but I felt the need to contact, if not Eliza herself, something in her world. The phone rang three times, then a pleasant-sounding woman picked up.

"Hello, Mrs. Harder, this is Jack MacLeod from Norman State, an old friend of your daughter's. I wonder if you remember my name?"

There was a short pause, then the woman's voice became instantly warm and kind. "Dr. MacLeod, of course I remember you. How are you?" (What, exactly, I wondered, for the millionth time, had Eliza told her mother about me?)

"Fine, thank you. I hope you're well too. I know it's been some time since I've spoken to Eliza, but I wonder if f you could tell me how to get in touch with her?"

This time the pause was longer, and, for the first time, I became afraid. Deep in my own miseries for so long, it had not occurred to me that anything bad could have happened to my Lizzie—for that is what I sometimes called her. Fear shot through my already throbbing head like a fiery arrow, and I thought, dear God, not *that*: that I could not bear. All those long months, a smiling image of Lizzie in her funny multicolored beret had illuminated my way. To think that she might have come to some harm filled me not only with pain and sorrow, but with the crippling guilt of the suddenly self-identified egotist. I realized I had been endlessly selfish, had thought only of myself all along. I was so relieved when Mrs. Harder finally spoke, I nearly dropped the phone.

"Well, I can tell you how to get in touch with her, Dr. MacLeod," she said, "but did you know that Eliza's married now?"

Although I suppose this piece of news was not really what I had wanted to hear, I was terribly relieved. Lizzie lived and thrived. I tried to sound avuncular and cheerful.

"Ah, no, I didn't know that. I'm so happy for her," I lied. "When did all of this happen? I'm afraid I've been really out of touch for quite a while."

Mrs. Harder must have bought my uncle act, because she opened right up. She told me that Eliza had married someone she'd known at NSU, a boy a few years her senior (not, then, the boyfriend she'd had when I first met her), and that they were living and working happily in a town a few miles from Mrs. Harder's own. There were no children "yet," she added, with a little smile in her voice. I wondered if Lizzie had changed her opinion about having children.

After a few more exchanges, which I suppose allowed her to convince herself of my benevolent intentions, Mrs. Harder offered me Eliza's phone number, which I pretended to write down. I knew I'd remember it anyway. I have a prodigious memory—a rather famous one, in fact. But more about all that later.

I thanked her, we exchanged a few parting pleasantries, and we said goodbye. I just sat there in my bathrobe, feeling like a complete fool. I turned on the radio. Then I turned off the radio and searched through the little stack of record albums I kept in the bottom drawer of my file cabinet. The one I was looking for was one Lizzie had left with me the last time she'd visited me at this apartment. When I'd first heard it, with my head resting on Lizzie's lap, I hadn't liked it much; I'd never heard anything quite like it before. But over time I'd come to love the songs and the eerie voice of the young woman my darling admired so much. I hadn't played it in a long time. I located the fourth cut, which seemed to me to echo my relationship with Lizzie, then carefully placed it on the turntable of my little stereo. The lyrics told the story of a chance meeting in a bar between the singer and an older man. She seemed to feel a magical connection with him, as well as a terrible premonition of chaos to come, but she was drawn to him, nevertheless.

I still found the song seductively disturbing, but I wasn't sure why. I wanted to talk to Eliza more than ever after I heard it. I was tempted to call her. Why not? I asked myself: what harm could come of it? In my heart of hearts, I could not name the harm, but I was quite sure there was one. Nevertheless, as George Eliot once wrote, "The fear of poison is feeble against the sense of thirst." I dialed.

A young man answered. He had a slight New York accent. "I'm sorry," I said, "I must have the wrong number. I beg your pardon."

"That's okay," he said.

I never tried to call her again.

2. I'm No Angel

When I realized I had died (it happened in January, 1974), I expected to be privy to a great deal of knowledge, expected to have the mysteries of the universe open up to me like water lilies in the sunlight, but, alas, that isn't what happened at all. Probably we give much too much attention to our physical bodies. I was alive, and then I was dead. I was the guru of nothing but my own life. That's saying a lot, though, really, as it included remembering everywhere I'd ever been, everything I'd ever experienced, everyone I'd ever known. Remembering everything feels like this: imagine a photograph of about fifty beautiful sky-blue rowboats floating on a sunny day in a pretty harbor. That's from one angle. From another angle, you can see the warships floating right next door. Everything depends on where you focus.

I couldn't feel my body anymore. It was just gone. No heaviness, no pain, no hunger or thirst or heat or cold. I was no longer lonely (that may be what is meant by "heaven"). And my entire, absolutely entire, life as John Tilford MacLeod unfolded before me, from the moment of my birth. I've tried to remember life before birth in my mother's womb, but there's simply nothing there—I suppose one mustn't be greedy. I found it was as easy to call up a day from my life as a one-year-old as it was to recall Eliza's face in Thompson Park when we fed the swans, or Don Rath's funny little laughing cough, or the doctors in St. Sebastian's as they stood chatting around my father's death bed, unaware that their words were being recorded on some celestial tape loop for future reference by the deceased son of the nearly deceased. Once in a while I catch sight of my sons, and they seem to be in their thirties. But I could be wrong; my perceptions have altered radically, and, as I've told you, I still haven't learned to understand them too well in terms of earthly time.

I now remember things I didn't even know had happened to me, and I've been re-viewing (as I call it) all of it ever since I died. I don't actually know how long ago I did lose my life, since I can no longer follow the events of living humans with any chronological accuracy, but I suspect it was about fifteen years ago. By the way, I don't think I really "lost" my life; I just experienced a radical shift of some kind. I also suspect that those theories about the flow of time being an illusion, with the past, present, and future existing simultaneously, are probably true. I'd always loved what Lewis Carroll's Queen said in *Through the Looking Glass*: "It's a poor sort of memory that only works backwards."

By the way, I'm no angel. I never was, of course, but I'm certainly not one now. No wings, no halo, no access to Jimmy Stewart. I don't know what I am. A soul, I suppose. How I can communicate with you this way is not something I understand. All I know is, it's not a hoax. I know what true means. I'm not going to disguise anybody or make things up. It's hard enough just to recount everything without doing anything like that. I'll probably skip around a bit though, since time is such a mystery to me now. I find the big picture more interesting than the details. Bear with me.

3. A Cheap Plastic Clock

I frequently see myself sitting in my office musing about Eliza Harder, or my Lizzie, as I liked to call her. A scene from the early days after my divorce recurs frequently. I felt those days were hell then, and I was right. Not even the gradually accelerating physical illness that would plague me in the following months and years would come close to causing me the pain that such intense loneliness had occasioned. I wasn't just missing my marriage; I was deeply missing my boys. It was devastating. I played with the idea of suicide daily, but never got very far. I think, predictable self-worshipper that I was, I was mostly just afraid that if I killed myself I would miss something. But this day, I was excited: Lizzie was going to visit me.

There I was, ensconced in what could truly be called a bachelor pad in a semi modern complex called Maplewood, about seven miles from NSU. I'd taken the first place I could afford. My world was shrinking, in every possible way. The new apartment was smaller than anywhere I'd ever lived. I tried to adjust. I tried to fit my body, such as it was, into its new environment. This effort was complicated by the fact that I had headaches often. To compensate, I would run a comforting hand across the crown of my head, slowly ruffling what I thought of as my remaining feathers; heredity plus months of sickness and anxiety had depopulated my roundish pate of all but a fringe of babyish down. The very feel of my skull, its smooth, reliable hardness, soothed me. It was ironic, this comfort, for all my troubles were deep inside that skull, flowering microscopically like some gorgeous but lethal underwater plant. Soon, I knew, there would be no more room for such flowering: something would have to give.

I looked around my weirdly designed "efficiency" living-dining room and was pleased in spite of myself. Ceiling to floor, along all six walls, and even extending into the area called the breakfast nook that had been much heralded by the real estate agent, my books lined the space like a beautifully crafted battle-shield that might protect me somehow from the forces without. I had splurged and commissioned specially designed shelves for them.

Their spines made a familiar, glossy mosaic. There were no paperbacks, except for a few on the little corner table—mostly gifts or items from the library. I was an inveterate book snob. Once I had been wealthy enough (and snobbish enough) to purchase only hardcover books, and once I had believed that even if I could not manage to live forever and enjoy them myself, that I might pass them along to my sons, and they to their sons and daughters, and so on: books like mind-edible candy jewels—gorgeous, useful jewels with juicy centers to be read and memorized and rearranged on their shelves like pieces of a perfectly crafted, ever-changing pattern.

Memorized. I'd memorized many of them—not just sections, not just favored passages, but entire books, and while I knew this was not a common practice, to me it was simply a deeper, even more pleasurable, reading experience. It was part of the way I read, in fact, the way another man might underline phrases or copy out words, lines, or paragraphs. I would often lose myself in the delight of recitation for hours, lying on my back on the sofa, my lips barely moving, my mind playing back whole chapters as swiftly as I wished, or as slowly.

There was no time for that now, however. I had only allowed myself half an hour for rest and contemplation; had I begun to recite a book, even a short one, like *The Old Man and the Sea,* the evening would quickly be gone. And also, although the idea did not terrify me as it once had, there was the certainty that someday soon I'd forget something—maybe everything. The more or less constant headaches reminded me that my celebrated brain was no longer entirely on my side. I had no idea how the disaster would happen. Before it did happen, though, I wanted to give over at the very least a whole day to recitation, and to plan with the greatest care which book or books would constitute this ultimate, sure, and holy performance. After that, I would not try it again. It would be like retiring from baseball immediately after hitting a grand slam in the final, victorious game of the World Series.

I continued to examine the room, trying to ignore a burgeoning headache. In one corner, and using up most of the available space, was my old piano, the one I'd had since childhood. I'd been forced to leave the new one, the budget-busting Bösendorfer, with my wife, who could not play. The old piano, my beloved Baldwin, had my brother Duncan's baby teeth marks on one of its legs. I could barely make them out anymore, but my fingers still knew just where to find them, and when I touched the tiny, notched indentations, I imagined I could smell Duncan's sweet, baby-moist, silky hair and feel his velvety, warm skin as I lifted him away from the piano.

The rest of the furnishings were new, ugly, rented; I passed my eyes over them as if they weren't there. I looked at the cheap plastic clock: fifteen minutes to Lizzie. The pain in my head was becoming hard to ignore. I reached into the desk drawer, drew out a bottle of Percodan, and swallowed a half-dose, dry. I would have to shave and change my shirt at least. I wanted to shower, but there was no time—or, possibly there was time, but if Lizzie should come early, if she should knock timidly and no one answered, she might just go away. I couldn't risk it. My loneliness bore down on me like a bag of heavy gravel. Besides its terrible weight, I could feel its filth seeping through the burlap and covering me everywhere. A shower. I would take the chance.

I got up slowly and turned off the desk lamp. Without turning on any lights in the tiny bedroom, I laid out clean clothes, arranging them on the bed in the order in which I'd put them on: a thin, beige, cashmere "Perry Como" sweater on the bottom, then a pale blue button-down shirt, then an undershirt on top. I chose new socks and shorts and decided the chino pants I was already wearing would have to do. I wished I had some jeans like Lizzie's, then I laughed at myself. Jeans for the young, the whole, the with-it. Not for me.

Then, in the warm dark of the bathroom, I took off my clothes. I ran my hands over my chest, which, like my skull, still pleased me. I found myself gingerly touching my body more and more of late, suddenly valuing it, finding it a blessing. I paid no attention to my skinny arms and legs. Where, I wondered, not for the first time, did all those swimming muscles go? "Gone to academia, one by one," I sang to the tune of a popular protest song, giggling. The headache was letting up, leaving the slightly drunken feeling I'd come to recognize, if not fully welcome. At least I'd remembered to break the tablet in half; Lizzie probably wouldn't notice any change in my behavior. I decided, in honor of my galloping anxiety, to take an incredibly fast shower, extremely hot. After that, I dressed as quickly as I could without making myself dizzy. Then I sat down on the bed and prayed.

I prayed for the pair of swans in Thompson Park: that they'd stay and make a home there; that their unquestioning fidelity to each other would reward them with peace, good health, and many offspring; that no one would offer them junk food that would make them ill; that no one would taunt them and risk their righteous slashing; and that someday, very soon, I would take Eliza there to meet them. She would like the swans, and, what's more, she would know what I had prayed for without my having to tell her.

Repeating "soon," I went back to my desk and checked the clock. Five past the hour. Maybe the clock was fast, or she'd had car trouble, gotten lost, or simply decided against coming at the last minute. But all of that was unlikely. Eliza seemed shy, but her will was unbreakable. She'd said she was coming, and she would come, I was sure of it. Any minute now she'd arrive, or else she'd call to say what had detained her. She knew I would worry. She wouldn't leave me hanging.

I thought about her last semester in my psychology class. To my initial amazement, this shadow from the back of the room had stood up for her point of view time and time again, courageously and unflinchingly. Sometimes, playing devil's advocate, I would instigate extra discussions, just to see her in action. Her classmates would become exasperated with her at times, but if she thought she was right, she would not budge; she would calmly state and restate her position until the others would grudgingly grant her if not their concurrence, at least a portion of their respect. This mysteriously quiet girl: who would have thought it of her? I never interrupted her once she gained some verbal momentum. I allowed her, as I thought of it, to do my work for me, to teach for me (she was unquestionably my brightest student in many years), and to amuse and deeply interest me as well. There was something of the young John MacLeod in her, and I was drawn to it gratefully.

When she wasn't debating some finely tuned point, however, Eliza was invisible in the classroom, as motionless as the tall-windowed classroom's afternoon light, a little long-haired figure in the back row, seated deliberately behind some broad-shouldered hulk, or next to one of the classroom's thick, four-sided columns, so she could lean against it and make herself even harder to see from the front of the room. I knew it was only because she liked me so much that she bothered to speak at all: that flattered me. I imagined it meant she knew how much she could help me, though she didn't know the nature of the help, or why I needed it so desperately. Eliza didn't have much use for school, or school as she knew it. I always wished I'd met her when I was younger and richer, when I could have plucked her out of this state penitentiary of a learning institution and helped her to attend some saner, more classical, and just generally sounder university. But here she was, luckily for me, and she seemed to really take to my field, to be truly interested in my lectures.

The pain in my head wasn't pain anymore, but it had taken over. It was like a stocking cap of thin, highly elasticized material pressed all around my skull. I imagined there were tiny lights in it, flashing on and off like starry pinpricks on a map of the night-roads of America. This made me laugh, and the sound of the laugh frightened me: it was a child's laugh. Suddenly I was on the street corner in Boxwood, New York again, and seven years old. I tossed handfuls of dirt into the twilit air to see the bats rush at the particles, as if they were insects, food. The strength of their instinct amazed me, how they never doubted the evidence of their senses, how they experienced what they needed to see. When the streetlights finally went on in my memory of Boxwood, I remembered to look once more at the clock.

Twelve after, and no Lizzie. The stocking cap of pain somehow kept my head from exploding, although that might have given me some relief. I remembered a time, not too long ago at all, when allowing myself strong emotions had been as natural as breathing; now I was advised to avoid them, and I'd learned that that advice was wise. I hardly noticed feeling sad—I'd become inured to sadness—but I imagined Lizzie slowly slipping away, and myself unable to stop her, unable to summon up the passion such a motion would demand. Was it worth it, or would it be better to plunge into so-called "normal" reactions, and give my dear Lizzie a taste of what my feeling for her was truly made of? I didn't know the answer, doubted if I even had the strength anymore to find it out. But one thing I did know: that if Eliza slipped away, I would not try to replace her. Even had there been a great deal more time left to me, the chances of again meeting someone so miraculously intuitive to my situation, so respectful and yet so sweetly mocking of my ways, were incredibly slim.

I decided to make some tea, to pass the time. In my new little kitchenette, everything was arranged precisely to my tastes and needs, a pleasure I had never before experienced. All mine. My first weeks in this place had been sad and monotonous, but I had to admit there were some compensations. I went first to the cupboard and selected two tall glass mugs with heavy bottoms—beer mugs, I suppose, but, in my view, the only perfect receptacles for tea. From the refrigerator I took, carefully, with two hands, the heavy plastic bottle of spring water, and poured some into a saucepan, setting that on the stove. I'd found that trying to direct a stream from the jug into the kettle's small opening was a waste of time and effort, and anyway, the water boiled so much more quickly, with so many large and satisfying bubbles, in the pan. I waited a few moments until the water started to heat up, then held my hand over the surface, delighting in the warmth and moisture. Then I went again to the cabinet and took down my tin of tea, the darkest, smokiest Chinese tea I'd been able to find in town. Costly, but I couldn't give up everything. And I took out the sugar bowl, which I had to refill, using up the last of the bag. I wrote "sugar" in large letters on the notepad attached to the refrigerator. Then I sat down, squeezing into one of the two chairs around the tiny table with its peach and grey boomerang patterned Formica. I was breathing heavily, afraid to look at the clock. Automatically, I began to take my pulse, then stopped, disgusted with myself. Who cared if it was racing? And why had I set out two mugs? She obviously wasn't coming.

Taking a very deep breath, a breath so deep it seemed to make the insides of my lungs stick together for a second, I forced myself to calm down. I closed my eyes and breathed that way for a minute or two, until, as I'd trained myself to do, I had directed a warming, relaxing flow of blood into my extremities and to the top of my head and the soles of my feet. When I'd first begun to practice this technique, I would experience a fleeting sensation of sexual arousal as I directed the blood to course throughout each part of my body, but no more. I told myself this was a sure sign of how I had refined the technique, yet I suspected and feared the real reason. Once again, at least, the technique was working. I managed to clear my mind, for the most part, of Eliza, the swans, and the head-ache. Then I allowed those images to seep back in again, but cleared, I hoped and imagined, of their worrisome edges. I opened my eyes, and then realized the pan on the stove was boiling raucously. Turning off the gas, and in one deliber-ately graceful, despairing movement, I placed one of the mugs gently back into the cabinet. No, she wasn't coming: I was sure of it, and I was right.

4. Cybèle, Luther, and
an Evening Surprise

My wife Frances and I, when we first began to pull in two salaries, had managed to purchase a little getaway cabin in New Hampshire. I had loved it unreservedly from the moment I first saw it and had more or less successfully (often by lying about available funds for renovations) stymied Frances in her efforts to turn this uncut gem into a piece of costume flummery. She therefore quickly lost interest in the place ("Who on earth could one invite there?"), and I went to the cabin as often as I could get away, which was not, of course, often enough.

One time, I'd managed a few days at the cabin to work on a paper I had to present the following weekend in Anaheim, California, at a meeting of the animal rights organization to which I had devoted as much time as I could manage. Shortly after arriving at the cabin that morning, I'd caught sight of a gorgeous little fox nosing around the falling-down shed out back.

I watched her (I decided it was a she-fox, though I had no way of knowing) for some time and became bewitched by her. I decided to make her my friend, but I had no idea how to do so—nor, in retrospect, had I any idea what I was doing, or whether it was a good idea at all. What might a fox like to eat, I wondered. Meat, of course, but I didn't have any in the cooler; there was an egg-salad sandwich—maybe that would do? Eggs: "the fox in the hen house"? I had already decided to call her Cybèle, after a character in a movie who had once enchanted me. The idea of naming her and befriending her made me ridiculously happy, as did the dust-laden smell of the cabin, the early morning sunlight on the cobwebs in the window corners, and the way my feet felt cushioned and warm in my new canvas boots.

I unwrapped the sandwich, laid it on a shiny red plate I found in the cupboard, and then, as an afterthought, removed the top slice of bread and placed it to one side. An open-faced sandwich for my little open-faced Cybèle. Maybe the smell of the eggs would reach her faster that way. I couldn't wait to see her again. Deciding not to put the food too near the cabin this first time, I placed the plate out beyond the car and driveway, making sure I'd be able to see it from the window before I set it down.

I could hear the telephone ringing as I returned to the cabin. I thought it might have been a mistake to give in to Frances and have a phone installed up here, but when she cited the actual possibilities of illness, death, or other emergencies, what could I say? I went inside slowly, removed the pile of clean flannel shirts I'd dumped on top of the phone, picked up the receiver, and said, dully, "Frances."

Her voice oozed sarcasm. "However did you know?"

"What's up?

"Well, actually, darling, your service called about five times last night and once this morning about some patient and they want you to call them right away."

"Why the hell didn't you tell me last night, Frances? Which patient?"

"I don't know. I forget. It was a boy's name. Fred or Ed or something. I was too tired last night. I'm not your secretary, you know."

I dialed the service immediately. As I listened to the familiar voice of the woman on the other end, I looked out the window and noticed the red plate on the lawn. Licked completely clean. Of course, it was possible some other animal had come along and beaten Cybèle to the goodies, but I didn't think so. I'd missed her, but at least now I knew she liked egg salad. And bread. I smiled. Then I dialed the number the answering service woman had given me, the number of Luther Edwards.

He picked up on the first ring, his voice timid and tired.

"Luther. It's John MacLeod. I'm sorry I didn't get back to you last night. I just got your message. I'm up here in the woods in New Hampshire, and they had a little trouble reaching me. How're you doing?"

There was a long pause. "All right, Doctor."

"What happened last night, Luther? Do you want to talk about it? I've got all the time in the world."

Pause again. "I guess I'm all right now, Doctor, really. I don't feel like talking. I'm all right."

"What are you doing today, Luther?"

"Not much. Going to the library. Going to the park. Not much. I'm okay, though, really; don't worry about me. I'm sorry I bothered you. I just got a little panicky last night. I had a bad dream. I had a dream about some Indians—not the wild-west kind, I mean Indians from India—and there was one of those funeral pyres and when I got up close to it you were on it, Doctor, you were on it, all wrapped in, you know, 'swaddling clothes' like in the bible story, and I don't think you were dead yet, but you were going to burn and burn, you were going to burn for my sins, and there was all this beautiful singing and swaying going on in the crowd and a gorgeous young woman whose voice soared out over all the rest and I think she was singing to me, to me, Doctor, but I couldn't stop to go to her because you were burning . . ." His voice trailed off.

By this time, I'd made myself a comfortable seat on the floor, padded by the stack of shirts. I listened and talked to Luther for almost an hour, until the boy had calmed down, promised he'd eat a good lunch, and said he'd call me in the morning. Then I spoke to his mother for a minute or two, to be sure she would watch him carefully. I thought the immediate crisis was over, but I wanted to be certain: to lose Luther now to a major setback would be a sad thing indeed—the boy had come so far. I liked Luther—he was more than just a patient to me—and I didn't regret having given him the precious phone number. Now when the phone rang it would either be Frances, Luther, or a wrong number. Of course, Frances might give the number out at any time, or let one of the boys call, but she'd probably forgotten about me already this morning.

It didn't matter. A shaft of sunlight was hitting me in the stomach as I lay there, and it felt wonderful. And Cybèle had had her breakfast. All was not exactly right with the world, but I'd seen worse days.

After spending the rest of the morning cleaning up the cabin's interior, driving into town for supplies (including some canned dog food for Cybèle), I began to feel the creeping fatigue that had been building in me for months. I'd set up the cot like a couch, with some pillows leaning up against the log wall, and there I settled, to think with my cup of coffee, watch the modest fire I'd started in the fireplace, and glance once in a while out the window for the little grey-red fox. I wrapped a wooly blanket around my shoulders; it was not particularly cold, but I felt comforted by it, more secure. I started thinking about Luther's strange dream. I'd felt it to be fairly transparent at first hearing, but I'd reserved my full opinion, knowing from experience that nothing was really all that transparent in Luther's case. The funeral pyre part was a bit worrisome, but I didn't spend too much time analyzing it just then.

Luther had been my patient for five years now, and we'd made tremendous progress together. When we started, the boy had been twelve, skinnier than a blade of beach-grass, and smarter than anyone knew. He was acting out violently at home and at school, and his parents thought they might have to place him in an institution, but in a very short time, through intense talk therapy, we were able to get almost past his deep anger. He was still unstable in some ways, and needed to do a lot more work, but gradually I had been able to win his trust and draw him out, and his new-found communicativeness brought to light all sorts of psychological complications with which Luther and I would do battle. I was convinced he would someday be whole, and looked forward to that day with great interest, since Luther's intellectual powers were, in my opinion, quite remarkable.

My opinion in such matters was based not only on my extensive research on gifted children, but on personal experience: I had been a so-called gifted child myself. In fact, both my younger brother Duncan and I were discovered to have unusually high IQ's, and were exposed, through our parents' gracious and knowledgeable attentions (they were both college professors: Mother in American history, Father in the physical sciences), to academic and artistic influences that helped us develop our abilities to what were considered astonishing degrees.

Duncan had fared rather better than I. As the second child, he was naturally more relaxed, and he was privy as well to the experience my parents had had while raising me, their first-born "genius," for five years. Duncan did extremely well in everything, but not well enough to be singled out quite the same way as was his older brother. I think, to a broad degree, this "just well enough" routine was deliberate on his part, and I always revered him for that: indeed, it convinced me that Duncan was, in all the ways that really counted, far brighter than I.

When my IQ was first recorded, at the age of six, it was brought to the attention of some people in my parents' university who were initiating life-studies of gifted youngsters. I believe that when approached with this project by a bevy of psychiatric researchers, my parents did not fully realize the extent to which they were offering up their offspring as a guinea pig for life. They were told that I would be tested periodically and followed in various ways to track my development. It did not sound to them like a cruel idea; and the experimenters themselves, while certainly aware of the possible deleterious effects their studies might have on the chosen children, most probably thought that they had the problem well in hand. I did not realize myself, until early in my teens, how much I hated them, but I never let anyone know. I cooperated and cooperated; I seemed a willing victim. I suppose I could have walked out on it all at any time, but I didn't. I was a kid. What did I know?

By the age of seven I had mastered the piano and was composing almost daily; everyone thought I was well on my way to a concert career. I gradually lost interest. For the next several years I did practically nothing but read, and it was during that time I discovered my strange ability to memorize literary material. It had to be something I liked a great deal: with other kinds of text, I was not a quick study, and I never showed any signs of having what's commonly called a photographic or eidetic memory. Many scholars don't even believe those types of memory really exist, but I think it's a matter of semantics; people quarrel over definitions sometimes as if there were hard and fast explanations of the mysteries of the mind. That approach leaves out so much. I'd learned from having my own brain studied that having a good imagination has a lot to do with having a good memory, and I did enjoy imagining things. While my "reading years" were in progress, my father wisely decided I should be forced to rest my eyes and exercise my body now and then, so he took me to a pool at his YMCA. After a few weeks there, I decided to become an Olympic swimmer.

I stopped reading. I did not have to do much schoolwork, since I was so far ahead of everyone already, so I devoted myself to my new obsession. I turned from a skinny little wimp into a finely muscled specimen of young manhood, and eventually was successful enough to reach the Olympic trials and qualify. I decided not to go. I knew I could not be a swimmer all my life, and I missed my studies, so I went back to school.

At that point, I decided to become a doctor, but I had not chosen a specialty. For so many years, the "psycho-studiers," as I called them, had interviewed me and reviewed my every movement at regular intervals. At first, when I was just a child, this following wasn't really bothersome—it was all for science, and, odd as it sounds, it seemed to be my destiny. But ultimately the team of researchers began to anger me intensely. They wanted to know about my eating habits, my dreams, my ambitions, my sexual inclinations. I told them, quite truthfully, whatever they wanted to know, but I was building a terrible case against the medical profession. I decided to forgo an MD and become a "simple" psychologist. I would specialize in childhood and young adult problems. I knew I could do well at that. Something at last felt permanently right. My brain was famous, but I was not. Not every gifted child invents a pollutant-free fuel, paints a masterpiece, or finds the cure for cancer. Some of us just live out our lives.

And that is the course I pursued. When I realized I would complete my studies too soon (no matter how brilliant, no "shrink" can qualify to practice at age sixteen, and rightly so), I picked up a couple of other graduate degrees to pass the time: a master's in English and a doctorate in education. And I began to write.

It was obvious I could not write fiction. I had some small success with poetry, but I was not driven to it, and therefore knew I did not have what it takes to be a poet of any high caliber. Nevertheless, I floundered happily for quite some time amidst the pages that issued copiously from my little portable Olympia. I never threw any of that stuff away either; in fact, I later foisted some of it on poor Eliza, who had more literary talent in her fingernails than I could ever hope to display. She took it, bless her, as a gesture of love (which is what it was) and did not stoop to critique it.

∞◦◦◦◦◦◦◦∞

That reminds me: Eliza did not show up that terrible night, but what I did not realize was that she was not due to arrive until the next evening. I'd gotten the date wrong—perhaps from mere impatience, perhaps from the Percodan—but I certainly suffered for my error.

I waited for her that night until 10:30 or so, when I finally fell into a fitful sleep on the sofa. My dreams were dreadful dreams of abandonment and physical pain (in one of them I was deposited on an ice floe, naked and freezing, by a gang of oafish sailors), and when I woke, although I did not recall immediately why I was in the living room instead of in my bed, I was grateful to be alive and awake in a world I could at least control to some small degree. My first thought was to call Eliza, but I could not do it. There were too many reasons to simply let things take their course.

I dressed and shuffled to my car to make my mole-like way to the school, fumbled and bumbled my way through my classes (I was attaining new heights as the lovable, absent-minded professor: an odd-edged humor had taken hold of my lectures, and my students seemed to appreciate it), paid attention to two troubled young persons who had come to me for psychological/academic advice, and moled my way home again in the Caddy. I was looking forward to a hot bath, a pizza (delivered), and an early bedtime. I had not allowed myself since waking to think of Eliza, and I was feeling the better for it. By nine o'clock I was snugly tucked in bed, a full dose of "Dr. P." (like Dr. J. of basketball fame, the drug could stuff my pain right through the hoop of infinity, leaving me a breathlessly grateful fan) settling itself into the half-pizza I'd devoured, which was resting comfortably in my stomach. I had a tape of Brahms on the machine, satin sheets on the bed, and an old, holey set of red flannel long johns swathing me in joy. I knew it was absurd to feel such happiness from warmth and comfort and freedom from pain, but I did. I felt almost elated. It was Dr. P. talking of course, but I did not care.

When the doorbell rang, I had been dozing, and at first I wasn't sure that what I'd heard had not been some peculiar sound effect from the stereo. Then it rang again. And again a few seconds later.

It took me, in my groggy state, what seemed like a year to find my robe and reach the doorway. I had not stopped to find my glasses, and so when I opened the door, I was uncertain for a moment whether it was really Eliza or just a woman who looked somewhat like her. Whoever she was, she took my hand and spoke.

"Jack! Are you all right?" she said. "I kept ringing the bell because I could see a light on and I knew you were in there and I thought . . . " She didn't finish the sentence. She dragged me inside and sat me on the sofa. She pulled her coat off and sat down beside me. It was so cold outside that her long hair crackled with electricity and stuck to her cheeks as if blown there.

It was my Lizzie. I could not believe my luck. I could think of nothing to do but reach out for her head, pull it towards me, and kiss her, once, hard, on the mouth. She kissed back softly, sweetly, like, I thought, Snow White would have done. The kiss stopped her little monologue about how worried she was getting when I didn't answer the door. I laughed.

"I thought so," I said, happily.

"What?" she asked.

"I thought I'd kissed you before," I told her.

She laughed then. "But you haven't," she said.

I kept on laughing; I was so foolishly happy I couldn't stop. "Then let me do it again," I said. And I did.

We sat there holding each other for a minute or two, then I took her out to the kitchen to make her some tea.

"Eliza, my dear, what are you doing here?"

She looked at me as if I were a madman. "What do you mean? You invited me, I told you I was coming, and here I am." There was a thin strand of hurt in her voice.

"Oh God," I told her, "I'm so glad to see you, Eliza, you have no idea. But the reason I'm all discombobulated like this is because it was last night that I was expecting you, not tonight. And when you didn't come—"

"No, no, you're wrong!" she said, jumping up from the table. "I'm sure you said Thursday, I'm sure of it. It's the last thing I'd make a mistake about!"

Then it hit me. She was right. Not only had I mistaken the day, but I'd accused her of doing the same. I'd suffered all the night before for no reason. And now that I allowed myself to feel the residual pain of what I had fancied to be her silent, deliberate rejection of me, I was nearly felled by the magnitude of it. I flopped into the kitchen chair opposite to hers.

I pulled her back into her seat and took her hands. "Eliza," I said, "I'm such an idiot! You' re right of course. I waited for you all last night, I thought you'd decided not to come, and I—"

"I would never do that; I wouldn't. I couldn't wait to get here."

I got up and dragged her, laughing, into a little waltz around the table. I hugged her close. She felt like a soft, flexible doll in my arms and her sweater had that amazing wooly smell that only happens in winter. "How do you like my outfit?" I said.

She took a step back and examined me: red long johns under a tattered white terrycloth robe. She pronounced me "noble and kingly." I hugged her to me again and felt dizzy. Then I put her back in her chair and proceeded with my tea making. We took our mugs to the other room.

It was a wonderful evening. We talked more than we'd ever talked before, and we laughed and laughed, Eliza seeming to take a true delight in my silly jokes and puns. I dragged out a bunch of family pictures from the piano bench: pictures of me in my swimming-champ days, pictures of Duncan, pictures of my various graduations, and then a picture that caught us both by surprise.

"It's your wedding," she said.

"Oh. I didn't realize those were in there."

"Your wife is beautiful. What's her name?"

"Frances."

"Frances. Nice."

"How do I look?"

"Very handsome," she said. "Very."

She put all the pictures back inside the bench, closed it, and sat down on it. "Do you have children?" she asked me. I'd forgotten there was so much she didn't know.

When Eliza and I had started seeing each other outside of school, which was only very recently, I'd told her only that I'd just gotten divorced. She didn't ask me anything more. And I'd told her I was ill, but not the full extent of the problem. I think she guessed but was too discreet to press me for details.

"Two sons," I said, "Ages eleven and thirteen. Harry and Mark."

"Not little boys then," she said.

"No," I answered, "I'll tell you all about them someday. I miss them."

∞∞∞∞∞∞∞

And that was the night that Eliza and I first made love. Or that is how I think of it, because the truth is that, for all our trying, the act was never consummated—not technically. That humiliating fact was the one thing I could never come to terms with while I lived, though I knew—I knew with certainty and gratitude—that Eliza and I did indeed make love that night and many others. I do not think we loved each other as "normal" lovers do anyway—how could we, amidst our peculiar circumstances—so perhaps my physical failure was a fitting accessory to our complicated passion. I tried to think of Abelard and Heloise and other exalted duos, but usually I failed to extract much comfort from that exercise. Eliza did not mind as much as I did; she said she minded for me, but it did not make any difference to the way she felt, and I believed her. I believed her because I loved her and because I knew her very inexperience worked in my favor: although she was not a virgin when I met her, she had not yet been trained by life to crave reliable physical love. I told myself she was like someone who had only been smoking for a little while: it would be easier for her to forgo the habit. Naturally I felt some guilt, but my need for her was great, and I suppose I never entirely lost the hope that a miracle would restore my physical powers. I was solaced only by the fact that I knew that after I was gone (or, I had to admit to myself, quite possibly even while I lived) Eliza would easily find a lover who would fulfill her as I was unable to do.

Oh, but that night, that night. It started off so joyously. I was so elated to realize my mistake about the date, and we were so relaxed with each other—so goofy and normal and unlike our usual half-nervous selves—that fate led us inevitably back to the sofa, where we lay kissing and touching each other's faces like children. I had not slept with a woman in what felt like a very long time—since a woman named Sarah Bowe, in fact (I'll tell you about her later)—and I was very excited.

I did not know, however, whether or not—or how—to proceed with Eliza. Our age difference (which I reckoned to be some eighteen years) and our odd friendship added up to a big question mark in my mind. While she was kissing me not inexpertly, I had no idea about her previous experiences with men. I wanted to find out, at least a little.

I maneuvered us both into a sitting position, and sat with my arm around her, her head nestled into my shoulder. She was innocent and kitten-like, I thought, but also immensely seductive somehow: she exuded some subtle sexual power that was almost palpable in the silent room. Looking back, I know I had always sensed that in her; I had just been too psychologically polite to admit it to myself. My chest was bursting with desire and confusion. "Eliza," I said, "Have you ever made love with a man?"

She nodded against me. "Yes," she said. "A few times. "

I was glad. I was jealous. "Do you have a boyfriend now?" I asked her.

Again she nodded, lifting her head from my shoulder and reaching for my free hand. "Miles," she said. "A guy from school. We've slept together on and off this semester." I could get no clue from her voice of how she felt about this Miles.

"Do you love him?"

"Well," she said, without hesitating, "In a way I do, but it's not that simple. Miles is still half in love with his old girl-friend. And I, I . . ." she faltered only for a moment, "am more than half in love . . . with you." She pushed away from me and looked at me strangely. "I'm sorry," she said, "but it's true. You probably didn't want to hear that. But please don't psychoanalyze it; don't spoil it for me. I know it's all wrong in the world's eyes, but it's made me very happy—you've made me happy, that's all."

I pulled her back and kissed her face over and over. "Lizzie," I said, "You are sweet and wonderful. You have no idea how happy you've made me by telling me that. You know I love you too, don't you? You've read those poems I gave you—you knew they were about you, didn't you? You silly thing. You silly, silly thing."

She was crying and laughing both. "Well," she blubbered, "I did think they were written for me, but I was afraid to be sure."

We kissed then for a long time. When I could wait no longer, I asked her, "Would you like to make love with me?"

She smiled. I had pressed my hand gently to her mouth, fearing she might say no. She put my hand aside. Simply, she said, "Very much." We went into my bedroom.

I was amazed to realize I was still in my odd, mostly flannel ensemble, but I was glad that the old satin sheets were still on my bed (relics of the early days of my marriage that Frances had sarcastically packed in with my things when I moved out). I did not turn on the lights; I was as embarrassed as a boy. Briefly and vaguely my mind flashed back to my final liaison with Sarah Bowe—how very different that had been.

While I fumbled with my robe and other gear, I noticed that Eliza had stepped out of her jeans, removed her heavy red turtleneck, and was standing before me in a silky little undershirt and some skimpy briefs. I ran my hands all around her and sighed; she felt so solid and serene. Her navel was flat, her breasts were small and firm, her buttocks were rounder than they looked in her jeans. She was shivering a little, so I put her under the covers, quickly finished removing my odd regalia, and joined her there: we were both trembling.

She was delighted with the feel of the sheets, saying she didn't think "average people" used such things. After some delicious foreplay, Eliza spoke shyly. "Jack," she said, "Do you have any protection?"

For a moment I had no idea what she meant; it had been a very long time since I'd heard the term. Frances had had a diaphragm. Sarah had never mentioned the subject. And other women, I assumed, had taken care of all that themselves—or had they? My age—all the repressed habits and general male stupidity of my generation—fell down around me like the proverbial wet blanket. I moved my body off my little love.

"Oh God," I said. "I don't. I'm such an idiot. You're right. We mustn't take any chances. Get your clothes on."

"WHAT?" she fairly shouted. "Are you throwing me out?"

I pulled her from the bed and held her by the shoulders. I hugged her. "Eliza, I thought you were an intelligent person," I said. "We're going to the drugstore, that's all. We've all the time in the world to get back to this. Get dressed. You're far too valuable to me to take foolish chances with, and I thank you for reminding me. I apologize, truly; I should have thought of it myself. "

Soon we were in the Caddy, the heater turned up full blast, shivering and giggling. I turned the radio on, and Frank Sinatra blasted out "Chicago." I had Eliza in convulsions of laughter as I crooned along with Frankie.

Not until I was out on the main road to town did I remember that I could barely see the road at night. I continued singing, not to alarm poor Eliza. I was terrified: I had spoken nobly about not taking chances with her and here I was, possibly driving her to an early death. I steered and prayed.

The night road, fortunately all but deserted because of the lateness of the hour, looked for all the world like a room full of jukeboxes seen through an oily lens. A few stars dotted the cold black sky—or were they stars? I relied on my memory of the area and drove as slowly as I could without alerting Eliza that something was amiss. She was so distracted by the immensity and plushness of the car's interior (she drove an ancient Volkswagen bug) that I hoped my driving would escape her notice. She exclaimed over everything: the deeply cushioned leather seats, the roominess, the hood ornament, the bevy of mechanical doodads on the dashboard, and when I lifted the little panel between our seats to show her the telephone, she was beside herself with wonder (in those days, don't forget, a car phone was truly a remarkable appliance).

"Jack, are you rich?" she asked, in wonder.

I laughed. "I was for a while," I said, "But no more. This car dates from fancier days."

"Well it's really something," she said, and then, frantically, "Watch out!"

I pounded the brakes, and we slid a little, then skidded to a halt. Eliza had leaped across the seat and thrown her arms around me. "My God, Jack," she said, "Didn't you see the red light? You went right through it! That car almost slammed into us!"

"Where are we now?" I asked her. I wanted to die. "Where have we stopped?"

She reached up to my face and found tears there, wiping them away with her soft hand. "I didn't realize," she said. "You should have told me." And then, "It's okay. We're fine. There's no one around. Do you want me to drive?"

"I'm sorry, Lizzie," I said, "I should have asked you to drive from the start. I'm a prideful old fool. I can't see worth beans after dark." I got out, felt my way around to the passenger side, and got back in. Eliza had already slid over into the driver's seat.

"Bet you never had a chauffeur quite like me," she said cheerily (I knew it must have cost her dearly to overcome her fright). "Even in your wealthier days." She was going to make a game of it; I loved her for her sweetness. I pictured Frances under the same circumstances: she would have still been screaming at me.

As we pulled out again into traffic, Eliza reminded me she didn't know where we were going. I asked her to describe the landmarks, then directed her to the parking lot of an all-night pharmacy in a shopping mall. She walked with me up to the door of the place, but I told her I wanted to go in alone. She did not laugh at me, but I laughed at myself. "Let's hope," I told her, "that there's some discreet and understanding old chap behind the counter."

"Silly," she said. "Would you rather I buy them?" That shocked me a little, I must admit, but I think I didn't let it show.

"Of course not. Can I get you anything inside?"

"No, thanks," she said. "See you soon."

⚭⚭⚭⚭⚭⚭⚭

On our way back to the apartment I asked Eliza if she'd like to stop for a drink. I wasn't planning on imbibing any alcohol myself (I thought Dr. P. might still be in my system), but I wanted a little pause in the night's activities. So much had happened in so few hours that I felt a bit unsteady. Happily, Eliza agreed, and I directed her to my favorite nightspot, a quiet, dignified little bar called simply "Tom's."

They knew me there; I guess I wanted to show Eliza off a little. Perhaps I'd be thought of as a silly old fool, but at least I wouldn't be pegged as pathetic and lonely. Our waitress, a wise middle-aged woman named Emma who had shared some of my lonelier evenings by sitting and having a drink with me just before they closed, was obviously pleased to see me with a female friend. If she was shocked by Eliza's age, she didn't let on. I think we must have looked the odd couple indeed: Eliza in her jeans, long hair, and wide-cheeked innocence, and I in my fedora and dark overcoat, with what was no doubt a mixed expression of wonder and fear on my own less innocent features. Emma chatted with us for a minute or two, then left us to our sherries. I don't know why I ordered sherry for both of us, but it somehow seemed the thing to do. Dry Sack. Warming. We didn't talk much, but sat very close together, our hands intertwined under the table, resting on Eliza's leg. She did not seem nervous at all, and the wine made the temperature of her hand rise just perceptibly—or maybe it was my imagination. I couldn't wait to get her home again.

My funny little chauffeur (I promised her an official chauffeur's cap) brought us safely back to the apartment, and we wasted no time getting back into bed. After some warmup activity, it was clearly time to don my new purchase. I expected some clumsiness with this; after all, it had been so many years since I'd used one, and I'd really only done so a couple of times in my youth. But I did not remember having any special problems in those days, so I approached the task with a certain dogged optimism. The first try was a disaster, and we had to warm up some more before I could try again. Eliza was patient and reassuring, but I was becoming irritated.

After the third try I lay down on my back and said, "Damn."

Eliza began to laugh. I had to join her. It was wonderful to see just how little all this bothered her. "Listen," she said, "I'm not laughing at you—you know that! Want me to make a cup of tea or something?"

But the laughter had loosened me up again, and I didn't want to waste a moment. I got the damned thing in place and was inside my darling in about ten seconds, occasioning from her a deep sigh of pleasure and surprise. And for at least sixty seconds more we were in heaven together; I had forgotten my dreadful rotting body and was alive anew in her young and healthy one. There was a pulse between us, a current so strong and beautiful, that I could have shouted for joy. I could not remember ever having felt so wholly good, so wholly impassioned. Then I lost my erection. Just like that—it collapsed like a sad old concertina. I rolled off Eliza and covered my face with my hands.

She tried to remove them. "Tea?" she suggested again, desperately. I needed to tell her it wasn't her fault, that she was wonderful and exciting to me beyond belief, and I started to do so. She stopped me.

"I think maybe you're more ill than you've told me," she said quietly. "Is that right?"

"Sweetheart," I said, holding her very close, "I'm afraid it is."

"Are you in pain? Do you have drugs for that?" she asked.

"I'm not in pain at the moment; I'm in depression. Eliza, this was all so beautiful, and suddenly I can't do a thing. It's the drugs and the wine and the excitement I guess; and maybe it's just the disease working in my head. I don't know. Maybe it's nothing. Maybe it's just first-night jitters. Please forgive me, Lizzie. Let me give you some pleasure anyway—at least I can do that."

But she wouldn't let me. She insisted on making the tea. And she brought it back to me in bed on a tray with some cookies she must have had in her bag, and we played at our tea party until I became excited again. "Try it without," said Eliza when I reached for the condom, but I simply could not think of it. I succeeded in putting the thing on, entering her, and then, once again, becoming instantly soft. Eliza crept down to my thighs and took my limp member in her mouth, astounding me. I felt so happy I thought I could easily die right then, and she drew from my idiot body an instant and enthusiastic response, but it subsided as soon as she stopped to draw a breath. I pulled her up to my chest again.

"No more," I begged her. "Have mercy on this ridiculous old wreck."

"There'll be lots of other nights," Eliza said, as I traced her smile with my fingers. "I don't want you to worry about any of this, okay? It's no big deal. I don't care. I feel wonderful just being with you. And I think you're right about first-night jitters—I mean, my God, I'm glad I'm not a man—there's always so much pressure on you."

"I too, goose, am glad you're not a man," I told her, "And besides being sweet, understanding, and brilliant, which I already knew, you are the sexiest thing on the face of the earth—did you know that?"

"Ridiculous," she said.

"No, no it's not," I responded, pinching her lightly. "But don't let it go to your head."

She laughed at me, got out of bed, pulled on her clothes and tossed me my robe. "I think I'd better go," she said. "I'll call you in the morning. "

I walked her to the door. "Don't you want to comb your hair or anything?" I asked her, remembering how women usually spent lengthy periods of time in the bathroom after any amorous encounter.

"Nah," she said. "What for? I'll be home in half an hour. Nobody's going to see me." Then she added, "And besides, this way I can go to sleep with your fingers in my hair." She kissed me and left. I went back to bed. I did not sleep at all until nearly seven that morning.

5. Frances, in Love and Disillusion

B ut what of my darling wife, you ask? I have already spoken
so poorly of her I'm afraid you might have the wrong
impression. Frances had many good qualities; still has, I'm
sure. She was not always a witch; perhaps she is not witch now.
Perhaps, when she *was* a witch, it was I who caused her to
become one. That's highly possible, in fact; I was not an easy
man in many ways. But Frances Buehr, when I met her in 1952,
was a walking dream. In fact, I used to hum that old song "Did
You Ever See a Dream Walking?" whenever I spotted her on
campus. Frances was a freshman at the university I attended
for grad school, going after one of my famous degrees. We
were the same age, but she was beautiful, mature, socially
successful, and sophisticated, while I was gawky, pimply, a
dedicated bookworm, something of a recluse, and a virgin.
I had no idea whether or not Frances Buehr was a virgin; I
didn't consider it my business in any way, present or future. I
only knew I adored her and that I hadn't a chipmunk's chance
in a shopping mall of meeting her, much less getting close to
such a perfect specimen of young womanhood.

One autumn afternoon I was in line in the cafeteria, anxious lest they serve pigs' knuckles again and wipe out my appetite for another two days, when I simultaneously bumped into my dorm-mate Fritz Nilsson and sighted Frances. She was lingering over the trays of lime and cherry Jell-O. Fritz cut in line in front of me and tried to be friendly.

"How're you, MacLeod? "

"Hungry," I said. "Let's hope there're no pigs' knuckles today." I spoke to Fritz, but I'd never taken my eyes off Frances, which of course he noticed.

"Hey, Mac, what're you looking at?"

"Oh, nothing. Just looking forward to dessert," I lied. I still couldn't stop staring at her. I rarely got up so close to her, and I could see individual strands of her gorgeous red-blonde hair flowing down the back of her fuzzy sweater. I was sweating profusely. Fritz put his head next to mine and followed my gaze.

"Holy mackerel, Mac," he said very loudly, slapping me between the shoulders with all his might. "That's Flabby Frances you're staring at, right?"

I was aghast, certain I'd misheard him. I turned on him so quickly he backed away.

"Flabby Frances?"

Fritz was laughing and slapping himself now.

"Good lord, Mac, you're a creep of sorts, but you sure don't have to sink that low. Flabby Frances . . ." and he continued to laugh.

"I think she's gorgeous," I told him, and pulled the last coveted piece of lemon meringue pie from the display in front of him. "So shut up, okay?" He sniffed and went on his way.

Now Fritz was no Einstein, but it was for that very reason I tended to trust his social instincts. I looked again at my dream girl: well, she was a little overweight. Okay, she probably needed to lose a few pounds. I simply hadn't noticed. Nor did I approve in any way of Fritz's slurs. All Frances's other sterling qualities had eclipsed this one minor physical failing from my view. I considered this all through dinner, which I ate alone, Fritz having lost interest in me when I refused to discuss the distribution of Frances's avoirdupois overload with him any further.

Shortly after that fateful dinner, I ran into Frances Buehr in my dentist's waiting room. The place always reminded me of a cocktail lounge gone wrong; even the potted plants looked slightly tipsy. Frances and I had never actually met, but I caught her eye as soon as I walked in, and I could tell she'd recognized me as a fellow student. We were the only two there. I swallowed a lump of fear the size of Gibraltar and walked up to her, hand extended.

"Jack MacLeod," I said. "I've seen you on campus."

She looked a little surprised but took my hand politely.

"Frances Buehr," she said. "Alpha Delta Chi."

"I know," I stammered, "I mean, I know your name; I didn't know your sorority. I'm not in a frat; I'm not a normal student—I mean, I'm a grad student, that's all."

"I'm pre-law," she said, "And how did you know my name?"

I decided to risk all. "Well," I said, "Let's say I've been admiring you from afar. I asked about you. I hope you're not offended."

Her face softened, then suddenly hardened into a sharp mask of pain. "Ooh," she said, grabbing one lovely cheek. "Toothache."

"I'm sorry. I hope it's not serious." I sat down beside her on the orange leatherette couch.

"Oh, it's serious all right," said Frances. "It's always serious with me. They tell me that, unless I change my eating habits, I'll be toothless and gumless by the age of thirty-five."

"Good grief," I said, with galactic stupidity.

"Good grief," she agreed. "I've really got to change. I'm a sugar addict. I'm ruining my mouth and my social life. I eat more garbage than a Dispose-All. I'm getting fatter by the week." Then she looked at me as if I were an alien from Mars. "What the hell am I telling you all this for?" she said, laughing.

I fell in love with her that day. I asked her if I could take her to lunch in the city when our dental tortures were over, and she agreed to come "if the Novocaine's not too bad." It wasn't. We had a marvelous time. I promised to help her diet, and she promised to help me "normalize" myself—she thought the word was hilarious. I thought it was grossly off the mark, but I didn't care.

Soon we lost our virginity together. Frances, for all her apparent sophistication, was a virgin too, and we continued loving each other for quite a few years; I know we helped each other a great deal too. Frances lost weight and gained confidence in herself. She became a successful lawyer and a loving mother. I lost some of my inborn pessimism and gained the joys of family life. But somewhere along the line, as the saying goes, something happened. Somewhere along the line our paths diverged, and Frances began to be disappointed in me. I think she'd always believed that my famous brain would become *really* famous—that I would do something or say something or write something that would catapult me and my entire family into the public eye, bringing fortune along with the fame.

But I was tied to my books, my teaching, and my patients, and I guess I wasn't really that exciting in general. Frances returned, after Mark was born, to her law practice, and began to compare me unfavorably to her snazzier colleagues and clients. In turn, I became disappointed in what seemed to me to be her changing values. Life turned hollow, except for our two boys, on whom we both doted. I know now that we probably should have separated long before we did, but who can really determine the perfect timing for such things? There were times in those last years, even as Frances was making me rue the day I'd met her, that I'd get a flash and an ache inside. I'd see her reddish hair glinting in a beam of light or hear a trace of some long-lost sweet inflection in her voice, and it would give me pause. If our life together had become a barren field, it's also true that once that field had flowered bountifully, and that even toward the end a few maverick blooms could be found amidst the dust. Perhaps we always love the ones we first love, even when love goes sour.

6. Lunch with Dr. Sarah

Wally Mussel had had it in for me since our first meeting. I don't know why. I mean I can guess the reasons he came to dislike me more and more as time went by, and I know why he ended up hating me, but I could never fathom his incredible and instant dislike of me the first moment we laid eyes on one another.

Not that he made such a good first impression on me either (and in truth I already had a bias against him—you'll see why soon), but I did not want to kill him on sight. Wally Mussel, head of the psychology department at NSU, was an obese man, short, with a pouty little mouth, and yellowish, pouch-endowed eyes that exhibited no intellectual luster whatsoever. He had a set of false teeth that must have previously belonged to George Washington, or possibly Martha. His voice was high and whiney, and everything he said sounded like the complaint of a dying monarch. He appeared to be about twenty years my senior, but I knew he only had five or six years on me at best.

I did not meet this neurotic little dictator until I had already been offered the job, a job I'd had my heart set on because Frances and I longed for something closer to civilization than Vermont, and it paid much better than my private practice. Northern New Jersey was so close to New York City. My one interview had been held with the provost, two psychology professors, and, wonder of wonder, two senior students. I say "wonder of wonders" because, in those days, students were generally considered a little higher than groundhogs in the academic hierarchy. They all liked me, and I liked them. I felt comfortable with them, and I was looking forward to some satisfying years of teaching and befriending my colleagues. One of the professors, a stunning thirty-ish blonde named Sarah Bowe (Dr. Bowe, that is), had been elected to take me to lunch after the interview. I remember she wore a pale blue tweed suit with a lacy little lavender blouse underneath that looked more like lingerie than outerwear. She was intelligent as well as sexy, and I was delighted to go off with her to a nearby inn, called the Sherwood, for what I hoped would be a pleasant little meal.

After the usual small talk, Dr. Bowe assured me she thought the interview had gone very well.

"If you want this job, I'm sure it's yours," she said, smiling. "That's quite unofficial of course, but I wouldn't say it if I didn't truly believe you were in."

"Oh, I'll accept all right," I told her, smiling back. "If they can match my present astronomical salary that is. I have an expensive wife and two enormous sons to spoil, you know."

Sarah laughed and said the salaries at NSU were terrible, but no more terrible than they were anyplace else. She hoped I'd sign up. I was buoyed by her enthusiasm and began to question her about the school.

"This is a state school, Doctor, as you know," she began. I interrupted to beg her to call me Jack and was asked to call her

Sarah. I noticed how delicately she ate, and with what obvious enjoyment. She picked an orange slice off the display of fluffy greens at the side of the plate and bent the rind downward, so the juicy little sections stood up like a row of soldiers. Then, instead of biting them off, she tongued each pointy morsel exquisitely, and noiselessly drew it into her mouth. I loosened my tie. I was not fool enough to imagine an affair with this good woman, but my all-but-nonexistent sex life with Frances had rendered me as bottled up as a Catholic teenager. I tried to concentrate on what Sarah was saying.

"In a state school," she went on, "one often finds an interesting blend of students, at least that's been my experience here. There'll be, of course, a certain number of rejects from more expensive schools, but for the most part NSU students are an able and enthusiastic bunch. They each have a personal reason for choosing this college, but I've found that at the bottom of it all lies a serious desire for learning. Many of them work their way through, so they have to want to be here. For the most part, I find them challenging and fun. Some of them are extraordinarily bright, too, which surprised me at first, and those brighter students often have quite fascinating reasons for choosing NSU."

This interested me, of course. "For example?" I asked her.

"Well, there's a boy in my intro class who's really a near-genius. I'm sure he could have gotten a scholarship to almost any school. But he mentioned once that he came to NSU because his brother had cerebral palsy, and he wanted to be within commuting distance of home. I thought at the time—I still do think—that that's too much of a sacrifice for a parent to allow a student of his caliber to make, but on the other hand I have to respect him for it. And he'll probably do just as well no matter where he goes."

"Possibly," I said. "I hope so. That's an intriguing case. You know about my interest in gifted children."

"Yes," said Sarah, smiling again, "I suppose that's why I brought it up. I'm curious about your background, Jack, as a child, I mean. We've all heard about the research project you were involved in."

"I'll tell you about it some rainy afternoon in the faculty lounge," I told her. "It's really too much for now."

"I hope you will," she said, "I'd love to hear all about it." She looked at her watch. "I still have half an hour," she told me. "There must be other things you want to know about this place."

"How's the boss?" I asked her.

We'd ordered white wine with our meal, but Sarah had hardly touched hers. She picked up the glass then and all but drained it. Then she gave me a sideways look.

"I like you, Jack," she said, "So I'll tell you about Wally Mussel. But I hope you won't let what I say turn you against the place. Keep in mind that we hardly ever see him."

"Forge ahead," I said. "I want to know."

"He's a miserable, pig-brained little bastard," she said, and waited for me to react. Although that statement was certainly more hostile than I'd expected, I didn't flinch, so she continued.

"I don't know how he got his position," she said, "But I wouldn't put anything past him. He isn't intelligent; he isn't popular; he isn't even crafty. He's just an old-fashioned bully." Then she paused and drank some water. "I'm sorry, Jack," she said, looking almost at the point of tears, "Wally really ticks me off."

"You needn't go on if you don't want to," I said. "I can see this isn't your favorite topic. I don't want to spoil what's been for me a lovely lunch."

"Oh, that's all right," she laughed a tight little laugh. "Actually, with me and Wally it's more of a personality conflict than anything else. I had a run-in with him early on, and I've never gotten over it. He's never given me any reason to get over it, I should say. But it is true that we hardly ever have to deal with him; he makes himself blessedly unavailable, and only turns up now and then at a faculty meeting when he has no other choice, or when he has something especially unpleasant to tell us."

"I did think it was odd he wasn't at my interview," I said.

She finished her wine, then the water, and smiled. She was looking more composed, and I was determined to end the subject quickly and make my own investigations regarding Dr. Mussel.

"Not odd for him," she said. "He rarely participates in such things. He'll look over your credentials and the recommendations of our search committee, take longer than he ever should to make his decision, and then have his secretary—or slave, as we think of her—offer you the job. I'll be careful to make my own report extremely staid, so he'll have no reason to think he could hurt me by rejecting your application."

"Jeez," I said. "He sounds awful. Thanks, but I'd rather have your unreserved approval."

She laughed. "You have it, you know that. And now I've got to go, I'm sorry to say."

She took care of the check, drove me back to my car in the faculty lot, and wished me luck. I was infatuated with her; I felt like kissing her on the cheek. But I merely thanked her warmly and shook her slender hand, which seemed to lie just a second too long in my own. I knew I was dreaming.

7. Sarah, Grace,

and My Knighthood

Just as Sarah had predicted, two months after my interview, when I had practically convinced myself to forget about getting the job, Wally Mussel had his secretary call to offer me a contract. I accepted. Then, before I told another soul, I called Sarah.

"This is wonderful," she said, "I'm so glad you told me. Will you be moving your family here during the summer?"

"I don't think I'll wait that long," I told her. "I'd like to come out soon and look for a house, and then get us all settled in as quickly as possible."

She told me she knew some real estate people in the area, and I made another luncheon date with her the following week so we could discuss the best way for me to start house-hunting. It wasn't at all necessary; I'm sure she knew that as well as I did. I could easily have done a lot of the initial fact-finding over the phone. I just wanted to see her. I was lonely, I had to admit to myself, for a kindred spirit, for some approval, for, simply, a warmer reception than the one I usually got at home.

I didn't even know if Sarah was married. Surely, I thought, she must be, a person like her—though she hadn't mentioned anyone at lunch. But then again, I hadn't really given her the chance. I guess I hadn't wanted to hear it.

After I called her, I told the family my news. The boys were delighted at the prospect of moving so close to New York City. We'd been living in the sticks as long as they could remember, and they needed a change. I preferred the country myself, but I wanted them to have a fair exposure to all kinds of situations while they were young. They needed some friends who were different from themselves. For example, there weren't any families of color anywhere around us, and I didn't want my sons growing up thinking the whole world was as homogenized as the milk produced by the nearby farms.

And Frances? Well, Frances was ecstatic. She even began to display (or was it feign?) a renewed physical interest in me that distracted me from thoughts of Sarah for a while. But it soon became obvious that Frances's main delight in my forthcoming professorial peregrination lay wholly in her fantasy that she would be able, at Norman, to inhabit the vastly superior social milieu to which, she was certain, she had a God-given right. I knew she'd be disappointed, but as long as she was so cheerful, I didn't try to disabuse her of the notion. Had I done so, she would have had still one more thing to hold against me. We slept together the night I told her my news and another night that week, and I told myself that we "made love." I tried to enjoy it without fussing over what to name our contact.

The morning of my lunch date with Sarah Bowe, I readied myself carefully for what I hoped would be a delightful day. I had visions of arriving at Sarah's apartment (she told me she lived in an apartment—that was a good sign—it made her sound single), whisking her off to that comfortable inn, watching her nibble her salad like a big, beautiful bunny, and then touring the neighborhoods of Norman in search of my dream house. I really didn't carry the fantasy on any further than that. I just wanted her impeccably female company; I didn't want to start up a big fat mess. I made the trip in about three hours, a whole hour short of the usual time. When I realized how I'd been speeding I tried to calm myself, calling myself a fool. I sang along with the radio in a deep baritone to prove that I was one. I was having a great time already.

I found Sarah's street easily; it was quite near the school. Her apartment was on the third floor of a very old, eccentrically styled house, bordered by orchards of what looked like dead pear trees and some rather splendid iris gardens. I rang the buzzer under her name several times before she came to answer.

As soon as I saw her, I realized I should have called the night before to confirm our engagement. She was dressed in a sloppy-looking old cardigan over what may well have been a pajama top, baggy jeans, and old moccasins, and her lovely blonde hair looked to have been stirred up by a Mixmaster. She wore no makeup, and her eyes were as baggy as her trousers.

Yet she did not look surprised to see me. She gave me both her hands and pulled me through the door. "Jack," she said, shaking her head. "I'm so sorry. I know I look a fright. I didn't forget our lunch; I've just had such a dreadful morning. Forgive me. Have a seat in here. I promise I'll only take five minutes to get ready."

She half pushed me into a funny little parlor and rushed off up the stairs before I could say a thing. I looked around me. Everything in the place seemed to belong in a Victorian museum: heavy cut-velvet-covered furniture, potted ferns, Oriental rugs one on top of the other, floor-to-ceiling bookcases crammed with dark leather volumes, a stuffed owl (oh no!), a stuffed squirrel (ugh!), and thick brocade drapes drawn only slightly apart with tasseled ropes, letting in dusty sunbeams and no air whatsoever. I went over to the bookcases, naturally, and was just pulling down what appeared to be a very old copy of *The Turn of the Screw* when a voice from behind me almost scared me into dropping the volume.

"Young man," the voice said.

I turned and peered into the dimness. There in one corner, in one of the chubby chairs, sat a plump elderly woman with a huge, orange, longhaired cat on her lap. She wore, of course, a crocheted shawl and slippers, and had little wire spectacles on her nose. A pair of canes rested against her footstool. She did not wear a lace cap, but she might as well have. "Madam," I said, "Forgive me. I did not see you there."

Her voice was childlike in pitch, but commanding. "And so you made free to pluck down my books," she said.

I decided to make a friend of her. "How could I resist such a devastating temptation?" I asked, then said, "My apologies. My name is MacLeod, Jack MacLeod. I'm a friend of Dr. Bowe's." I walked over and offered this apparition my hand.

I was not sure she would take it, but she did. Her own little paw was surprisingly smooth and warm, and she grasped my hand firmly. At that, the cat jumped off her lap with a peevish cry. "Foolish thing," she scolded, with great love in her voice, "Nobody's going to molest you," and she brushed some long red hairs off her lap, pulled herself up straight in the chair (which obviously caused her some pain), and gestured for me to take the one opposite hers, which I did.

"Do you like cats, Dr. MacLeod?" she asked me, looking into my eyes piercingly to drive home the importance of the question. I assured her I did, very much, and could tell that I'd pleased her.

"Friend of Sarah's, are you?" she went on, but did not wait for me to reply. "Good for her to have some friends. Taking her out, I hope. She's been up there all morning crashing around like a wounded moose. I called up and asked her what was the matter, and she said she was cleaning closets. Well, I don't believe it. Anyway, a young woman like that needs to get out more. She shouldn't come down here and sit with me of an evening—not that I mind the company of course. Forgot to tell you: I'm Grace Rinkette, I own this place. Those are my iris gardens outside; did you like them? President of the Iris Society of America, I am. Don't tell me you didn't notice my iris?"

Here she paused, but only for air. I was able to assure her I'd thought the iris delightful, and then, just as Grace Rinkette was about to launch another conversational ocean liner, Sarah came in looking like Her Serene Highness and smiled calmly at both of us. She was wearing the blue suit again, but this time with a white scoop-neck sweater underneath the jacket, and toweringly high heels. Her hair, which had been a tangled nest a few minutes ago, looked like one of those ads for Prell shampoo, though it was impossible for her to have washed and dried it in so short a time. She had little pink pearly things in her pearly ears, and just a touch of pink on her cheeks and lips. I was astonished. I momentarily considered the idea that it had been some poor, bedraggled twin sister of Sarah's who had answered the door a few minutes before. The fairytale atmosphere of the parlor and Grace Rinkette was making me lightheaded.

"I see you've met Miss Rinkette, Jack," she said. "I'm glad. You two will like each other—you're both such book nuts." She turned to Miss Rinkette. "Jack and his family are moving here, Grace. He's going to teach at the university."

Grace was pleased to hear it and invited me to stop by any time. She asked if my wife were interested in iris. Then

Sarah bustled me off, stuffed me into her Ford Falcon station wagon, and took off like a maniac down the hill to the Sherwood Inn. She did not say a single unnecessary word until we were settled in our seats.

Then she smiled at me, took up her napkin, and burst into tears. I held her one hand while she dabbed at her eyes with the other. When she was finished crying, I went to the bar and brought us back two bourbons, neat.

I said, "I thought this would do better than white wine."

"Bless you," she said, and took a long sip, then another.

The waiter appeared and we ordered. When he had gone, Sarah looked over at me sheepishly.

"Not everyone at Norman is as crazy as this," she said, "Please forgive me. First I meet you at the door looking like a bag lady, then I cry at you and drink your bourbon too quickly. I'm sorry, Jack."

"Don't mention it. Anything I can do?"

"No. I don't know. This was supposed to be a meeting to discuss your real estate options. Seems to be going all wonky." She gave me an abashed smile.

I decided to take an honest tack with her, since clearly we'd been catapulted, by circumstances as yet unknown to me, onto more personal ground.

"Sarah," I said, "I think we both know that was an unnecessary excuse to get together—at least I did. If I can help you with whatever is making you so unhappy, even just by listening, I'd be delighted to do so." I took her hand again. "No extra charge," I kidded. "You can tell me who to call about a house any time."

I couldn't believe it, but she blushed. Then she sneezed and took her hand away to wipe her eyes again. "Thanks, Jack," she said. "You're right. I just wanted to be with you again. I don't want to start up anything funny, believe me—I just need a friend." She smiled up at me, the blush receding into the low neckline of her sweater. "Is that okay with you?" It didn't require an answer. "Are you hungry?" I asked her. By this time the waiter had delivered two huge plates of pasta and a gigantic basket of bread. I couldn't imagine why we'd ordered it. I mean, it wasn't even an Italian restaurant.

She looked at the vast pile of comestibles on the table and laughed. "I'd rather have a beer and a hot dog," she said. "I know a great place for that sort of thing."

"Good idea." I threw some money on the table, grabbed her arm, waved to the waiter and called "Ciao," and we were back at the Falcon, Sarah fumbling in her bag for her keys. I took her hands, held them to my face, and kissed her quickly. She looked astonished, but not unhappy.

"Now we can relax," I told her. To my delight, she seemed quite pleased.

⤙⤙⤙⊶⊷⤚⤚⤚

We drove, not talking. Sarah took me to her apartment. She parked on the street about a block from the house, explaining to me that if we went in the back way, quietly, we would avoid another audience with the amazing Grace. As much as I liked the old dear, I too was eager to slip past her. The rear entrance to the house, almost entirely masked by the thick vines of an ancient wisteria, was a private route to Sarah's apartment, and as we carefully tiptoed our way to the third floor, past closed doors with lace-curtained windows on each landing, I felt a mixture of impending adventure and threatening doom. I sensed that whatever was upsetting Sarah must be something deep, and while I knew I was soon to learn the secret behind her distress, I was also thrilled and frightened by this chance to be alone with her. Sometime during the short drive from the inn, I had stopped fooling myself about my intentions, and I worried that I would frighten Sarah off. She had asked for my friendship, nothing more, and I had to be careful not to take advantage of her troubled state of mind. On the other hand, she had accepted a slightly-more-than-friendly kiss from me, and she had taken me back to her apartment. What was a boy to think?

"My kingdom," she said, waving me through the door. Sarah's place was small, but tastefully appointed and perfectly neat. There was a kitchen area extending into a small living room, and a large, old-fashioned bath off the hall. I saw another closed door, that must have led to her bedroom. The living area was dwarfed by a huge roll top desk, full to its very edges with books and papers, all in tidy piles. There was a radio in evidence, but no TV, and I wondered if she kept a set in the bedroom, conjuring up a cozy picture of Sarah with her hair combed out like a '40s movie star, lolling in a pink bed-jacket while taking in the evening news with her dinner on a tray. While I washed my face and hands, Sarah fixed the hot dogs.

She soon presented me with a Heineken and a plate containing two frankfurters on toasted buns, a mountain of potato chips, a large slice of kosher dill, and, oddly, a banana. I couldn't help but laugh.

"A banana?"

She didn't seem to think it odd. "For dessert," she sensibly replied. She kicked off her heels, peeled off her jacket, and settled into an old armchair across from the couch where I was sitting. Then she got up again and turned on the radio, low, to a classical music station. "For background noise," she explained. "I find it difficult to unload on people in total silence." The smile she gave me then made her look about twelve years old. She picked up her pickle and began to eat it daintily, first licking some juice off its side. The way she ate made me crazy. I had to look away.

I took a bite of the frank. "Delicious," I told her, "Exactly right," and then, "So what's the problem?"

She giggled nervously, then sighed, then put her plate down on an end-table and tucked her legs up under her. She gripped the arms of the chair as if bracing herself for an explosion. "Jack," she said, "I don't think you're going to like me much after this."

"Impossible. Tell me."

She took a very deep breath, as if there were not enough air in the world to satisfy her aching lungs. "It's that slime, Wally Mussel," she said. "I'm sleeping with him."

I could do nothing but stare at her. I was utterly shocked and confounded. I waited for her to go on.

"I mean I'm sleeping with him, but it's not my choice. He'd just left my place this morning when you arrived. He dropped in unexpectedly while I was cleaning: that's why I looked the way I did. I wanted to get ready for lunch, and I couldn't get rid of him. I even picked a fight and threw a chair at him—that's when Grace called to ask what was going on."

"Does he hurt you?" It was all I could think of to say.

"No, oh no, Jack, never. I mean, that's not the problem, he doesn't beat me up or anything. *I* threw the chair at *him*."

"Good," I said, idiotically. I still could not believe what I was hearing. Although I had not met the man, I remembered Sarah's hatred of him, and I could not make the puzzle pieces fit.

"Jack," she went on, "I want to explain. I can't imagine what you think of me. I'm sorry. I'm such a mess. Look, Jack, he's blackmailing me. If I don't have sex with him, Wally's going to tell the whole world that I had an affair with a student. I'd lose my job. And I'd probably never get another one."

She began to sob. She reached out for her beer and sent it crashing to the floor. I went over to her and held her.

"Jack, I'm so sorry. I shouldn't have told you. I must disgust you. I just can't hold it in anymore, I feel like I'm going to go crazy, very quickly." She cried a little more and then wriggled out of my arms and sat up straighter in the chair. She wiped her eyes on a Kleenex she'd retrieved from under a cushion. I remembered my mother stowing tissues in such places: women are always prepared for sickness or grief. I was perched on the arm of the chair.

"Poor Sarah," I said, resting my chin on her head.

She laughed a little then. "Get up," she said, "I need that beer." I got her a fresh Heineken from the kitchen and she fetched a towel and sopped up the spilled one. Then we both went and sat on the couch.

"Better?" I asked her, when she'd had a few gulps.

"Yes, thank you."

"So when did all this start?"

She looked at me dolefully. "Five years ago," she said.

Five years! I had a sudden violent desire to vomit, but I held my breath until it passed. Five years. Sarah Bowe—this lovely, sweet, most charming and intelligent woman—Dr. Sarah Bowe had been raped repeatedly by a fat rat-maniac for five years. I tried to make myself calm so my voice would behave, but before I could speak Sarah took my hand.

"Jack," she said, "I know this is shocking. Let me fill you in a little—it might take the edge off."

"That bastard," I said, shakily.

She gave me a shy look of gratitude. "Five years ago, there was a student in one of my classes who touched my heart. I was young and lonely, he wasn't much younger, and before I could get hold of myself, we had a brief affair. Very brief—not more than two or three nights over a whole semester. Then I did get hold of myself, and I broke it off, and Jim—the student—quite wisely transferred to a west-coast school. I've never seen or heard from him since. I thought I'd gotten away with it, and I vowed it would never happen again." She went back to her chair for her hot dogs and returned with them to the couch. She ate ravenously, all delicacy gone for the moment. "Jim was a sweet kid," she said. "I hope I didn't do him any harm."

"I wouldn't worry about that," I told her. "How did Mussel find out?"

"That's just it, Jack, that's the awful part: I don't know. He must have spies. I have my suspicions, but no proof. There aren't that many people who like him enough to be his snitch. All these years I've tried to get him to tell me, but he won't. I should have called his bluff when he first approached me, but I was scared and inexperienced. Now it's too late." She shrugged. "How can I get out of it now, short of moving? And how could I get another job without the chairman's recommendation? I'm stuck. It's my own stupid fault. I'm the prisoner of a slimy little fuckhead."

I had to laugh at her language, and so did Sarah. "We're going to get you out of this," I told her. "How often . . . I mean when . . .?"

"Whenever." she said, shyly. "It's not all that often anymore. At first it was horrible. He used to come here all the time. He used to try to get me to respond to him, but when that failed, he just did it quickly and left. I'd just lie there like a dead thing. For a while I even thought he was getting tired of me altogether, but recently he's started up again demanding all this 'response' stuff and . . . God, Jack, it's too embarrassing. You don't know how I hate myself."

I took the plate out of her hands and made her stand up. "That's got to stop," I told her. "I hereby appoint myself your personal shrink and knight in shining armor." I wanted badly to make her laugh, because I felt so close to tears myself. I picked up the tray she'd used for our lunches and held it before me like a shield. "I shall beard the slimy fuckhead in his den," I declared. "And bring you the head of Wally Mussel on a garbage-can lid!"

She was laughing and motioning for me to keep quiet. "Grace," she sputtered, "Grace will call. Oh Jack, you're crazy, stop it, stop . . ."

I stopped. "It's good to see you smile."

"Thanks, Jack, you're a dear. And you don't think I'm repulsive?"

"I think," I said, "You are fabulous. You're a victim, and that's got to stop. You also break my heart with this story. I want to kill that asshole, but I'm going to think of a better plan than that. I'm glad you told me: we're going to fix this. But for now, the question is, how do we protect you from Mussel until he can be stopped for good?"

"I don't think he'll be around for a while," she said. "Today he said something about a trip."

"Good," I said. "I'll check on that. If he's really out of town for a while we'll have time to work on a plan. As for now, I think I'd better go. Are you going to be okay?"

She gave me a brave grin. "Fine. I'll be fine. I can't tell you how much you've already helped."

I kissed her again. I had to. Then I made my way stealthily down the back stairs.

8. Don at Howard Johnson's

I did not go directly back to Vermont after leaving Sarah's. I went to a diner. I wanted to think. After three cups of coffee, I called the university and spoke to Mussel's secretary, Dottie, who confirmed that the good doctor was off to a conference and would be gone all week. That cheered me a little; at least Sarah was safe for the time being. But how to help her? How to expose Mussel while saving her job and reputation? For some reason I started wondering about Dottie, the same person who had called to offer me the job. I had only met her once. She was a tall, slightly stooped, breathlessly stupid woman, probably in her forties, always on the verge of saying something you never wanted to hear. I had taken an instant dislike to her, based on nothing, and I was slightly ashamed of myself, although usually my first impressions proved to be correct.

Finally, I hit the road toward home, and on the way back I formed many a plan but rejected each of them. It was becoming quite obvious to me that this mess was a deeper one than my initial rage had allowed me to see. If only we had something on

Mussel—something so appalling that not only could we force him to leave Sarah alone, but force him to vanish forever from the department. I also considered simply confronting him with the idea that if his blackmailing was made public, he'd go down in infamy, but naturally Sarah's fate wouldn't be too dissimilar to his, so that was no good. What I really wanted to do was punch his guts out. And I was slowly (how slowly, considering my own professional training, was truly surprising) beginning to admit to myself that Sarah's real problems weren't professional ones. Once this nightmare was over, once she no longer had to endure Wally Mussel's unwanted attentions, she would have years and years of confronting her vanished self-esteem, her guilt, her fears, and her feelings for the entire male sex. It was promising that she had allowed me to get close to her so quickly, but I knew I had to tread carefully with her and forget any romantic ideas I might have had. She obviously saw me as some kind of brother or uncle, someone whose affections were safe, and that was how I'd have to treat her. I promised myself to put my galloping lust on a back burner, or to extinguish it completely, for Sarah's sake. She was so warm, so sexy, so seemingly comfortable in the world—I was mystified by her double life. How was she able to control it? For one horrifying instant I entertained the idea that Sarah secretly got off on Mussel, but then I remembered the sincerity of her tears. I also found myself recalling her blush, and turned on the radio to distract myself from that image.

I called her from my study when I got home that evening and told her she could relax for the week. She was grateful and relieved. I promised to call her again in a couple of days. Then I looked up Donald Rath's number and called him.

Dr. Rath, a young psychologist on the NSU faculty whom I had met briefly on my initial tour of the department, was a friend of a friend of mine, Paul Myers. I hadn't known that until I got the job, but now I was counting on it to gain some entree into the secrets of departmental goings-on. I needed a viewpoint other than Sarah's: I needed to assure myself that my infatuation with her hadn't blinded me to some obvious loophole in her story. I did believe her, and it felt a little traitorous to think otherwise, but I had to, for both our sakes. After all, I was just a newcomer to this scene; I couldn't just rush into this hurricane without some sort of raingear. My plan was to pump Rath a little and perhaps learn from him whom next to pump. My friend had given me reason to believe that Rath was a decent fellow.

⌒⌒⌒⌒⌒⌒

He did appear to be one. He seemed pleased to get my call and pleased to learn I'd be joining the faculty. He wanted to get together for lunch, he said, whenever I was again in the area, but although I accepted his invitation warmly, I asked him if we might chat a few minutes on the phone. I told him I wanted to pick his brain a little on a possible problem I'd uncovered. Don, as he immediately asked me to call him, agreed instantly, but when I brought up Wally Mussel's name (in a way that did not involve Sarah) he all but clammed up.

"Mussel," he said. "Not one of my favorite people, but there's not much I can tell you about him. Keep out of his way, that's my advice, but that won't be hard—he's virtually a ghost in the department anyway."

"So I've heard. But I've also heard he can be a formidable nay-sayer when it comes to special projects, and I've got some rather delicate research in mind. I'm worried that he'll put up some roadblocks, and I want to be ready to deal with him." I knew I was being ridiculously vague, but I was simply feeling out the territory.

There was a pause, and then Don said, "Listen, MacLeod, I'm sorry, but I don't believe you. I mean I believe you want to know about Mussel, but I don't think it's got anything to do with your research. Am I right?" He gave a little half-cough, half-laugh—a unique sound, and something I would quickly identify as a signature noise of his.

I laughed myself. "Okay," I said. "You're right. Paul told me you were perceptive. If this topic makes you uncomfortable, I'll lay off, but I'd really like to hear what you know about Mussel."

He told me then that he didn't think we ought to talk about it on the phone, and we arranged to meet the next day in Connecticut, since Don was going there to visit his sister and it was a convenient halfway point between our two states. After I hung up, I wondered about all the secrecy. Was the telephone really that dangerous an instrument in this case? Was it because I'd called him in his office at the university? What were we dealing with here? I decided things were either a lot worse than I'd suspected, or that Donald Rath was a bit of a paranoid fellow. I really didn't feel like taking another drive, but my curiosity was piqued, and anyway, I only had a week before Mussel got back within reach of poor Sarah.

I met Don at the Old Lyme exit on the Connecticut Turnpike and we drove, in both cars, to a nearby Howard Johnson's. I loved the familiar orange and turquoise color scheme, which reminded me of going there as a kid with my parents, and also of taking my boys there for ice cream when they were small. Don and I ordered what we discovered to be a mutual favorite, HoJo's greasy fried clams, and I sat back to take another look at Rath. He was shorter than I, somewhere in his early thirties, and impeccably dressed and groomed. I could not imagine going for an ordinary visit to one's sister in a suit and tie, but that was what he was doing—and a very natty suit it was. Facially, with his little goatee and pleasant, though pointed, features, he resembled nothing so much as an actor portraying some modern-day incarnation of Mephistopheles. When he smiled, he showed small, uneven teeth. But he was so pleasant a chap, and so obviously eager to please, that we had little trouble beginning our conversation. Rath, in fact, started it off right on target.

"I hate Mussel," he said, stirring his coffee energetically, "And don't mind telling you so. You'll come to hate him too—everyone does in time. But as for why I hate him, that's pretty complicated."

"Go on," I said. I knew he would tell me everything if I didn't push too hard.

"Well," he went on, "Let me put it this way. If I were on the sinking Titanic and there was only one lifeboat left and there was only one seat on that lifeboat and it was next to Mussel, I would just stay on the Titanic."

He then emitted one of his laugh-coughs, "I hated him, I'm ashamed to admit, on sight. I have this terrible thing about fat people, men especially. It's irrational and stupid, I know, but there it is. I struggle with it. Most of the time I get over it as soon as I get to know somebody, but not this time. Heavy women don't bother me all that much, but then again, women don't bother me all that much in general. What I mean is," he continued, fixing me with a searching stare, "that I love women, but I 'like' men. Maybe Paul didn't tell you I'm gay?"

I said truthfully, "He didn't mention it, no."

"Well, why would he, I guess. And you've probably figured it out for yourself." He smiled at me, charmingly.

"Okay," I said, "It crossed my mind. But why tell me at all? Does it have some bearing on the Mussel story?"

"Absolutely. Mussel judged me instantly and made my early days at NSU a living hell. He's like some vicious teenage devil. My first week I received a dildo, in the school's colors, in the interdepartmental mail, with a note attached that said, 'Not our boys!'"

"Good lord," I said. "But what made you think it was Mussel?" Then I had to laugh. "And where the hell did he get a dildo in the school colors?"

"I don't know," Rath said, with a huge smile. "Isn't it amazing? Maybe he commissioned it. Anyway, I can't prove it was Mussel," he went on, "but I just know it was. I got creepy phone calls too—vicious ones—and I easily recognized his voice, though he pathetically tried to disguise it. He assigned me all the worst classes, at the worst times, and continually ridiculed me at meetings and even in front of the students when he got the chance. It's only because I survived those first months and managed to hang on all these years that he's lost interest, for the most part, in torturing me. But I know he'd like nothing better than to get me ousted on some trumped-up charge, so I watch myself very carefully. I've lived with the same partner for the last five years, but Wally thinks I live with my mother—because," and he paused here to laugh a very satisfied laugh, "I actually do live with my mother. She rents an apartment on the third floor of her house to me and Denny."

"Neat," I said. "But don't you hate living that sort of lie just because of someone like Mussel? Why bother? Especially these days—probably very few people even care that you're gay."

"I know, I know," said Rath, shaking his dapper head, "But it's just a habit now for me . . . and for Denny it's a very necessary evil." He paused for a gulp of coffee, "Denny's an executive in a very uptight company. He believes he needs to stay in the closet." Don sighed and smiled. "It's different for everybody."

"You love him dearly." I didn't know why I said that, to a veritable stranger, but Rath's sincerity had touched me.

"Yes," he said. "You see."

After a momentary embarrassed silence, both of us began to speak at the same time. I begged him to continue.

"Well, to get back to our topic supreme," he grinned, "now that I've upchucked my grisly story all over our clams, are you going to tell me the real reason you wanted the dirt on the old boy?"

"God, Don, I wish I could. I'll tell you as soon as I can. It involves another person, that's the only reason I can't let it out now—it's not that I don't trust you."

"Okay," he said. "But I hope you'll be careful, whatever you're up to. Christ, Jack, you haven't even started work yet and you're already up to your neck in muck!"

I hoisted my coffee cup in a toast. "To muck," I said.

Rath grinned at me, raising his own. "To muck and its rakers!"

9. Sleeping with Edith Wharton

My illness was formally diagnosed shortly before Frances decided to divorce me, but I had known for months what was happening. Even though I'd not pursued an MD, I knew a great deal about medicine, and I was pretty sure there was no hurry about getting the official word. I dealt with the knowledge that I almost certainly had a brain tumor privately, gradually, and with a certain amount of wonder mixed in with the anger and pain. The only thing I didn't know was whether it was malignant, but it probably didn't matter. In those days, treatments and surgeries were primitive compared to what became available in later years. I remember feeling, at first, like a character in a sad novel, like all sorts of fictional characters I'd enjoyed—most of them heroic, if tragic, and stiff of upper lip. I did not tell Frances my secret until the divorce was over and I'd moved out of our house, knowing that she would feel obliged to care for me until the end, and knowing that, scorning me as she did, no loneliness or hurt could be worse for me than being imprisoned under her roof when I became helpless.

It started slowly. Always nearsighted, I began to need stronger and stronger prescriptions with increasing frequency. Sometimes there was a dull pain, like an ordinary sinus headache, and sometimes a shooting, piercing one that would momentarily cause me to gasp. Occasionally I would have a little trouble with my balance, or I would suddenly experience a peculiarly bitter taste in my mouth, or a sickeningly sweet one. Now and then I'd hear loud noises that weren't there, or a memory from my childhood would, like a hologram, transfer itself to the world in front of me for a moment or two, blanking out all else.

But after a month or so, the more bizarre symptoms ceased, and only the nagging headaches and some vision problems remained. While I utilized various self-hypnosis techniques to diminish the headaches whenever I could, I knew I needed something I could take when I was unable to work and couldn't stop and take the time to meditate. So I took a trip to see Dr. Gerald Hamilton. I planned to stay in New York at least a couple of days, telling everyone I would be attending some lectures at Columbia.

Gerry and I were buddies from college, but I hadn't seen him in years. When I went into his office he said, "What have you got, Jack?" and I told him. He nodded. He sent me to the hospital for the needed tests, but both of us knew what they'd tell us. The tumor was not malignant, but it was inoperable, and there was no telling how long it would take to permanently humiliate, incapacitate, and kill me, in that order.

"This sucks, Jack," Gerry said. "Did you come all the way to me in New York because it has to be a secret?" He was wise and direct, as always. He was also sweet; while I sat in his leather office chair looking over the test results, he stood behind me and kneaded my neck muscles like a concerned lover.

"For a while," I said, "A secret for a while at least. What can you give me for pain?"

He sighed, and I returned his chair to him. "If only we could operate, but the optic nerve is too involved: no surgeon would touch you the ways things are now. I wish you had come in sooner, but by the time the symptoms appeared it was probably too late already. I only say that so you won't torture yourself about letting things go."

"I know," I told him. "I know. I came to you for secrecy and for affirmation of my suspicions, but mostly for medication. What have you got that will take the edge off the pain but leave me able to function as normally as possible?"

"We'll work up to the really hard stuff when you need it. For now, take this prescription to the pharmacy downstairs. When you run out, call me. I take it you don't want to get refills locally. When you need something stronger, call me then too. Call me whenever you want to."

He got up and stood with his back to me, looking out the window, and there was a long silence. I figured he was crying, so I threw my shoe at him.

He laughed and called me a fucking idiot and we embraced. Men who first meet each other as boys remain so, when they are together, all their lives.

"Thanks a million, Gerry."

"Take care. Don't drink with the pills. Don't drink at all if you can stand it. I'll pray for a miracle."

"Me too," I said. I then went out to my car and cried myself, for the first time, about my situation. It didn't seem real until just then—until someone else knew about it. I thought about Harry and Mark, and how I would never go to their graduations or weddings, and I wondered if, had I tried harder, I could have, at some point, won back the Frances I had once so loved. I thought of all the things one would naturally think of under a finally realized death sentence, and then, for the first and last time, I got deliberately drunk.

I don't even like to drink all that much, and I had never done what I did that night, but perhaps it was the unreality of it all that prompted me to behave like a character in a made-for-TV feature. There was a friendly looking little saloon right around the corner from Gerry's office, and I took up residence in a comfortable booth and tied on a big one. I knew I was going way over my limit, but, interestingly, the liquor seemed to have very little effect on me, except for cheering me up a little. I was able to move to the bar and watch the last half of a Mets game like any normal guy. It was a bizarre evening.

But I did wake up the next morning with what I dubbed "The Last Hangover." I'd been to the edge and looked over, and I wasn't going to drink anymore. When my symptoms began to subside, I took myself off to the New York Public Library, and stayed there most of the day, reading a book I'd been meaning to get to for some time. I had a copy at home, but suddenly there it was on one of the library tables, under one of those lovely, green-shaded lamps, as if it were waiting for me to stop by: *The Age of Innocence.* I fell asleep in the brilliant and understanding arms of Edith Wharton.

10. Eliza Accepts Two Books

Sometimes I got really tired. Even before I allowed myself to admit that I was ill, I found myself becoming wearier and wearier, until sometimes, alone in my office on one of those grey, damp, seagull-filled winter days, I would nod off like big goofy dog, right in the middle of something I was reading or writing. One of those times, I'd napped off somewhere in the middle of an article on bipolar disorder in adolescents and had wakened with a start to an entirely silent world. I shook my doggy head and limbs and wondered what had roused me. Leaning over to the window and parting the venetian blinds, I realized it had been not a noise, but a presence: Eliza was walking quickly along the long path from the library to the main quad, her head bent down (she was wearing the funny multicolored beret with the big tassel again—something she once told me she had crocheted herself "in a whimsical mood") and her stack of books clutched close against her chest. No one else I knew walked as fast as Eliza; she seemed to be, like the March Hare, perpetually late for some "very important date."

The truth was that she was so well organized she was really very rarely in a hurry. I guess she was simply a driven soul, but I never really found out what was driving her; indeed, there was so much about Eliza I really never was able—or had time—to discover. She ate quickly too; and read quickly, and probably drove too fast as well—too fast, but very carefully. I often thought I had her pegged, but I know now I was quite a fool to think so. Sometimes I would wonder if Eliza made love with the same intensity she showered on everything else; then I would tell myself that was purely an idle question.

I knew if I put on my coat immediately, I would be able to plant myself casually outside the humanities building just as Eliza passed by, and we could have one of our "accidental" encounters. I felt I had a right to do this: after all, hadn't she willed me awake? I smiled to myself; I really believed that so-called nonsense—that is, I believed that the psychic bond between Eliza and myself was not nonsense at all. It really existed. I pondered that miracle as I rushed down the back stairwell, pushing my arms into my coat sleeves and trying to decide whether I should ask her to coffee or merely chat with her for a few moments before taking myself off on some bogus errand. But, alas, I had missed her.

I had discovered the link that Eliza and I shared early in our acquaintanceship, when she was taking my intro to psychology class. One day, early in the term, we were discussing various types of creativity, and students were offering examples of creative individuals. Someone said Picasso, someone said Leonard Bernstein, someone else said "all poets." Eliza had been even more silent than usual that day, so I decided to draw her out. "Who's your favorite poet, Eliza Harder?" I asked her. She never seemed surprised to be called on, always lifted her head, flicked back her curtain of thick unruly hair, and said something quickly and definitively, as if she'd been the one to volunteer a comment. She looked at me and smiled. "Kenneth Patchen," she said, without even taking a breath.

I still remember how it felt to hear that. I couldn't believe it. I don't think anyone else in that room even knew who Kenneth Patchen was (it's true there were only a few English majors in the group, but even so . . .), and certainly, even if some student had heard the name before, it was extremely rare to find any person who had even read one of his works, much less someone who would name Patchen as his or her favorite poet.

As for me, I'd been strongly attracted to his writing since my early youth and had collected almost all of his strange and beautiful books in hardcover first editions, when they were easy to come by. I considered that Patchen had initiated me into the world of true imagination, and I held his writings closest to my heart. That this Eliza, this student to whom I was so inexplicably drawn, but about whom I as yet knew next to nothing, should name him her favorite as well, was something of a miracle to me. It made me shiver, and I must have given Eliza a very funny look indeed, for with a charming and quizzical smile she said to me, "Wrong answer?" The class, which had fallen silent, laughed, as did I.

"Not at all," I said. "A very good choice. I'm a Patchen fan myself. I have some rather rare books of his you might be interested in; I'll bring them next week."

Eliza beamed at me. I don't know what the rest of the students were thinking; I should have considered that. And I should have introduced the class to Patchen there and then, but I couldn't—I was feeling too stricken with delight at the recognition of a kindred spirit, so I merely continued our original discussion, although it was hard to concentrate on anything but Eliza. When class was over, she scooted out invisibly, as she'd always done.

The following Tuesday, I lugged my entire Patchen collection—some ten or eleven books—to class, and when Eliza was taking her seat, I asked her to wait for me when class was over. I was very excited. I had already decided to make a present of the books to her; it never crossed my mind that she wouldn't accept them. When I emptied my satchel onto the desk after class, Eliza's eyes lit up like twin votive candles; I had not seen such an expression since my son Mark saw a butterfly emerge from its chrysalis one spring morning long before. She handled the volumes carefully, saying things like "Oh, I've never seen this one," and "Oh, this is a first edition," and often, simply "Oh!" Finally, after she had laid out the books across the desk so she could look at them all at once, she looked at me shyly. "May I borrow a couple?" she said.

"They're yours," I told her. She simply stared at me; I could read nothing in her expression.

"Oh no," she said. "No, no, Dr. MacLeod. But I would love to borrow one or two—the ones I've never seen. I promise I'll be very careful with them."

I decided not to argue with her; I wanted her to feel at ease. "Of course. Take as many as you like. And keep them as long as you like. I love him myself, as you can tell, but these books have sat on my shelves untouched now for a long time. They'd be pleased to go home with you and be appreciated again." I didn't tell her I'd memorized several of them, though I'd wanted to: she didn't know me well at all, and I didn't want to scare her off. Of course, that wouldn't have scared Eliza at all—she would have been fascinated by such a thing—but I didn't know it then.

She selected two prose works, *The Journal of Albion Moonlight* and *Sleepers Awake*, and I convinced her to take two volumes of poetry as well, and after some shy thank yous and goodbyes, she took herself away to wherever she'd come from. I found out later, from Eliza herself, that she'd fairly sprinted to the boarding house where she was staying, so eager to examine the books that she'd forgotten about her evening meal, which she usually took in the dining hall on campus. I had planned to tell her of my passion for Patchen, of how I had discovered him, of the influence he had had on my life, but oddly, although we had exchanged but a very few words, I felt she'd understood the whole story. It would not be the first time I'd get that feeling.

The very next week Eliza returned my books. I pleaded with her to keep at least a couple of them, and she finally accepted. Her gratitude was humbling; I was so delighted to have made her happy. I asked her to come talk to me about them sometime, and she said she would. I remember going home that night feeling as though I'd kissed her, but never imagining that someday I really might.

11. Dinner with Al Capone

I was getting undressed for bed one night, during the week's grace from her persecutor that had been granted to Sarah Bowe, when Frances mentioned casually to me that she had invited Wally Mussel to dinner. So bizarre was her statement that my mind was catapulted for a moment or two into something like complete confusion—a state I can only compare to that curiously vivid instant between waking and sleeping that one experiences now and then when overly tired or feverish or drugged. When full consciousness returned to me, I had already formulated some rather grand, if obvious, questions: How did Frances know Mussel? Why was he here in Vermont? When was this dinner to take place? Was I glad of or terrified by the prospect of meeting him, knowing what I knew?

I turned on Frances with what must have been startling intensity.

"WHO?" I asked, my voice crumpling a little under the weight of my emotion, and then, without waiting for an answer, "How did this happen?" I stood there in my undershorts feeling both ridiculous and on guard. Frances gave a short laugh.

"Well now, Jack," she said. "I thought you'd be pleased. What's that look for?" She picked up some items of clothing from a chair and began folding them. "Actually, it's a very funny story. I went to lunch at The Blue Cafe today with Margaret and Anna, and we chatted in the parking lot for a while before leaving. They'd just driven off together when I realized I'd locked my keys in the car; I could see them lying on the seat inside, in fact. I was just standing there trying to decide what to do next when this nice gentleman asked if he could be of any assistance. I told him the problem, and he got some kind of nifty tool from his own car and had the window open in no time at all. I thanked him profusely of course, and we chatted for a minute, and then I noticed his license plates were from New Jersey. I said we were all about to move there, mentioned NSU, and . . . voila! He revealed himself to be your very own department-head-to-be, in this neck of the woods for a conference." Frances stopped for a moment. "Isn't that odd—what kind of conference does anyone have up here? But anyway, Jack, what else could I do but invite him for dinner?" She looked at me coyly. "You should be thanking me, dear, not acting as if I'd invited Al Capone."

"You might as well have," I wanted to say, but I had to muster all my wits to avoid putting Frances on the defensive; one thing I certainly didn't need was a lot of questioning from her.

"Sorry, Frances, I was just so surprised" I said. "I'm glad you were rescued. When is he coming?"

She smiled at me almost sincerely. "Tomorrow night," she said. "As I told you, he's only here a couple of days, for a conference." And then, in an extremely odd tone of voice, "Such a nice man."

I climbed into bed feeling as though I were climbing into a coffin. Everything was just too crazy all of a sudden: Sarah,

Wally, Donald Rath, and now this weird side Frances was displaying. Could her last comment really have meant she liked this guy? I wasn't in love with Frances anymore, it's true, but neither did I consider her a fool. She'd always shown good judgment with people before. I was thoroughly confused. I thought I would never fall asleep, but strangely enough I did: I fell immediately into a deep, dreamless state that sailed me effortlessly into morning. When I woke up, Mussel's name was already on my mind.

~~~~~~~~

I was so busy all day that, fortunately or unfortunately, I hardly had time to give Mussel a thought. It was difficult trying to tie up the loose ends of my practice and hand my patients on to other therapists; each case required special care and lengthy consideration. With only about six weeks left before we moved to New Jersey, I had to take care of all the house-selling and house-buying problems as well, and my days were filled to the brim and beyond. So that night I raced home, showered quickly, changed, fixed a quick drink for myself and Frances (who was fluttering over her wardrobe like a debutante and simultaneously trying to organize things in the kitchen), and paid a speedy visit to the boys who, already fed, were cleaning up the garage in preparation for our move. Then all of a sudden, the doorbell rang. Frances commanded me to answer.

I don't know what I expected, exactly. Don Rath had told me Mussel was fat, but that was all I really knew about his physical appearance. Because of what I knew about his infamous personality, I was prepared for a certain amount of repulsion, but almost never before had I reacted so viscerally to any mere human. Suffice it to say the man was a mountain of flesh topped off by a highly unpleasant little head and face and two of the beadiest, deadest little eyes one could ever imagine. I definitely suspected a toupee. Also, he was wearing some kind of shiny, ill-cut suit, and a shirt that looked a great deal less than fresh. I took a deep breath and was relieved to note that I could not smell him. That made me think of Sarah, and of kicking Mussel instantly in the groin.

I extended my hand to him. "Dr. Mussel," I said, smiling. "How remarkable that our first meeting should be in my home." I was trying to establish my territory before the monster set foot in the place.

He pumped a smushy little handshake my way and said, in his uber-creepy whine, "Dr. MacLeod, how kind of you to invite me."

I wanted to say, "I didn't invite you, you gigantic spill of filth, my foolish wife did. And you'd better be careful tonight if you want to get out of here alive." But, of course, I simply stepped back and allowed him to enter.

Frances appeared out of nowhere and glued herself to his arm. She had settled on a floaty chiffon number that would have been more appropriate at an outdoor summer wedding reception. I suddenly wished for the kind of wife who wears plaid shirtwaists and ruffled white aprons—someone like Margaret on *Father Knows Best*. Mussel patted Frances's hand, and, as she led him toward cocktails on the patio, the two of them began a running conversation that lasted for the better part of three hours. I could barely get a word in anywhere. Occasionally it would occur to one of them that I ought to be included, and then they would draw me in for a moment or two in some minor way, cast me off again quickly, and resume their exclusive dialogue. I don't even know what they were talking about, it was that boring: an endless string of meaningless, unconnected observations on the state of the world.

What irritated me most of all was that I was unable to find out anything more about Mussel than what I already knew: that he was a disgusting sort of chap indeed. He seemed to find me disgusting as well, for though he managed to remain polite and even unctuous at times, he eyed me with unmistakable contempt. I could not tell if it was simply the fact of my being married to Frances that annoyed him, or if he were picking up on my hostile vibrations. Whatever it was, by the end of the evening, just thinking about it had exhausted me. After Mussel left, drooling his gratitude for a "fine, fine dinner" all over my wife, I went directly to bed in the spare room. I did not want to listen to Frances talk about what an interesting man he was, and I knew she wouldn't miss me.

12. A Priest, a Barber,

and a Psychologist . . .

I mentioned, way back, that now and then I would "catch sight of" my sons. This phenomenon, which I enjoy with ever-increasing frequency and precision is, like my limitlessly back-filled memory, a happy perquisite of death that never ceases to amaze me. Maybe it has something to do with the common expression "My life flashed before me" that people frequently say when they've had a close call; maybe what seems to me like infinity is really just a moment of reality. It happens this way: suddenly I will simply "see," like the proverbial fly on the wall, some scene, past or present, in which someone close to me figures prominently. These scenes, more often than not, seem to point out some previously mysterious aspect of my own existence, although I am not always immediately aware of their significance.

In this way I have followed the lives of my sons. Harry and Mark, I am pleased to report, did not seem to suffer unduly from the rather bumpy family life they experienced during their teenage years, and have grown, both of them, into remarkably likable, capable, and seemingly satisfied individuals. Mark, oddly enough, became a Catholic priest. At first, when I dropped in on his ordination ceremonies and saw the archbishop bestowing what I considered rather ridiculous religious powers upon my boy, I was appalled. Neither Frances nor I had ever succumbed to the temptations of any organized religion, and while we had, I hope, allowed both boys to satisfy their natural curiosities about such things and also instilled a sense of tolerance into their malleable young psyches, I think we must also have conveyed to them that Mom and Dad had little use for religion in the ordinary sense. Thinking back, however, I suppose Mark always was the more spiritually inclined of my sons, and while I do not exactly know what road he had traveled to arrive at his vocation, since his ordination I have seen evidence of his genuine happiness and usefulness to others on numerous occasions. Had I continued to live, I do not doubt that I would have had a great deal of trouble with his choice of career and faith—but then, had I lived, he might have pursued a different career entirely.

And Harry. Harry, my darling. All parents, in their truest hearts, have a favorite, and Harry was mine. As a tiny child, he was like a little man: funny, eccentric, peculiar looking in an engaging way, and full of a natural wisdom the origins of which defied all scrutiny. I doted on Harry until Mark came along, at which time I attempted to divide my attentions equally between them, I hope with some success. So, Mark became a priest . . . and my Harry became a barber.

Harry was fifteen when I died, Mark thirteen. Both boys were quite intelligent, but we never did them the disservice of having their IQs tested. Harry always shone a little brighter somehow—perhaps it was his wit, perhaps just that

all-comprehending light in his eyes. He was physically superior to his brother as well, with Frances's reddish golden
coloring and a slender though muscular build. He excelled in
math and science, pitched a mean season of baseball for his
high school team, swam competitively, and showed all the
signs of becoming a junior league ladies' man, much to the
delight of his mother. I suspect, though I cannot even now
be sure of this, that Harry was Frances's favorite as well; I
think she saw in him the well-rounded, handsome devil her
husband had never been. I'm sure we both expected Harry to
excel in some profession, if not one of ours, and I admit I used
to fantasize about taking him along on trips to psychology
conferences when he was older, thereby gently steering him
in the direction I had taken myself,

But, of course, that is not what happened. Harry did go
to college, he did wow the ladies (how many of them were
wowed amazes me), and he eventually did marry and start a
family with a lovely young woman who looked a lot like his
mother. But somewhere along the line our golden boy dropped
out of school, and somehow, he drifted into hair-cutting—and
not the fancy salon-type either. One could by no stretch of
the word call him a hairdresser or stylist: a simple barber is
what he had become. The first time I saw Harry in his white
tunic rubbing tonic into the scalp of a half-bald elderly man
I figured my sight had gone wrong in this afterworld as well,
but it had not. Harry seems, like his brother, very happy, and
that makes me glad. I truly wonder what his mother thinks,
although I can well imagine.

⚬⚬⚬⚬⚬⚬⚬⚬⚬

Weather is something I don't experience anymore, of course,
and, except in rare instances, when the weather had some

enormous effect on events, I seldom even remember anything about it. In my favorite sighting of Eliza, however, the weather played a very important part: I saw her shoveling snow.

I cannot say precisely how old she was when this scene took place, but she might have been about thirty, judging more by the clothes she was wearing than anything else. Her hair, which had been very long when I knew her, and all of one length (those were the flower-child days), stopped short of her shoulders, and there were a few strands of grey showing through the dark at the front, where long bangs escaped from the funny old beret. She still had that hat—it was the first thing in the scene to bring me a kind of possessive joy, though not the last.

Instead of her old formerly ubiquitous jeans, she was clad in plaid woolen pants, and instead of the Navy surplus pea coat I had grown accustomed to seeing her wear, she had on what appeared to be several layers of sweaters, giving her frame an oddly unbalanced silhouette.

She was shoveling the end of long, curving driveway, and it was obvious from her high coloring and from the long breaths she was taking that she had shoveled the entire length of the thing herself. I wondered whether she lived alone, and why there was no one to help her. It was early morning. A fluffy, large-flaked snow was still falling, and there were about six inches on the ground. I had never seen the location before—indeed I do not even know what part of the country it was—but there was a certain familiarity about the scene just because Eliza was there. I focused in on her face and hair, eyeing the old hat lovingly and wishing greedily for the impossible physical happiness of reaching out and touching her cold, burnt-red cheeks. Aside from the fact that there were bags of fatigue under her eyes, she looked wonderful. She looked dreamy and exalted and very, very womanly. I felt suffused with her, and at the very moment this feeling reached an almost unbearable peak of intensity, Eliza pushed her shovel into a snowbank and gazed up at the sky.

She was not, I suppose, looking for me in those snow-laden clouds, but something did stop her and make her look up. Her face took on, for just a moment, the look of a woman's face after love. She let the snowflakes gather on her upturned face until she had to close her eyes, then she shook her head and reached out her tongue to them like a child might. After that, although she had some ground yet to cover, she did not continue her labors, but picked up the shovel and headed slowly up the drive. It was then that I noticed the object that exploded my reverie into gratitude and felt that sense of possessive wonder I'd tasted when I saw Eliza's hat. Halfway up the little path she had cleared on one side of the lawn stood a small signpost suspending a nicely lettered placard from two little chains. The sign was covered by flakes of the wet, sticky snow. Eliza reached out a mittened hand and wiped it quite clean in one motion. DR. ELIZA HARDER, it read, and, under that, CLINICAL PSYCHOLOGY. She looked at it with great pride—as if she'd lettered it herself.

I "froze" that frame of the scene until my composure returned. To say that I had never expected Eliza to take up psychology as a profession would be an egregious understatement. I had suggested to her, time and again, for my own selfish reasons, that she should apply to graduate school in that field, that I would help her with her studies, and that, under my tutelage, and with her literary gifts, she would be able to plan out and execute a thesis that would make her success a certainty even before she left the university. But although Eliza never came right out and said no to this idea, it was always quite clear to me that it didn't quite suit her. I think she was too independent to want to take on something so reliant on my accompaniment, and also, I'm sure, she instinctively wanted to avoid a daddy/daughter or Higgins/Eliza association with me. She was, I knew from our many discussions of her past, acutely aware that because her father had passed away when she was in high school, she was more vulnerable than most to a relationship of that sort. I did not want that either, of course, but so needful was I of her presence at the time that it seemed any plan that assured her continued attendance in my life was worthy of serious attention.

So imagine my delight at seeing that little wooden sign. Eliza, like me; Eliza, like me . . . the phrase repeated and repeated itself in my mind like the lines of some chorus, sung by angels. I don't believe in angels, and yet, I really did hear strange and glorious voices; they were all around me. Their music obliterated all else for a space of time that seemed endless.

And when I remembered at last to look for Eliza again, in her snowy, glistening landscape, she was gone.

I was born in the winter: I have always loved the snow; and if ever there was a bit of weather that changed me, dead or alive, it was that little winter scene in Eliza's world that brought her that much nearer to mine.

13. Hansel and Gretel

Another time I saw Eliza with her lover. Of course, she had told me about Miles DiGrazia, and she had also intimated that Miles was not the boy with whom she'd lost her virginity, though I gathered from her oblique references to that event that Eliza's "first time," while not unpleasant or meaningless, was less than completely fulfilling. When I say fulfilling, however, I do not mean physically: Eliza was, judging by my experience of women (and by a not insignificant amount of reading I have done), very responsive on the physical plane. I only mean that her first lover seemed to have been a man from whom she broke away rather quickly, and about whom she seemed somewhat confused—which no doubt furthered her desire not to talk about him, especially with me. I never even learned his name.

Anyway, I happened in upon Eliza and Miles in Thompson Park. They were sitting in an old beat-up brown sedan, which I assumed to be Miles's, since Eliza, to my knowledge, had owned only her old green Dodge station wagon all through her college years. They were sitting on opposite sides of the wide front seat, Miles behind the wheel. The car was running, and the heater had steamed up the inside of the window. This was my first real glimpse of the DiGrazia boy, and I was very curious. I didn't know much about him. He was popular on campus, a talented classical guitarist in the music department, and a leader of one of the "peacenik" groups to which Eliza and many of her friends belonged. Now, at my leisure, I examined him closely. I must say he looked kind and serious that day, and he gazed at Eliza with real love—and real pain. He was muscular, quite tall, and had long, straight black hair pulled back into a ponytail.

His complexion was ruddy, but his eyes were remarkably large, blue, clear, and honest. Best of all his features, I think, were his hands: strong, long-fingered hands, smooth skinned, and steady. I could easily see why Eliza would be attracted to them.

"Miles," Eliza said, reaching out a hand and laying it along his thigh, "What's the matter?"

He looked at her for a long time, then bunched his thin plaid coat around him tightly and looked away from her at the steamy side window. He cleared off a space on its surface.

"Grazzie?" she said, pleadingly. It must have been a pet name.

He spoke very quietly. "Billy told me something," he said. "I was wondering if it's true."

"Something about me?"

"About you. About me. God damn it, Eliza!" he suddenly erupted, switching his position and drawing one leg up underneath him so that he was facing her, wedged between door and steering wheel. I was suddenly afraid for Eliza—the kind of fear one would have for a character while watching a film—but her calmness did not waver.

"What?" she said simply.

There was a long pause, then he spoke down into his coat. "Billy said you've been seeing MacLeod," he said.

This shocked me. I didn't know who Billy was, or how he'd come into this knowledge, but I'd always been comfortable in my belief that my relationship with Eliza was a complete secret. I really did not believe she'd told anyone about me; in fact, she'd assured me she hadn't. Neither of us really had any reason to keep such a silence—Eliza was no longer even a student of mine by the time things became serious between us—but I think we both felt self-protective about it all.

Eliza shifted a little in her seat too, until she was facing Miles. She let out a slight guttural sound. "Oh," she said.

"What do you mean, 'Oh,'" said Miles. "Is it true?" He still spoke down into the collar of his coat. He looked so young and afraid.

"Well," Eliza finally said, pulling one mitten on and off slowly, over and over again, "Yes. It's true, Grazzie. I'm sorry. There's a lot more to it than you think, Miles, really, but I don't think I want to go into it all. Don't be so hurt, Miles, please. Let me tell you what I can, if it will help you understand."

Miles slumped against the car door. "Thanks a heap," he said.

"You see," she said, her voice grainy and soft, "It's not about sex, Miles; I mean, I'm not just certain what it is, but it's not just that. And you and I weren't really tight, you know. I mean we didn't really have an agreement not to see other people."

Miles stopped her with an explosion of words. Out of the very center of her bittersweet monologue he had chosen the one word that disturbed him the most: sex.

"Not just sex!" he said loudly, lifting up his head and piercing Eliza with his clear eyes. Then, more quietly, "Shit.

Oh, God. My God, Eliza, Billy just said you were 'seeing' him, that's all. I didn't think—"

Eliza took his gaze and turned it back on him. She sounded a little angry, but it was the kind of anger one would feel towards a child. "Didn't think what?" she said. "I don't believe you. Of course you thought I might sleep with him, didn't you? How could you not think it? We're not talking about going to a prom or something. If we're going to talk about this at all, Miles, I think we'll have to be honest."

I thought she was being a little hard on him, but I told myself I didn't know the whole story. After all, Eliza had told me once that Miles was still "half in love" with his old girlfriend. Maybe he'd hurt her too. God, they were so young.

Miles was valiantly fighting back tears. He pulled his face into his coat again, turtle-fashion. "Yeah," he said.

Eliza was blushing. "I'm sorry that I hurt you," she said again. "This is a very hard time for me, Miles. I know you don't understand it—I barely do myself—but you must at least know I never set out to hurt you." She reached out to him again and he took her hand, then she moved over and sat leaning against him. They looked like Hansel and Gretel in the forest of evil.

"No," he said, "I never thought you set out to hurt me. It just does."

They didn't say anything for a long time then, and after a while the scene faded from me. This usually happened when the useful part of a vision was over. Most of the time I learned something, whether practical (like the fact that other people actually knew Eliza and I were lovers), or psychological (like the fact that, in spite of my monumental neediness when I knew Eliza, I was never her only lover). Sometimes my visions merely served to underscore what I already deeply realized, like the fact that the masses of things Eliza and I never knew about one another could have easily filled the pyramids of Egypt. This scene had unnerved me. Had I been alive, I would have recited a book to calm myself. I guess I always believed that a book could deflect a bullet.

14. Sarah, Lost and Found

Although it seemed quite endless at the time, my affair with Sarah Bowe really only lasted a few months. It did not begin beautifully, so I do not know why its supremely un-beautiful ending should have surprised me so.

It did, however. I was, for however brief a time, completely crushed. I thought I had found in Sarah the woman of my dreams: that blend of softness, toughness, intelligence, and pure intuition the pricelessness of which I had been too green to appreciate when I was courting Frances. I was careful with myself when I first fell for Sarah; I suspected, I think, that I was riding for a fall, but I never dreamed I would fall so hard or be so severely injured.

Let me return, briefly, to earlier days. For a time, after the mind-boggling Wally Mussel dinner party, I somehow lost touch with Sarah for a while. I did call her, of course, to tell her of the vile event that had taken place in my home, but, to my astonishment, this seemed to ignite her paranoia in a rather dramatic fashion. Perhaps she suspected me of being some kind of spy from his camp, or perhaps it was simply that my innocent proximity to him for one evening was enough to taint me irrevocably in her eyes. Whatever it was, I felt a cool breeze immediately. I was not able, as I had hoped, to discover anything more about Mussel that Sarah could use as armor against him, and when I suggested to her that she leave town for a while (even offering her the cabin and promising not to bother her there) she greeted my idea with something approaching hysteria. When she finally calmed down, she apologized to me, told me she was sorry she'd involved me in her problems, and begged that I not concern myself any further with the whole mess. It was appalling. She drew back from me as if I had waved an unsheathed sabre in her direction; I had no idea what had ignited such fear.

My family was moving house, however, at that time, and that project so engulfed me, physically and mentally, for so many weeks, that I was unable to dwell on Sarah's predicament. Whenever it did come to mind, I pushed it away. I always ended up seeing the same horrendous picture: Mussel approaching Sarah and sliding his puffy, greasy palms over her finely sculpted shoulders and breasts. I knew I would see her again and try anew to help her, but I put it off and off, grateful for the distractions of the move and the mysteries of settling Frances and the boys into a new town and myself into a new job.

We had found a pleasant if somewhat humbler house (prices were so much higher in our new state), and the boys seemed to be adjusting nicely to the neighborhood. Frances was not thrilled with the place, but she tried to be cheerful and speak of the "possibilities." This frightened me a little, but I ignored her for the most part. I knew that soon enough her "possibilities" would make me miserable: no need to hurry things along. When the fall semester began, I found my classes stimulating and the rest of the faculty agreeable if not exciting. Don Rath was, of course, right down the hall, and that arrangement was truly a boon to me. We began to visit one another's lairs quite often, and I grew fond of him quickly. He was always up on things; his lively imagination never flagged; and he was very, very clever and funny. Little did I know in those early days at NSU how faithful and valuable a friend Don Rath would prove to be.

It was not until the day before the Christmas break that I had my next real encounter with Sarah Bowe. Oh I had run into her many times, but she had always made it clear that she was (a) in a big hurry to be somewhere else, and (b) unwilling to have any conversation with me more meaningful than one she might share with the UPS deliveryman. I was saddened by her attitude, but I did not press. There was, I think, an air of danger about her—the sort of thing one feels from certain patients on the edge of a shattering breakthrough—and I did not want to push her in any direction at all. I surmised that, like my pretty little Cybèle, she would come closer when she was ready. But Sarah, as it turned out, was really not the person in my life who would prove to be like Cybèle at all.

It was an oddly warm day for the twentieth of December in New Jersey, and I could see from my office window that the few students who had not yet left the campus for the holidays were frolicking about on the green in front of the student union building as if it were May. There was no snow on the ground (this amazed me, having spent so many years in Vermont, where December was always as white as a luxury liner from stem to stern), and they wore bright scarves, their long hair flying in the breeze like carefree flags. It looked, in fact, like a jolly sort of postcard, and I decided to chuck my reading and go outside. I felt fine, but a little lonely. Frances was, at that very moment, decorating the house for

the holidays as if it were Rockefeller Plaza, and while I knew
she wanted me to come directly home and do things like nail
evergreen swags along the tops of the windows, I could not
bear the idea. If I left the office, she would not be able to reach
me. Her last phone call, when she demanded that I bring home
more mistletoe, had left me somewhat depressed. I decided to
go to the cafeteria, acquire a foamy hot chocolate, and bring
it outside to one of the benches in the sun. That is where I
found Sarah, and to my surprise she looked really glad to see
me. She lifted her own paper cup to mine in a toast and smiled.

"Happy holidays, Jack," she said.

"And to you, Dr. Bowe."

She laughed. "Please sit down," she said, "Unless you've
got a better offer."

I sat. I didn't know what to make of it, but I wasn't com-
plaining. Fifteen minutes before I had been cold and lonesome
and now there I was sitting in the sun sipping a delicious drink,
accompanied by a friendly, beautiful woman. I did not speak; I
thought she should set the ground rules. We sipped on silently
for a few minutes, then a young student couple walked by, arm
in arm. They looked blissful. Sarah sighed, and I looked at her.
In spite of my decision not to talk, I had to ask her.

"How have you been, Sarah?" It was not a rhetorical question, nor did she take it as one.

She looked at me, hard. I noticed that her previously flaw-
less complexion was marred slightly by a dry tightness around
her mouth and a puffiness under her eyes that bespoke spiritual
weariness more than physical fatigue. Her eyes were filling up
with tears. And all I had done was ask her how she was.

"Okay," she finally said, with a rueful smile. And then, "Not
too hot, I'm afraid, if you want the truth."

It was some kind of opening, however small. "I've wondered

about you a lot, Sarah," I said. I decided to be terse, to let her do most of talking. After all, I told myself, she had withdrawn from me after some startlingly personal confessions, much the way a patient will, for a while, after a particularly revealing session. It was my training to wait.

"I'll bet," was all she said. We sipped our chocolates for a while longer.

"Sarah?"

"Oh, Jack," she said, staring down into her cup. "I am so truly sorry." I started to interrupt her, but she went on quickly. "I've been horrible to you. You were very, very kind to me, and I dropped you cold. I won't ask you to forgive me, but I beg you to believe it was nothing personal." She stared into her cup and said nothing for a moment, then went on.

"I've been a very screwed-up lady, as my students would say. I guess I don't know what I'm doing half the time. I just felt like I had to stay away from you for a while, not involve you any more in my sordid story.

"But," she said shyly, reaching out a soft, gloved hand in my direction, "I did miss you a great deal."

I met Sarah's hand in midair and held it tightly with both of mine. My heart was thumping so hard I was sure it was audible inside the nearby buildings. The fact that my feelings for Sarah had leapt so immediately to the fore at her slightest bidding truly amazed me. She began to cry a little. I made a stupid joke, hoping it would distract her.

"I believe this is where I came in," I said. She laughed; it was a good sign. I held her hand for a second or two more and then I asked her, "Does this mean we're friends again, or is it simply a little Christmas cheer you're spreading, Doctor?"

"Friends?" she said, a little, I thought, flirtatiously, and then, "Yes, absolutely—friends."

"That's wonderful. I always buy my friends a cup of holiday eggnog," I told her. "If you wish to remain my friend, you will have to oblige me on this point."

Sarah looked at her watch and made a face. Then she said, "The hell with it. Okay, yes, thank you, Jack. I could use a drink… I mean, you're speaking of grownup eggnog, I hope."

"Extremely grown up," I told her. "Let's go."

On the way to the inn, Sarah suggested we buy the ingredients for our drink and go to her apartment instead. Grace Rinkette, she told me, was away for the holidays: we could enjoy the fireplace in Grace's wonderful old rooms all by ourselves. I took a long breath, hesitating only long enough to fortify myself for the temptations I knew were coming.

Sarah took my hesitation as a question. "He's out of town too," she said.

"Good," I said. "But actually, that isn't what I was thinking." I could tell she didn't believe me, but she set about concocting our drinks, and after a couple of heftily laced glasses of nog, none of the past seemed to matter. Within an hour or so I felt I could lie happily in Sarah Bowe's arms for the rest of my days. After a while we pulled ourselves reluctantly back into our clothes (out of respect to Grace Rinkette, I suppose, whose vintage sofa we had blessed with our modern-day lovemaking) and lay sprawled on cushions before the last of the roaring fire I had so hastily created. All the weariness had left Sarah's face; she looked like a Christmas angel. I told her I wanted to put her on the top of a tree. It was a foolish thing to say, but she kissed me for it.

She kissed me for almost everything, in fact; she seemed truly starved for affection, and I suppose she was—starved for someone to whom she might give her affection even more than for someone to spend his affection on her. I teased her. I told her she'd have to keep her hands to herself in the hallways at school and not be mauling me all the time in front of the students. She laughed and kissed me for that too.

"I'm not sure I can," she said.

"I don't think I really want you to," I said. She kissed me again. The next thing I knew it was very dark outside. I had to go home. It wasn't at all easy.

15. Eliza's Inheritance

I left nearly everything to Eliza in my will. The fact that I had not seen her, spoken to her, or even heard from or about her in years did not matter to me at all. Although I had no proof whatsoever, I knew in my heart of hearts that Eliza had been thinking of me all through that time.

I had had dreams in which we had spoken to each other, and they were as real to me as any everyday conversation. Perhaps I was simply an old, sick fool, but I didn't think so. Just before I left NSU, I had the document drawn up by a local lawyer who had never seen me before and therefore had no reason to cross-examine my motives. I asked a friend to witness the thing for me and assure me that it did indeed say what I had intended it should. My priest son and my barber son were left a few personal mementos, of course, but neither of them really needed anything from me anymore. There was no one else. Except for a small bequest to my favorite animal-rights group in memory of Cybèle, the bulk of my estate was to go to Eliza Harder. Now I know, unfortunately, what a bleak and fruitless gesture that was. I did have some money when I died. In spite of the large chunks my illness had forced me to cull from my accounts, there was still quite a bit of money there, and I knew that if Eliza did not need it for herself she would find a good place for it. Maybe she even had children, (though I somehow felt I would have known if she did) and she could spend the money on them. At any rate, this bequest would let her know she was never forgotten.

I suppose it did do that, but recently I happened in on a strange scene in my lawyer's office. At first, I could not understand what I was seeing, or why it had been brought to my attention; then Eliza came into the room. She looked very serious and was dressed up oddly in a long skirt and out-of-fashion blouse; I imagined she had hastily thrown the outfit together for this peculiar occasion. The lawyer, a nice-mannered fellow in his fifties, asked her to sit down.

"As you know, Miss Harder, from our phone conversation, Dr. John Tilford MacLeod has bequeathed almost his entire estate to you. Before I read you the parts of his will that pertain to your situation, I'm afraid I have some unsettling news."

Eliza gave him a sarcastic look. "What could be more unsettling than his death?" she said. I had to chuckle. She was being a naughty girl.

Lawyers rarely reveal imbalance. "As you say," he assented. "I regret, as I told you on the telephone, that I had to be the one to deliver that sad news. But the unfortunate fact is, Miss Harder, that although you were named beneficiary to what Dr. MacLeod no doubt believed to be a rather sizable estate at the time he signed his will, it now appears that your inheritance really amounts to very little—next to nothing, in fact, except for some books, papers, and photographs found in the late doctor's apartment."

Eliza said nothing.

"And," the lawyer went on, "I must tell you that Dr. MacLeod's sons, Father Mark MacLeod and Mr. Harry MacLeod, have asked me to inquire if you might be kind enough to share with them some of the family photographs their father left behind."

"Of course," said Eliza. She said nothing more. The good lawyer was obviously baffled.

"Do you have any questions, Miss Harder?"

"What kind of books did Jack leave me?" she asked him.

"I am sure we can supply you with an inventory very soon," he told her. "But what I meant was, do you have any questions regarding the disposition of the funds that were to have made up the bequest?"

"Not really," Eliza said. "Money gets used up. I suppose there must have been a great many bills to pay after Jack died. Was that it? Never mind, I don't really need to know. I don't have any right to any of his money anyway; that should have gone to his family. Please tell his sons I will send them, through your office, if I may, almost all the photographs. I'll only want to keep a few, I think. I will keep his papers. And the books—or as many as I can make room for. I'd appreciate that inventory as soon as possible."

She had begun speaking slowly but had sped up towards the end until her last words were something of a blur. She was quietly crying.

The nice lawyer fellow slid a box of tissues across his desk. She thanked him. "This is still all very surprising to me," she told him. "I'm sorry."

"No need, no need," he said kindly. "I don't have to know your story to see how this death has upset you. I will send you Dr. MacLeod's papers and photographs as soon as his rooms are formally closed, and an inventory of his books as well.

Until you decide about them, I think we can probably store them here. Will that be satisfactory?"

"Oh, yes," Eliza said, smiling at last. "And thank you so much for your help. You've been very kind."

They shook hands. "Do call me if you think of any questions later," he said. "People often do, you know, and that's what I'm here for."

Eliza left his office and started slowly down the street, weeping quietly as she walked. The fact that my money had somehow been eaten away after my death shocked me, but it did not upset me as much as the fact that Eliza had been told of my demise by a stranger. I should have thought of that. At least she would have all my Patchen books now, and all the poems and letters I'd written to her those last years that she had never seen. Maybe it would make up a little for my going. Maybe she would know—even more fully than she already must have known—that I would always be available to her, even after my death. Maybe she would understand my death a little better; maybe it would help her somehow, sometime.

16. I Listen to Eliza's Dream

Even more amazing than the fact that I am able to eavesdrop (if one can use that word without the restrictions of time—meaning that I eavesdrop on the present and the past with equal clarity), is the fact that I have been able, a few unforgettable times, to see what a person has dreamed. I should say to see what Eliza has dreamed, because so far her dreams have been the only ones accessible to me. My still-extant, still insufferable ego allows me to imagine that this gift has been given to me because of the unusual, extrasensory bond that Eliza and I shared—that little mystical pull our spirits exerted on one another—but it may simply be true that these dreams, like the more normal scenes I have witnessed, are meant to teach me things I ought to learn. I wish I could say I am always certain of the particular meaning I am supposed to discover.

What follows is one of Eliza's dreams, told in her own words. That is how it was revealed to me, with the accompaniment of her very own voice, soft and unaffected, as if she were speaking it privately into a tape recorder. I have not developed

far enough on my present plane to understand how this voice-
over came to be, or if Eliza herself, on some mysterious level,
was conscious of creating it. How wonderful to learn that
she did not, in fact, forget me—that she was or is still able to
receive some kind of spiritual tidings from me, even after the
passage of so much earthly time.

∽∽∞∞∞∞∞∞∽

> "I dreamed of Jack in a blue silk hat.
> Death had made him very tall and wise.
> He'd come to tell me it was time to go,
> but I would not follow, though it made me cry."

I woke up with those lines in front of my eyes because last
night I had a very vivid dream about Jack MacLeod, the first
such dream in quite a while. He's been dead for about twelve
years and I still sometimes have these incredibly clear dreams
about him. I know it might seem crazy, but I do believe he is
my patron saint or guardian angel, and that he comes to me
in times of stress with these dreams for me to solve however
I can, though I must admit his messages are often puzzling to
me. Puzzling, but never troubling. They are always something
of a comfort, and I am always thrilled with them, and grateful
they have come to me.

Here is my dream. I am getting out of a car with a family
of strangers: a woman, a man, and a little girl of about ten. The
parents are dressed up as if for church; they are nice-looking
middle-class types. The girl is dressed up too: a fitted spring
coat, navy blue, with a flared skirt, white buttons, and white
collar. She's wearing a round white hat with an upturned brim
and a wide band of dark ribbon. We're in a very crowded train
station, like the kind one sees in old European movies. Jack

gets off the train. He seems about seven feet tall and is dressed in a camel hair coat and a tall Mad Hatter silk hat of a beautiful light turquoise color. He's wearing thick round glasses, wire-rimmed, and looks quite well, but serious.

I run to give him a welcoming embrace, but he tries to turn it into a passionate kiss. I know he's very glad to see me too, but he still looks so serious, although I am smiling. He pushes himself into the back seat of the car next to the little girl.

My husband Lou is sitting on the other side of her. Jack has one leg still outside the car and I have to push him over to make room for myself. Jack is whispering to the little girl and she's shaking her head gently. She looks at him with sadness and whispers back, "I don't want to go now." Suddenly it hits me that the little girl is me and I feel, absurdly, slightly jealous of myself. I want her to disappear, but at the same time feel very close to her.

We're on our way to a restaurant. I've been holding Jack's hat. I'm spellbound by its formal shape and beautiful color. I go into a long meditation on the hat, and it makes me very happy. I realize the hat is the same color as Jack's eyes. At the restaurant, I sit next to him and keep trying to introduce him to my husband, who's sitting across the round table from us. I long for Lou to move closer so that I can reassure him that nothing is wrong, but he seems oblivious to me. Jack and I talk, and in spite of the fact that we only speak of trivial things, our conversation is charged with importance and deep feeling, and again the great seriousness on his side and the unfettered happiness on mine.

Silent, turbaned waiters in white outfits serve us a marvelous dinner: delicate fish filets wrapped in something apricot-colored and one other interesting greenish dish. I am very hungry, nearly starving; the food smells wonderful, but

I do not eat. I notice that Jack is not eating either, and I think, "that's because he's dead." Then suddenly we're at a long picnic table outside on a high terrace instead of being inside a crowded restaurant. Jack and I are at the end of the table, across from each other. Off to my right, and below us (we are very high—treetop level) I see something floating in the air beyond the trees: a large and semi-transparent flying squirrel, drifting on the breeze. I call to everyone to come look at this apparition and we all go to the railing; then the squirrel turns first into a baby and then into a cloud. The sky is the same gorgeous blue as Jack's hat and eyes.

I woke up then; though the images were vivid I couldn't get back into the dream. I felt a tender love for Lou and another kind of deep tenderness toward Jack, but I couldn't quite reach or understand him in the dream: his gravity was puzzling and somehow sad. When I knew he was dead in the dream (and for the second time in one of these dreams) I didn't know how to treat him. Is his spirit not at rest? Or, more likely I suppose, is he trying to teach me something I'm not yet ready to learn? I do long for him sometimes. Oh Jack, we were so unfinished.

17. I Steal an Ashtray

Someone once told me an old folk tale. A man, searching for truth, finally finds it in the form of an ugly, wretched, but very wise old woman who lives in a hovel on a remote mountaintop. He spends a year and a day with her, and then the time comes that he feels he is ready to leave, to carry her message back to the world. When he is about to start back down the mountain, he asks the woman what she would like him to tell people about her. "Tell them," she says, "that I am young and beautiful."

That story always touched and mystified me. I thought of it the morning I learned that Sarah Bowe had married Wally Mussel. "Take my word for it; I'm a compulsive liar." Sarah never said that, but she might as well have. I couldn't have been any more confused if she had.

Fortunately for my sanity, I did not learn of this unholy union until after she had broken off our affair. Sarah and Mussel were married a few months before we broke up, but I did not know it: if I had, I cannot say what I might have tried to do. While I was alive, and up until the day I died—and yes, as you will see, I certainly did think of Sarah that day—I held the opinion that Sarah Bowe, for all her outward manifestations of health and sweetness, was a severely troubled person. I hesitated to slap any psychological labels on her, but I held some in reserve. However, after my death, I was suffused with a peculiar certainty that Sarah was, not "troubled," but simply not *good*. I know that's a strange thing for a psychologist to say, and I'm afraid I cannot precisely tell you what it means, but it has less to do with whether or not one accepts the usual guidelines of what a good person does and does not do, and more with a pervasive feeling one identifies within oneself regarding the existence of good, or, more to the point, evil. This feeling—this inner knowing—had begun to grow in me even before I started to catch sight of scenes from Sarah's life. I don't want to describe those scenes in detail here; they just make me sad, and no purpose would be served by recounting them. Suffice it to say that Sarah sowed unrest everywhere she went.

The terrible truth is this: Sarah married Mussel of her own free will, having eventually, I suppose, come to enjoy his attentions, which were nothing at all like the attentions she'd described to me. She was not only caught in but one of the chief weavers of a web of drama and falsehoods, and I don't understand exactly why—maybe I will someday.

It is also true that after I'd left NSU, having told Mussel about my relationship with his then wife, that Sarah told him I had beaten and blackmailed her during our relationship. She told him I was a violent, devious man, and that only my illness had saved her. Mussel of course swallowed this whole, since it was the very kind of behavior he had invested in all his life. I'd always known that there were people who believed in the power of evil, but I suppose I called them religious, superstitious, or even hysterical. I never really believed a person could be "possessed by the devil," or "infused with the spirit of God," or any of the other clichés people generally use. When I encountered persons whose actions seemed inexplicable in the light of what we know about the human mind, it confused me mightily. The horrifying cases of small children who murder, for example: how does one explain those away? And myriad other cases, criminal and otherwise, come to mind—cases that involve persons seemingly wholly without morals (we call them sociopaths, for want of a better label), persons who seem to take inordinate joy in causing pain, or sometimes even persons who seem inexplicably unable to cause anything *but* pain.

Perhaps it's the soul, and not the mind, that is involved in such cases, and perhaps that is why I understand it all a little better now that I'm no longer living. In any case, I find it difficult now to see Sarah Bowe in any other light. She had me, at least, entirely fooled—fooled to such a lofty degree that I fell head over heels in love with her. If anyone should have been able to see the signs of her mental or spiritual decomposition, it was I, but I never did. I guess I wasn't in such good mental shape myself—or maybe I'm just not as smart as everyone says I am.

While I was living, I thought Sarah was troubled, nothing more. I thought, optimistically, that although there was no doubt she would eventually require some kind of professional assistance to straighten out her life and restore her good opinion of herself, she would someday be completely well, and my vision of a Sarah wholly well was a vision of a very remarkable and lovable woman indeed. When Sarah and I started up our affair, I became instantly and deliriously happy. Far from entering into the problem-ridden relationship I would have imagined for us, we were able, almost effortlessly, to slide from what might have been an affair beleaguered by sordid, weary discussions of Wally Mussel and my family obligations into a world that seemed created just for us. All lovers have such a world, of course; but most lovers, thank goodness, don't have such enormous and maleficent hellhounds crashing at the gates.

I know now, and indeed I knew at the time, that I should never have allowed Sarah to push the Mussel problem so far under our rug, but I simply could not bear to hear too much about him: it made me feel powerless and enraged. I preferred, idiotically, to ignore the subject whenever possible. I knew that Sarah was probably still under his thumb at the same time that she spent so many hours in my arms, but unless Sarah mentioned him we did not broach the subject at all.

I was still searching then, of course, for the key that would unlock Mussel's comeuppance, but I had nothing solid to go on, so my search was more or less a psychic one; I suppose I thought I would someday simply happen upon the answer and all would be well. And it did, in fact, happen almost that way—it happened upon me, that is, though all was not well—but I will explain that later.

A red light should have gone off somewhere along the way for me owing simply to the fact that Sarah seemed not to mind my being married. We would, on occasion, fantasize about how lovely life would be if we were married to each other, and I did, on occasion (although it made me feel oddly cheap and disloyal), explain to her how Frances and I were no longer at all in love, but, unlike most women who have serious affairs with married men, Sarah never tried to find out if I intended to get a divorce from Frances in order to marry her. Had she asked it of me, even casually, I think I would have accomplished both feats in a minute. It might have even solved all our problems—who knows? She never even asked me if I were still sleeping with Frances, a natural question I always expected to hear. It did hurt me a little, this avoidance of such a looming topic, but I assumed it had something to do with the Mussel problem—another looming topic, and one that I was guilty of avoiding assiduously. Two psychologists, both in deep denial. We were quite a pair.

And yet I was so happy when we were together. We'd steal away from our offices sometimes and drive to a little isolate woodland stream we'd discovered in nearby New York state. The bird life there was almost deafening, and the clarity of the cool water, racing along toward some distant sea, made me remember a favorite place of mine in childhood—another hidden stream where sometimes we children would wade and even bathe in the icy water in our shorts and tee shirts. When the sunlight was able to make its way through the vast curtains of leaves, it would light up the dragonflies and water-striders as if they were neon.

In the colder weather, Sarah and I would walk around and talk for a while until it got too cold, then we'd go to a motel and make love. When it was warm enough, we'd have lovely picnics there, then go to a motel and make love. One time, just before our breakup, we made love to each other in a billow of fallen leaves, with leaves still falling around us. It was cold and uncomfortable; it was bliss. We then proceeded to our motel.

So the months went by, and the months went by. I found Sarah infinitely attractive, interesting, and sweet. She seemed to care as much for me; in fact, I would have sworn to it. The whole thing was slightly marred of course, as these things always are, by the clandestine nature of our union, but it seemed to me, after years of feeling more or less unfulfilled, a small price to pay for the happiness that loving Sarah brought me. I thought we were successful enough at school in keeping our relationship secret; perhaps the only one who guessed was Donald Rath, with whom I had become rather close. I never came right out and told him, but I know he knew.

When Sarah came to me one rainy afternoon in my office, I was more delighted to see her than ever because the bit of sleuthing Don Rath and I had done on her behalf had yielded some remarkable results. I was bursting to tell her that what we'd found out about Mussel might eventually free not only her but all of us in the department from his unsavory influence— and that this fabulous feat could easily be pulled off without involving her at all. I whisked her into my office and closed and locked the door (this was unwise, and would have made our meeting a little awkward to explain had anyone knocked, but I was so happy to see her that I'd thrown that particular caution to the winds). But instead of returning my embrace as she always did, she walked slowly to my bookshelf, turned on the radio, took a seat across from my desk and lit a cigarette. Sarah smoked only when under extreme stress. I knew she had turned on the radio to eliminate the chance that anyone outside might overhear our conversation. She looked around distractedly for somewhere to put her ashes, so I offered her my shoe. Normally, Sarah found my shenanigans quite amusing. That day she did not laugh; she did not even acknowledge my gesture. She pulled the wastebasket over to her, selected a used paper cup from its contents, and flicked her cigarette into that. "Jack," she said, "I've something terrible to tell you."

Here it comes, I thought, she's going to talk about Mussel. I steeled myself. I told myself I had it coming; the poor girl had probably been storing up awful stories for months, afraid to tell me anything at all that might bring her down in my eyes.

Why should she have to carry such a crippling burden alone? Wasn't I, her lover, supposed to soothe and succor? I had been selfishly allowing her to hide her worst moments from me and she had finally broken under the strain.

"What is it, dearest?" I said, very slowly and kindly. I pulled my desk chair out, rolled across the carpet, and sat facing her. I took her hands, which were limp and cold. She shrugged me off. I stood up.

"Sarah, my poor duck," I told her. "It can't be that bad. Tell me what's bothering you and then I'll make it all go away: I've got some terrific news that'll make you feel so much better."

She gave me a despairing look. "I don't think you can make this go away," she said.

"Mussel?" I asked her.

"No."

In spite of my resolve to bravely confront the worst, I was relieved; I felt almost happy. The thought flashed through my mind that she might be pregnant, but the joy of that idea was instantly lessened by the crushing fear that any pregnancy Sarah might embark on could be the product of a less pure love than ours. I couldn't even say the word Mussel in my mind in connection with the whole idea, so I banished the thought.

"Then what's so terrible?" I asked her. "Let me help you. I can't bear to see you feeling so sad."

She brushed some damp hair off her forehead and looked me straight in the eye.

"I can't see you anymore, Jack," she said.

It did not really register.

"Don't be ridiculous," I told her. "What's wrong?"

But she was already standing up, and when I reached out to her she nearly pushed me over trying to get away. It was then I panicked. I think I yelled.

"Sarah, NO!"

She turned up the radio. She said, "Keep your voice down." She sounded tired, but worse than that, she sounded cold. I hardly recognized her voice; all I knew was that the earth was slipping out from under me. I sat down on a corner of the desk.

She leaned against the filing cabinet. I had to get her to talk to me.

"What is it, Sarah? Don't say these things to me. Tell me what the trouble is—we can fix it . . ." I started to get up to go to her, but she extended both arms and held out her hands palms forward and fingers spread as if she were fending off a predator. The look on her face was foreign to me. I sat back down. I just stared at her.

She did not cry. She did not try to comfort me or soften the blow in any way. She offered no explanation, nor would she allow me to question her; whenever I tried, she would raise her hands again in that gesture of refusal. I hardly remember what she said, but I think she simply repeated, over and over, "I can't see you anymore, Jack. I just can't see you anymore."

The shock was too great: I began to weep soundlessly, huge tears plopping rapidly onto my tie and jacket as if shot from my eyes. Even my tears, which she had never, I think, seen before, did not move her. She seemed to be wearing a mask of white clay; her lovely eyes had hardened so that they looked like the fixed, blank, staring eyes of a marble statue. I went back around my desk to try to find some tissues, and when I looked back she was gone. I had not heard the door open or close, but she was gone.

That afternoon I told the department secretary I felt suddenly ill and asked her to post my classes as cancelled. I drove out to our woodland stream. I sat down on a fallen tree close to where Sarah and I had made love the week before. It was a very warm day; a group of starlings had established themselves in the surrounding half-naked trees and were making an insanely loud, angry racket, of which I approved. The stream trickled lazily over its rocks. The sun made knife-sharp shadows. I sat there unmoving, in my suit jacket, for several hours, sweating copiously and feeling utterly blank. I could not "think straight"; in fact, I could not think at all.

When I looked at my watch it was close to six o'clock. I rinsed my face in the icy water and drove to our motel. I rented our room. I went in and sat on the bed, turned on the television, and watched the end of the six o'clock news. A man in south Jersey had murdered an elderly woman and stolen three dollars from her purse. The picture they showed of the dead woman reminded me of my mother, whom I had not seen in some time. I suddenly wanted to see her badly. I considered driving to her house in Connecticut, then remembered she was on a cruise. I noticed that Walter Cronkite looked quite tired. I wondered how old he was, if he were married. A heavy, dreadful feeling, as if I had forgotten something, was giving me a headache. Suddenly I realized I had forgotten to tell Sarah what we'd discovered about Mussel. Would it have changed anything? I tried to use the bathroom, but I didn't need to, so I simply sat there for a while gazing at the overly bleached, stiff white towels. One of them had a small, rust-colored stain along the edge that I at first took to be an insect; I stared at it for quite some time, until I was sure the stain had moved. Back in the bedroom, I took an ashtray from the bureau and put it in my pocket. Then I drove home.

18. Listen to My Nothing

As I've told you before, the poems I wrote to Eliza (I gave her only five or six of them while I was alive, but there were many more among the papers I left her) were pretty dismal altogether as poetry, but every now and then I'd hit a few lines I wasn't ashamed of, like "There was a time/ in the wake of winter/ when we were less better off than we are now." There was something formal and sad and *me* about that sentence that I always found appealing, and thinking about it makes me remember how I began my memoirs, for I began to record them around the same time I wrote that poem.

It was while I was seeing Eliza that I began this project, and I intended the tapes to go, eventually, to her. There was no one else I needed to tell my story to, and I certainly did not consider it literary. There were too many memoirs out there in the world already, in my opinion. To expedite matters, and to spare my eyes, I spoke my memories into a tape recorder, a huge, clumsy machine I'd picked up at a discount place. Each evening—or whenever I could—for several months, I would talk to the machine, and each night it became easier and easier for me, until memories and thoughts began to flood out of me in a steady and fairly articulate stream. I made no effort to edit anything—for one thing, I was afraid to tamper too much with the recorder, which came with a little booklet of instructions in print far too tiny for me to read—but mostly I didn't want to interrupt the flow. It was fascinating to me; I had never attempted anything like it before, and I had never had the chance to spin out the whole of my life without feeling as if I were overwhelming someone. It was also greatly fatiguing, and sometimes I felt like the Ancient Mariner, "stuck, nor breath, nor motion;/As idle as a painted ship/Upon a painted ocean," but I persisted.

I did not fear that my story would overwhelm Eliza, for I knew her to be sensible enough to take it in small doses—or not at all, if that suited her better. This spinning out of my life's tale went on, as I mentioned, for some months, and then I became careless. I had never wanted Eliza to know what I was doing, but one night she almost caught me in the act. I had given her a key to the apartment at her request, in case of an emergency, but she had never used it. That night, however, she had planned to surprise me. I'd told her on the phone, earlier in the day, that I was planning to stay late at school for a departmental meeting, but as the afternoon dragged on I found myself too weary to risk a drive home in the dark, and so had left the office at my usual time.

After dinner I turned out the lights (it loosened me up, I felt) and began to speak to the machine; it had a trance-like effect on me. So consumed by my task that evening was I that I did not hear Eliza come in, and when she turned on the light in the living room I nearly had a seizure. She too was frightened: there she was, standing frozen in an arena of light, her eyes as huge as those Frisbees my boys used to play with, with one hand clapped over her mouth. Once we recognized each other we began to laugh. She dropped whatever it was she had been holding, let out a whoop of dismay, and fell doubled up onto the couch. I went over to her and fell upon her with kisses. She sat up suddenly.

"My God, Jack," she said. "Oh Jack, this is so funny. I mean it's terrible—I dropped my cake!"

She went over to the box she had dropped in the middle of the rug, opened it, and howled with horror. "Oh, no!" she said. "It's completely ruined—I dropped it on its head!" I then realized that she'd also been carrying some flowers wrapped in a flounce of tissue.

"Never mind," I told her. "What on earth is going on here? You're certainly the nicest burglar I've had in some time, and I'm delighted to see you, but would you please tell me what this is all about? Is it your birthday or something?"

Eliza sat down next to me and sighed, still laughing a little. "It's nobody's birthday," she said, "but when you told me you'd be late coming home tonight I decided to surprise you. Remember when you told me how you'd loved pineapple upside-down cake as a child? I made one for you! And there it is on the floor—really upside down! Oh, poor cake. Poor Jack. I'm so sorry I scared you!"

"You're too good to me, goose," I said, truly touched. "What a sweet thing to do. And flowers too?"

"That was an afterthought." She stopped for a moment, then reached out a hand to me, very shyly. "Peonies. I wanted you to open the door and smell them when you came home tonight." She stopped again. "I thought it might make up a little for some of the things you can't see."

I reached up and found some tears on her face and kissed them away. Then I tickled her until she begged for mercy; I was so shaken by her kindness that I was afraid we'd both go on a crying jag if I didn't jolly us out of it. Suddenly I realized the tape recorder was still on and got up to turn it off. Eliza was very interested.

"What's this?" she asked, and then, "Oh, I mean, you don't have to tell me. I'm sorry I interrupted. Never mind; I can't stay anyway. I promised to take my mother shopping tonight." She pulled on her hat and started to pick up the cake box and flowers.

I stopped her. "Just a minute here," I said. "Not so fast. First of all, I don't care what that cake looks like—I mean to have a piece. And I hate to eat alone. And my peonies need some water, and arrangement by a feminine hand. And speaking of feminine hands . . ." I picked up her hand, turned it over. and kissed the palm. "Thank you, love," I told her. "You've cheered me immensely."

"You're welcome," she said, solemnly. "And I'd love to stay, but I really do have to go." Then she bent down over the recorder and flicked some switches. "Jack," she said, "I hope you weren't doing any important work just now. This machine isn't recording anything. It's going around and around, but the tape is unhooked from the reel."

"Nuts," I said. "I guess it pays to read the directions. Never mind, I wasn't that important. I can do it again."

"Would you like me to rewind it for you?"

"No, thanks. I think, if you really have to desert me, I'll just take a bath and go to bed . . . unless you can be persuaded to join me?"

She laughed and kissed me, very, very nicely. "I wish I could," she said, "but I'll see you tomorrow," and she made her exit. I remember feeling cold; it was as if a charming spirit had left the room.

I had a piece of the delicious, mangled cake (it was still, miraculously, rather warm) and then went back to the machine and loaded into it, one by one, all the previous tapes. They were all blank. I carried the tapes into the bathroom, put them in the tub, and ran scalding water over them from the shower. I knew that action was unnecessary and weird, but it felt correct and ceremonial. Then I shoved them all in a plastic garbage bag and set them outside my door for the trash collector. I looked hard into the bathroom mirror.

"You blasted fool," I told myself. "You poor, sick, pitiful fool."

The world would have to march forward somehow without my memoirs. What a shame.

19. Like an Actress
in a Silent Movie

I think I can say without exaggeration that there was never a single day while I was working at NSU that I did not spend some time thinking about Wally Mussel. It was less of an obsession than a necessity. Don, Frances, Sarah—they were all involved, in one way or another, with this blowhard from academia.

I don't know when I began to suspect that Frances was having an affair, but I'm sure I ignored all the signs until it would have been obvious to any other dead man that something was going on. She and I had finally stopped even making a show of sleeping together a couple of months after the move from Vermont. The new house had two extra bedrooms and I moved into both of them; that is, I alternated nights between them depending on my mood. One room was a little cooler than the other, very pleasant on summer nights, but the second room was larger, and I moved quite a few of my books in there to keep me company. Harry and Mark, of course, were somewhat confused by all this, but I explained to them that Daddy had strange habits like reading all night or tossing and turning like a crazy person that kept Mommy awake unnecessarily. They were just boys. Lying to them was the only unpleasant part of the arrangement; other than that, I found that having my own space apart from Frances was the greatest thing that had happened to me in years. And the months when I was with Sarah were made all the sweeter, of course, by the fact that I could come home and be alone with my feelings and not have to spar with Frances or let her see the lovelight in my eyes.

And yet, somehow, she did see it. I suppose one never loses the ability to see through one's long-time mate, even when love has gone. One night I came home very late after being with Sarah. All the house lights were out, and I assumed that Frances had long since turned in. But as I was making my way to the cooler of my bedrooms, I ran smack into her as she blocked my way in the dark corridor. I let out a little "Eek," but she silenced me right away.

"It's only I—your wife," she said imperiously.

"You startled me, Frances," I said. "Why are you lurking about in the hall?"

"Keep your voice down, please. The boys are asleep."

"Okay," I said, more softly. "May I pass now?"

She stood in front of me, a wall of palpable scorn. She was wearing a caftan sort of thing and had a towel draped over her shoulders as if she'd just washed her hair. Her hair was still very lovely.

"Why don't you just bring the little slut home with you, Jack?" she said in a syrupy voice. "You have so many cozy little bedrooms here in which to screw her." I could see her red lipstick and white teeth reflecting what little light there was in the hallway. She looked like a vampire.

I felt a chill of fear, but it passed in an instant. "Frances, please," I said. "I don't know what you're talking about, but I'm very tired. I want to go to sleep. If we're going to have a big argument, let's have it in the morning."

"Fine," she said. "Fine. But you certainly do know what I'm talking about, and don't you deny it. I don't know yet who she is, but I'll find out. And when I do, I'll divorce you in the ugliest possible way. Not one of your little student geniuses, is it, Jack? That would be simply too cute for words." She laughed a cruel but pain-laced little laugh, then stepped aside for me to walk by her, but I grabbed her by the wrist and marched her into her room—the room that technically belonged to both of us.

I half dragged her over to a chair and sat her down in it, not roughly, but firmly. She looked a little scared. That was good; she was hard to impress. My one thought was that she would find out about Sarah and make the poor girl's already miserable life more miserable still with a scandal. I had to bluff Frances out of it. I had to win this time. I'd gotten so far into the habit of ignoring all Frances's little barbs and bites that I'd nearly forgotten how to deal with her. I had to start remembering fast.

"Frances," I began. "I don't know what put this particular bee in your bonnet, but let me tell you it really pisses me off. I have nothing to hide from anyone except the pain I feel every day when I come home to this wretched, empty farce of a marriage. Maybe you ought to divorce me. Maybe I should divorce *you*. Well, let's do it, I don't care. I didn't turn out to be the big fancy success you wanted; that's been clear to me for years. I'm not enough for you, socially, and I don't make enough money to keep you happy. The boys will be better off in the long run; we've been fools to stay together like this.

"Do it tomorrow if you want to—I want to move on. It's fine with me; in fact, I wish you would. But please don't start staging these moronic little dramas in the middle of the night. For your information, I'm not having an affair, but even if I were, what of it? You and I haven't exactly been cuddly for a long time, have we? Do I have to remind you that you were the one who finally turned me out of this room with your bitter, sarcastic criticism of my last desperate attempt to make love to you?"

I was just beginning to get up a head of steam when I noticed Frances was trembling. She looked absolutely cowed. I did not know what she was afraid of, but I was prepared to do some serious fishing. She did not speak, so I continued.

"You know, Frances," I said, turning to look out the window, "you really take the cake. You don't want me, but you want me to want you. You don't want me, but you don't want anyone else to have me. You don't want me—do you want someone else yourself? Is that it, Frances? Are you trying to make me feel guilty for something *you're* doing? Is that it? Is it?" When I turned back to look at her, I could see I'd reeled in the big one on my first cast. She'd gone absolutely white and was clutching and twisting her hands together like an actress in a silent movie.

"Don't be absurd," she said in a tiny voice.

"Well," I said, "Absurd or not, I just don't care. I don't care what you do, as long as you leave me in peace. You think I'm some kind of wimp, I'm sure, but that's only because I've let you gobble and gabble at me for a long time now without talking back. But it's not because I'm a wimp, Frances—it's because I just don't care." My voice was rising in spite of myself. Part of what I was saying was an act, but part of it was true. It was scary. My marriage was really over.

I looked at Frances to see if she would say anything, but she was still looking down at her lap and twisting her hands, so I left the room. I did not slam the door. I did not even close it after me. I went to my "cool" room, undressed in the dark, and got into bed in my shorts. So, Frances is having an affair too, I thought. It was oddly, quite oddly, surprising. It never occurred to me to wonder who her lover was.

20. Don Tells a Story

I ran into Don Rath the next morning, and we walked over to the cafeteria for coffee. Rath could really put me in a good mood in a few minutes; he was a very clever fellow and could turn the most mundane story into a hilarious tale with the twist of a phrase or two. That morning he began telling me something about an encounter with his mailman that had me in stitches very quickly. It felt wonderful to laugh after the previous night's set-to with Frances. I had awakened feeling soiled and sad.

After our second cup and a cursory discussion of a problem student who was taking classes with both of us, Rath got an uncharacteristically grim look on his face. "Mac," he said, "I've got something to tell you."

He really looked peculiar. He even sounded peculiar. He'd never called me "Mac" before, but I liked it.

"What's that?' I asked him.

Speaking down into his paper cup in a very low voice, he answered, "It's about Mussel."

"Ah." I didn't know what to expect. We hadn't spoken of him, except in jest, in a very long time.

"I think," Don went on, "though I am not positive, mind you, that I've happened on a bit of information that might interest you . . . that is if you're still interested in uncovering Mussel's past?"

I didn't answer him right away. A great many thoughts passed through my mind; I knew this could be a very important conversation. I tried to replay in my mind the talk I'd had with Don in the Hojo's before I'd started teaching. Something odd occurred to me in that connection.

"I am," I answered. "But Don, tell me something. Remember when you and I talked about this over fried clams in Connecticut?"

He smiled. "Sure," he said. "Of course."

"Well, correct me if I'm wrong, but I don't exactly remember telling you that I wanted to 'uncover' Mussel . . . or did I? "

Don smiled again; it was a smile of commiseration teased with a glimmer of mischief. "No," he said, "you didn't exactly tell me that." He paused. "But it's true, isn't it? You want to expose him?" He paused again, and, still smiling but more compassionately than anything else, said, "Because of Sarah?"

I heaved a great sigh and smiled back, ruefully. There was something I truly loved in the man, something I trusted. "Yeah," I said. "How long have you known?"

He patted me on the arm. "Don't worry. I'm pretty sure I'm the only one who knows. I've known for a while—a couple of months, I guess. It was just a hunch at first, and then somehow I felt sure." He got up and went over to the concession counter and brought back a couple of doughnuts, handing me one that was oozing red currant jelly.

"I think it's great." he said. "I mean, I like you both an awful lot, and I can only guess about your home situation—which is none of my business—but I just think it's great that you're making each other happy, that's all. I'm sure you know what you're doing."

I hadn't realized until that moment how lonely keeping secrets could be. It was wonderful having someone know and approve. It was all I could do not to divulge to him right then all the wonders of Sarah Bowe—I wanted to talk and talk and talk about her—but I knew it was more important at that moment to find out what he was going to tell me about Wally Mussel.

"Thanks, Don."

"Don't mention it. And don't worry about me mentioning it, either. I know it's got to be hush-hush. I'm very good at that, as you know." He chuckled.

"Yes, and thanks again. And I want to know everything you know—about Sarah's situation that is—but not right now, okay? What were you going to tell me about Mussel? "

"Oh, him. Do you remember reading last year about a fellow named Richard Collins-Spear?"

"No, I don't think so. Who's that?"

He gave one of his little laugh-coughs. "Richard Collins-Spear is an Englishman who performed open-heart surgery on some of the richest and most noble figures in Great Britain, including, if memory serves, some minor member of the Royal family. A few years ago, it was discovered—1 forget how—that Collins-Spear had never even completed grade school!"

"You're kidding."

"Nope. All of his patients lived to tell the tale too. Apparently, he was just some kind of a bright unscrupulous guy who'd picked up a lot of medical knowledge in the army and on odd jobs in hospitals, and was able to concoct a bogus vita and references and land a surgeon's position in a country hospital. No one ever bothered to check up on him. He succeeded there, gained some experience, and worked his way up to the top. When the story finally came out, of course, he was arrested, but I think he got off with a strangely light prison term. I forget the details, sorry. Isn't that amazing?" Rath looked at me with a satisfied gaze, as if he'd just told me exactly what I wanted to know. It confused me, the whole thing.

"Crazy," I said, "but every now and then a story like that pops up. What's that got to do with Mussel? Aside from the fact that I'd like to have someone who's never even seen a scalpel perform a little surgery on him?"

By this time, we'd left the cafeteria and were sauntering slowly back across the quad. Don stopped next to the library; it appeared he intended to go inside. He laughed hard at my last remark. "Mac, Mac," he said, shaking his head. "I'm trying to tell you that I sincerely suspect—no—I pretty well know— that . . ." and here he pulled me down suddenly by the necktie and whispered in my ear, "Mussel doesn't have an academic degree! Not one! Not a single fucking college degree!"

He let my head snap back up, slapped me on the back, ran up a couple of steps toward the library, ran back down, slapped me again, and gasped through his laughter. "Isn't that a kick?" He looked like a faun leaping jauntily through fountain waters.

"Wait a minute, wait a minute," was all I could get out. I was stunned by his statement. "Wait, Don, you've got to tell me more!" I tried to follow him, but he was already running up the stairs again.

"Can't now," he called over his shoulder. "I've got a research-methods class in the library lounge, but I'll call you tonight, okay? Okay? Hey, Mac, are you all right?"

"Yes, fine. Call me tonight. I can't wait!" I had a huge smile on my face. I turned and, as the gods would have it, ran smack into Wally Mussel, who gave me a sneering grin. He must have been delighted to see me cavorting so publicly with his favorite homosexual.

"Wally," I beamed. "Gorgeous day, isn't it?" and left him in my smug and happy dust.

21. A Lousy Proposal

It's hard to say how Eliza and I separated, for the simple fact is that we really never have. But we did lose earthly touch, and I find that a particularly difficult thing on which to meditate. After our initial unsuccessful attempt at lovemaking, there were several more similar encounters, all ending ignominiously for me and with the greatest confusion for Eliza. I was afraid lest she begin to blame herself for my physical limitations and decided to have a frank talk with her about my illness—for that reason, and for the more general reason that I felt it only fair that she know the whole story.

We had never had real "dates," Lizzie and I. On those sunny, cumulus-bedazzled New Jersey afternoons, when I had no classes and when she was free (she had a somewhat flexible schedule too; she had just graduated from NSU and was substitute teaching in a local high school) she would sometimes drive us around in the Caddy until we'd found some quiet spot to explore or some scenic area we both enjoyed. I could still see fairly well, but I loved hearing Eliza describe things; she talked about everything in a highly original and almost impressionistic way and seemed to enjoy the process. We visited my Thompson Park swans many times, feeding them pieces of the ice cream cones or popcorn we often bought to make our little excursions more festive. It wasn't until many years later that I learned that kind of food wasn't good for them.

We'd sit on the shore of the pond, or in the car if it were cold, my head on Eliza's lap and her fingers smoothing away what had become an omnipresent, though as yet not crippling, headache. We talked a lot about Eliza's past—her family and her years in school—but I don't feel that I should report much about her. Both of us believed that one of the true tenets of love was that you kept each other's secrets. Sometimes we just got silly, and Eliza would make up stories for me about "the lavender swans," childhood creations of hers who inhabited a castle-laden landscape and who derived their unusual color from eating violets and wisteria and "little pots of lavender eye shadow pilfered from the pocketbooks of princesses." I know it sounds saccharine and ridiculous. If you haven't been deeply in love like that, you will think us demented. I loved her so much then that I could not imagine dying.

But it was true that I would die in the not-too-distant future, and we had to discuss it. After one of our Thompson Park excursions, we went back to my apartment for a rest—not a real rest of course, although we did end up on the couch. Eliza and I had long passed the point of trying anything romantic in the bedroom but spent a lot of time "necking" in the old-fashioned sense. In an unexpected way, it was very satisfying: there was a closeness to it that was indescribably sweet, and sometimes, cradling Eliza close to me with her head under my chin and her young hips nestled into my traitorous lap, I found it hard to imagine that a sexual encounter would have brought us any closer—except, I suppose, for those fleeting moments of sharing an exquisite physical pleasure.

While we sat there that day, I said to her, "Lizzie, my love, we ought to have a serious talk about my illness."

I knew she would make it easy for me if she could, but I had no idea how easy.

"I know you're very ill, Jack," she said. "I worry about you all the time: I wish I could help you. Tell me whatever you need to tell me. I've been waiting for you to be ready. I didn't want to hurry you."

I felt a little rocky. I couldn't see Eliza's face where it rested on my chest, so I checked for tears with my fingers. Her eyes were dry. I moved my fingertips down over her nose and lips, and she kissed them. She said, "This isn't going to be about sex again, is it?"

"No, not exactly, but you know how bad I feel that I can't—"

"Jack, don't be boring—we've had that discussion a hundred times." She pulled my arms around her and held them very close.

"All right, I know. You're a dear, and I love you."

"You too, MacLeod." She smiled. In the back of her mind, I know I would always be "the professor," and she would always get a little kick out of speaking to me "disrespectfully."

"I've never even really told you what's wrong with me," I said, half holding my breath. I suppose some part of me thought she might bolt for the door.

"A brain tumor?" Her voice was very small.

"How did you know?"

She shrugged, and turned, and hid her face deep in my shirt. "I don't know," she said. I just put things together. I guess it wasn't too hard to figure out."

"I've had it a long time now," I said, "and there's no telling how long it will go on like this."

"Tell me the worst part."

"The worst part?" I was happy to let her keep questioning me; I found it impossible to ad lib.

She sat up and pulled away from me gently and clutched a fuzzy throw-pillow to her chest. "Can they operate?" she asked. "Is it malignant?"

"They can't do surgery, dear; it's in a tricky place. The tumor is involved quite deeply in the brain tissue," I said, sounding as if I were giving a medical lecture. "Right behind the optic nerve. That's why I have all this trouble with my eyes, and the pain."

She sighed. "And what else?"

I let her hand go. I knew we each had to be alone for this. "And then, sooner or later, I'll die of it, Lizzie."

"When?" Her voice sounded the way sand looks after the tide's gone out.

"There's no telling. A few years at best, I'd guess, but the doctors don't much like to make predictions. I'll become gradually weaker; the pain will increase—but don't worry so much about the pain, sweetheart, they can control that pretty well, and—"

Eliza suddenly interrupted me with a sort of low howl of grief. She'd finally begun to cry into the pillow and pulled away when I reached for her.

"Darling," I said. "I'm so sorry, I really am. It should have been different for us—for you. You're young and strong and healthy and wonderful. You deserve better, you . . ."

She hit me with the pillow, hard, and then began battering me, weakly, with her fists. All it took to stop her was to hold her wrists for a moment; she collapsed then against my chest and cried wretchedly for a long time. I just let her. I didn't try to soothe her. I held her as one holds a child who's having a bad time. I knew she would exhaust herself soon.

When she did, her recovery was sudden and complete. She sat back, reached for some tissues in her sweater pocket, dried her eyes, blew her nose, then excused herself to go to the bathroom. I heard water running noisily, some clattering of brushes and combs (she'd begun keeping a set of everything at my place, accusing me of "mussing" her up all the time), then, in quick order, she was back at my side.

"I think," she said, "I've finished feeling sorry for myself, for you, and for both of us. We're just going to have to take it one day at a time I guess." She was speaking very rapidly, as if she were afraid I would stop her. I didn't.

"What worries me most," she went on, "is the pain. I don't want you to be in pain. I want to know everything we can do to stop it. What are you taking now? You've got to tell me everything, Jack, you know? You've told me this much, so now you've got to keep me informed. What are you doing for the pain? How bad is it? Is it constant?" She took a no-nonsense tone that I'd never heard before.

"Percodan, at the moment," I said. "It's really pretty effective. Also I do a little self-hypnosis, which helps in between pills. I'm pretty good at that. And there are stronger drugs, or higher dosages, they can give me when things get worse."

"We'll have to look into acupuncture and things like that," she said, sounding very businesslike. "There are always a lot of remedies regular doctors don't explore."

"We'll see," I said, wearily. "I'm not really up for a lot of experimentation."

"You just leave all that to me," she said. "Now, what about lunch?"

Without waiting for my answer, she went out into the kitchenette and began preparing something or other. I felt a little lost. I knew her bounce-back from the tears was a necessary mechanism that allowed her to go on functioning in the face of all this terror, but I wasn't sure we'd really finished the conversation I'd intended to have. I followed her, cornered her up against the refrigerator, took a spoon and dishtowel out of her hand and kissed her repeatedly. She more or less melted then.

"Ooooh," she said, sinking into one of the stupid little chairs. "What a terrible world."

"I need you, Eliza," I was horrified to hear myself say. "Lizzie, I need you now, and I'm going to need you more and more."

"I'm not going anywhere," she answered.

"But no, darling girl, it's much more than that." I had to turn away so she could not see my face; I was ashamed of my need and my panic. I could not control what I was saying any more than I could control the pain behind my eyes, which was suddenly raging out of control. The doctors had warned me repeatedly that allowing myself to get into highly emotional states would only exacerbate my problems. But what the hell did they expect? That a man would just lie back quietly and die? I felt as if I were exploding, as if I couldn't breathe, as if I had to say terrible things to Eliza that would save her from me—things that would push her away forever so she wouldn't have to stand by me out of what could eventually, inevitably, become pity alone.

Instead, I said, "Eliza, I need you to marry me."

She said nothing. I was so darkened by pain I could barely see her shape at the other side of the table.

"It's a lousy proposal," I said, "and if you've got any brains at all you'll run for your life. It's a crappy hand you've been dealt, old girl. You ought to just spit in my face. Why don't you say something?"

Her voice was level. "It's not a romantic proposal, no," she said, "but it's a perfectly good one. I knew it was coming."

"And?" I said. But then at last I caught hold of myself. Was I really going to allow myself to sacrifice this girl to my illness, to ruin her best years, to saddle her with sorrows better wrestled in old age, to force her to confront what she ought, by rights, to avoid? I knew she loved me on some level—some truly glorious level—but I could not keep her with me. It would be the one thing for which I could never forgive myself. I wheeled around and grabbed her off the chair and leaned her up against the counter again. I spoke softly into her hair.

"Forget I said all this, Eliza. I apologize."

"No," she said, "of course I won't forget."

Some time went by while we simply held each other, standing there. Then she said, "You are going to need me. The question is, are you going to want me? I don't think there's any way to answer that now. I don't think talking about it is going to help much—I think we'll just have to live through it and see what it's like."

"No," I said, absurdly. I had no answer that made any sense.

"I know what I'm doing," she said, in that sure, quiet voice. "You think I'm too young, but I know what I'm about."

"Do you, really?"

"I think so," she said. "I do. Sit down and have some soup."

22. Lined with Pine Boughs

Poor Cybèle: my fox-child, my little girl, my wild friend. The whole of my life, animals had meant a great deal to me. I held them in almost sacred regard; what money I had for charity I nearly always gave to humane societies and the like, a fact that infuriated Frances, whose alleged allergies precluded our having a pet at home—something I'd always wanted for the boys. It's not that I felt coldly towards human causes— quite the contrary. My heart often bled for the foibles and plagues that beset my fellow man, and I struggled every day in my profession to better the human lot in some small way. But to my mind the animals had the worst of it. All their problems were our fault: human beings had beset them in every possible way since time began and had all but ruined the natural world for them, so that I felt the least I could do to offset my sense of universal guilt and to make up in some small way for the sins of the human race was to donate what I could of my time and money to animal rights and animal welfare causes.

When last I mentioned Cybèle to you our friendship was only a close call; we had not yet established a true connection. But in succeeding visits to the cabin I had been able, with the greatest of patience and respect, to almost tame the little beauty (not that I ever wanted to truly tame her—taming can spoil so much), so that she would watch for my arrival from a post beyond the driveway on Friday nights. This vigil so touched my heart—her intelligence, her faithfulness, her quiet dignity—that seeing Cybèle soon became my main reason for frequenting the cabin. Perhaps you are thinking that it wasn't me she waited for, but the food I would put out for her. Perhaps.

I would pull slowly into the drive on Friday nights whenever I could get away, and there in the bushes would be two bright little eyes gleaming in the darkness. I did not know how she knew I was coming, but she never failed me. I would go directly inside, open a can of Cybèle's favorite dogfood, and arrange it on her red plate. This I would set out in a little clearing under some bushes in the side yard. I'd turn on the yellow bug-light—just enough for me to see by—and, can of beer in hand, settle down on the steps to watch for my friend.

A delicate, silent figure would step carefully from the shadows, lifting each foot daintily and carrying her gorgeous tail level with her back so that its full glory could be seen. Sometimes there would be leaves or other debris caught in her fur, but more often than not the yellow light from the bug-bulb would cast a coppery sheen on her beautiful coat, lending a mystical air to the already dreamlike scene. Just before reaching the plate, she would always stop and look directly at me for a moment, as if to say, "May I?" or "Thanks, Jack." I was careful never to move at that moment. If there was a breeze, I'd be able to detect her sharp scent, which was quite remarkably and precisely "fox"—not like a doggy smell at all, or like anything else I could think of. I suppose there was blood in it, or simply the primitive wonders of the forest, forever unfathomable to man.

After her Friday night feast, Cybèle would not appear again until late the next afternoon. She was nocturnal, but I fantasized that she rose earlier on Saturdays just for me. It was then I would set out the red plate again, this time laden with canned tuna or salmon, which I had discovered she adored, and I would place it a little closer to the cabin. It took her longer to approach, but she never really seemed afraid. It was just a little game we played: she pretended to be wary of me, and I pretended some fear of her. But neither of us believed it. It was a ballet of politeness between the species, a private little dance we danced only for each other, with all the sure-footedness of enchanted beings.

When she had finished her fish, Cybèle would sit like a puppy and lick her lips. Sometimes she would roll around on the plate, then spring suddenly up and dart off into the woods. Once I broke the silence as she ran and said, very evenly, very softly, "Cybèle." I heard her leaf-pattering foot-steps stop, then begin again. I nearly expected her to say my name in return. And early each Sunday morning, just before I left, I would look out the kitchen window and see a little patch of dusky red amidst the foliage near the car. I'd load my gear and pretend not to see her. Then, last but certainly not least, just before I locked up the cabin, I'd set out Cybèle's final weekend feast: chicken, usually, and a great deal of it. I'd put the plate on the steps right in front of the door, then get into the car, put it in neutral, and back slowly and silently down the hill. By the time I'd slid into the shadowy part of the driveway, Cybèle would trot trustfully up to the door-step and begin to eat. I loved it so. I loved so to have my last glimpse of the cabin each week blessed by her beautiful little figure on my doorstep. The next time I returned, the plate be would be there, whistle clean.

But one Friday she did not appear. I didn't worry too much at first, but when I didn't see her Saturday either I decided to take a little walk in the direction Cybèle always headed when she left my yard. I didn't have to walk far to stop my heart—to break it.

Cybèle was dead. I found her poor body about twenty yards or so from the steel-jaw trap that still contained her right front paw and elegant ankle. She had chewed it off, as many animals will do when there is no other way to free themselves, but by doing so had lost so much blood that she did not have the strength to reach her den. She probably would have died there, in any case, even if she'd managed to limp back. I vomited into the bushes and sat down next to her body and wept.

It was a long time before I could look at her. She wasn't the same Cybèle. With the life gone out of her, with her dancer's body disfigured and gory, with her own dried blood still staining her mouth, she was only a bleak line-drawing of a fox. I could hardly bear to see her dead, button eyes; they were flat licorice, instead of the black star-sapphires she had once shown me. I struggled to close them. I touched her fur; it was coarse and dirty. Her scent, now thickened with death, filled my nostrils; I thought I would retch again. I went back to the cabin for a shovel.

And on my way back I realized that Cybèle had probably been on her way to the cabin too when she met her fate. I was consumed by a rage unlike any other I could remember. I was filled with a hatred for hunters and trappers and vivisectionists and fur-coat-wearers and riders of bicycles trailing fox tails from their handlebars and carriers of lucky rabbits' feet. I think I was possibly capable, at that moment, of murder—or mayhem at least. I found a stout shovel and drove the point of it insanely again and again into the side of a tree, making hideous gashes.

I could not stop crying. I told myself I was crazy, but it didn't help a bit. Finally, I went in the house, downed a beer and two aspirin, washed my face and hands, and sat still for a moment. The phone rang, but I didn't answer it. The doctor is out, I thought; he is very out indeed,

I knew I had to bury Cybèle. I dug a deep hole in what I thought was the very spot where she would wait for me each Friday night. I lined it with pine boughs. I went into the house and brought out the red plate, placing it on the branches in the grave. Then I carried her body from the woods and placed it gently next to the plate. She weighed next to nothing. I went back to the trap, forced it open with great difficulty, and carried her foot back to her. It hardly looked like a foot at all anymore. I covered her with more branches, and then with earth. I tried to make the grave look the way it did before I'd dug there; I wanted it to blend in, as she had. I did not want to mark it in any way. Then I sat down on it and said a sort of prayer, more to Cybèle than to any kind of god.

"Forgive me, my beautiful friend," I prayed, "for I never thought that knowing me would have led you to so cruel, so premature, an ending."

23. Sherlock Takes a Case

I had to find out if what Don Rath had told me about Mussel were true, and I knew that wouldn't be easy. Right after he said goodbye to me on the library steps, I went back to my office to think. All afternoon I sat there, pretending to read, and keeping my door open in case Sarah should come by. I had decided not to tell her anything in case it all turned out to be a mistake, but I wanted badly just to see her. She did not appear, however, and it was probably just as well: my festive mood would have been hard to explain, and I did not want to lie to her about it.

Don called me that night, as he had promised. I'd been, as my mother used to say, "sitting on the phone" in my cooler bedroom. He did not say hello when I picked up the receiver; all I heard was some suppressed giggling and his little cough-laugh.

"You devil," I said, "How long have you known all this?"

"Oh, Mac," he said, "Not long, not long at all. That is to say, I've had my suspicions for a long time, but I wasn't certain until last week." Then he stopped and started laughing again.

"I couldn't believe my eyes," he continued. "I turned around just as I was going in the library door and saw you run into Mussel! Jesus, Mac! Who the hell is writing this wild script, anyway?"

I joined in his laughter. "I don't know," I said. "Somebody up there has a great sense of humor, I guess. It was crazy. When I turned to go, Mussel was just there. It was all I could do not to blow you a kiss, just to amuse him!"

"You should have, you should have!" he said, delighted. "That stupid prick! But I think we've got him now, I really do. It's going to take some detective work though. Are you up for it?"

"What do you think?"

"Have you told Sarah?"

"No, I thought it best to wait until we had everything in line."

"Right-o. Here's the story. Mussel, without ever coming right out and saying so, has for years dropped little hints here and there that he went to an Ivy League school. I never cared enough to even be curious about which one. But a couple of months ago at that reception for the new faculty members, there was a guy there I'd met before whom I happened to know had gone to Harvard. Mussel was at the reception too, oddly enough—he usually never shows up at those things— and after this poor guy—Ted Sachs, his name is—spent a few minutes chatting with Mussel, he came over to talk with me.

"He asked me whether Mussel had gone to Harvard as an undergrad or for his doctorate, and I said I had no idea, and why did he want to know? Ted said it was funny, but that Mussel kept mentioning Harvard, saying that he missed the old place and hadn't been back there since graduation."

Don went on, "My curiosity had been aroused, and, odious as it always is for me to talk to Mussel, I decided to engage him in a little conversation. Maybe I'd had too much wine. I went up to the little group of ass-kissers he had assembled around him and waited for an opening. It was the weekend of a big football game between Yale and some other school; I'd seen it in the papers but hadn't paid much attention. I know nothing about that grotesque sport, but I asked Mussel if he were going up to New Haven for the big game. He seemed a little puzzled at first, then, surmising that I thought him a Yale alumnus, patted me heartily on the back and said, 'Would that I could, Donald, would that I could. You never lose your feeling for the old alma mater, do you?'

"Then I was really confused. Had he gone to Yale *and* Harvard? It was possible, of course, but I doubted it. For one thing, he hasn't got a brain in his head. I got out of the group as gracefully as I could and began to circulate among our colleagues. Here and there I'd artfully turn the talk to college days, and, what do you think? I got three different opinions about Mussel's schooling; someone even thought he'd gone to West Point. So my suspicions took a firmer shape. What do you think I did then?"

I was growing weak with the desire to get to the heart of this tale, but I sensed Don's happiness in telling me all the details and I didn't want to spoil it for him.

"You consulted a fortune-teller?"

"Very funny. No. I decided I had to have a look at his file."

"His personnel file? Aren't those things kept under lock and key?"

"Of course. But I like to feel that nothing is impossible. So, whenever Mussel wasn't in his executive suite, I began hanging around with Dottie—you know, his secretary. I have a theory about her, but I'll save it for later. Dottie's always liked me, anyway, and I think she was glad to have some company when the czar was out. Over the course of a week or two I was able to find out where everything in that office was kept—just by watching Dottie while she was fetching things for people and answering phone calls."

"Are you sure you weren't called Sherlock in a previous life?"

Don laughed. "I admit, it was fun. My plan was to wait until some day when Dottie had to go on an errand or something, then offer to babysit the phone for her. I didn't have to wait long. One day she got a toothache, poor thing, and I convinced her it was ridiculous to wait until quitting time to see the dentist. She was afraid to leave, it was obvious, but I told her that if Mussel should return that afternoon (and she was almost perfectly sure he wouldn't) I'd make her toothache seem like such a matter of life or death that even he couldn't begrudge her a few extra hours of freedom.

"She was terribly grateful. The phone did keep me busy for a while, but soon I was able to locate Dottie's set of keys to the file cabinets. I quickly found the folder that bore Mussel's name, and what do you think?"

"WHAT?" I burst out, my patience deserting me.

Don shouted back, gleefully. "There was NOTHING in it!"

I was crestfallen. "So we still don't really know."

"My God, MacLeod," Don said, "You really don't think that's the end of the story, do you? Have a little confidence in old Sherlock, won't you? "

"Okay," I said. "I'm sorry. But hurry up. I'm going crazy here."

"Right-o. I put the empty file back and thought for a moment, then went back to the drawer. Everyone else's files were in their proper places. There were no other empty folders. I figured Mussel must have taken his and hidden it in his office. There was always the chance he might have destroyed it, but I figured him to be too cowed by the wheels of bureaucracy to risk having someone important ask for it someday. So I decided to break into his office."

"Good God."

"Yeah. But it wasn't that hard, actually. I found a letter opener that worked to get the door open, and his desk, oddly enough, was unlocked. I'd locked the door to Dottie's outside office and put a sign up saying she'd had to leave early because of an emergency and to please come back the next day. My only fear was that some other secretary might have a key and let herself in for some reason, but that didn't happen. I couldn't find the file at first, but then I remembered the old desk-blotter trick and lifted up Wally's. There was the folder. All his official papers were inside, topped off by an old yellowing letter from the university president congratulating him on being made chairman of the department. At the bottom of the pile was his vita. I skimmed it, then read it more slowly. I was afraid to write anything down, so I tried to memorize a lot of the information so I could check it out later. There were three pages of publications and another one of speeches and the like."

"What did it say about his education?"

"I'm getting to that. It said he had a BA in psychology from Cornell, and an MA and PhD from Columbia. Nothing at all about Harvard or Yale. What a jerk that man is: he can't even keep his own lies straight!"

"Wow."

"And it gave the dates. I finally did jot it all down, including the names he'd given as references, from two previous teaching jobs, at NYU and Northeastern. The resume itself was quite old, of course, since it was the original one he'd submitted when he came here, but I figured very few people would be able to forget Wally Mussel."

I was mesmerized, but also losing patience with the length of Don's story. While he rambled on, I stared at a couple of the house plants I'd brought into that bedroom to cheer it up a bit. As I was watching, a fat leaf on a fat stem fell off the begonia.

"The first thing I did was check out the publications. That was easy: a half-hour in the library reference room was all it took to ascertain that he'd made up all but two of his citations. The next day I tried to contact the two references. Dead end. I knew it was possible those people were long gone and forgotten, but it did seem odd that no one I talked to even seemed to find their names familiar. I got absolutely nowhere with the folks at NYU—they wouldn't give me information on past employment over the phone and without permissions—but at Northeastern, with a little sweet-talk and a lot of bullshit, I was able, after three attempts, to find a willing pigeon. A woman in the records office told me she could find no trace of a Mussel-man ever having had a position there, at any time. So I proceeded to try Cornell and Columbia."

"Any luck?" I started to fantasize about going out for a snack.

"That's the sad part. No. I hit the same dead-end with the records people as I did at NYU. Seems you have to have an officially documented written inquiry of some sort before they'll divulge that kind of information. But I figured that between the two of us we could get around all that somehow. What do you think?"

My mind was awash with hope and confusion. "I honestly don't know," I said. "I guess we can try."

Don rallied to the cause. "Mac," he told me, "I just know this guy is not on the level. I know it in my heart. If he lied about his teaching experience and his publications—which is bad enough, you know—the chances are very, very good that he's lied about the rest. Let's just put our heads together and think about how to find out for sure."

"You're right," I agreed, "but it's not going to be easy. If we're wrong, and if anyone catches wind of our nosing around, we're going to have a lot of fancy explaining to do."

"So what? Come on, Mac. Put your thinking cap on. You're the genius around here, not me! I'll supply the guts and the footwork; you supply the brains."

I was already formulating a plan; Don's enthusiasm buoyed me. "How about this?" I said. "I'll write to the two schools saying I'm heading a secret committee to honor Mussel for his many years of selfless service to NSU, and requesting copies of his diplomas so that we can concoct some kind of nostalgic little presentation—sort of a 'Wally Mussel, this is your life' kind of thing. The chances anyone here would ever find out are very slim, and even if they did, I could just say I really had been thinking about such an event. Do you think that would work?"

Rath breathed his admiration heavily into the phone. "You *are* a genius," he sighed. "It's beautiful! It's priceless! It combines a dastardly criminal mind with a rare creative talent! Of course, they'll go for it: there's nothing a true academic loves more than the promise of another meaningless ceremony. I love it! They'll never refuse! Can you do it tomorrow?"

I laughed along with him. "Thanks, Sherlock. That's high praise coming from the likes of you. Yeah, sure, I'll get on it first thing. I'll bring the letter by your office before I mail it, so you can take a look. Will you be in tomorrow after lunch?"

"I will," he said. "Got to go now, though. Denny's waiting for me. Sleep well, old boy."

24. A Lucky Doggie

I had been a devotee of magical thinking all my life. I knew it was just a silly game that fed false hope—a close cousin to superstition in fact—but it gave me an illusion of controlling my fate that I often found necessary for survival. When I was first dating Frances, for example, I remember thinking, "If she's wearing her hair up when she comes to meet me tonight, we will sleep together before the week is out." When I was suffering dreadfully from the pains in my head, I used to tell myself something like, "If I eat my sandwich with a fork, the pain will be better this afternoon." Many times it worked, and many times it did not. I am not quite sure there isn't an element of magic in the practice after all, though of course on a reasonable basis it is all completely ridiculous. But who is to say that the continual harboring and nurturing of a fervent desire is not akin to concentrated, continual prayer, the power of which even atheists are unable to discount? By keeping a hope constantly alive, constantly on the tip of one's consciousness, might it not be possible to kindle a small flame of possibility into an actual blaze?

A month or so before it became obvious that I would have to leave NSU, my finances were in a terrible mess. I was paying out large sums every month to Frances, both for alimony (which I felt was unfair, since she was pulling in a large salary herself), and for child support for Harry and Mark. I had been ill for some time, and while insurance covered my few medical bills (there wasn't much the doctors could do for me, so it didn't cost that much, except for the painkiller drugs), my illness was draining my bank account in other ways. For one thing, as I've mentioned, I'd initially had to cut back my teaching load because I couldn't drive after dark, and so my salary was diminished. And the increasingly poor state of my eyesight occasioned many other expenses: there were so many things I could no longer do for myself, so many services of one kind or another that I had to pay for. While these expenses were mostly small on a day-to-day basis, they certainly mounted up. I had to do all my shopping over the phone and have everything delivered. (Eliza ran some errands for me, but I usually didn't let her know the full extent of my need.) I was paying a graduate student for many hours a week spent reading to me, helping me grade papers, and typing my class notes and such on a special large-font typewriter (a pricey item). I suppose I could have cut some of these costs by applying for the many types of aid offered by various agencies, but I was afraid that what I suspected to be my already failing credibility at NSU would only be fueled by the discovery that I was certifiably disabled. It never occurred to me that anyone there would take pity on me.

Eventually I had to stop driving altogether. Moving closer to the campus was out of the question (my apartment was too cheap to give up), so I had to pay for transportation as well. I hired another grad student to ferry me back and forth in the Caddy (I still clung to it as a reminder of happier times), and although he, a kind and intuitive soul, tried to charge me practically nothing for this service when my unfortunate circumstances became clear to him, I forced him to accept a reasonable wage.

I was close to despair about this money shortage. At times I would imagine myself ending up in some kind of welfare hospital, doomed to live out my days without privacy, dignity, or even much comfort. Comfort. I found myself craving things I'd never before much cared about, like special foods, and lots of them. Had my metabolism not been so churned around by both my nerves and the medication I was taking, I probably would have gained twenty pounds during this period. I also loved clothing that soothed my skin and required little upkeep; records and tapes, both musical and literary, to fill the blank spaces wherein I used to do my omnivorous reading; and many other little things that simply, I suppose, made me feel somewhat more alive. It was difficult to sustain my greedy new lifestyle on my present salary, but I felt powerless to control my habits.

One morning I was sipping my mug of tea and listening to the radio when I heard the announcement of a fabulous contest. By simply filling out a postcard with one's name, address, and phone number, and printing the words "I listen to WKRD" in block letters underneath, one could enter into a drawing for the unbelievable sum of fifty thousand dollars. At first, I thought I had misheard: how could a radio station, even one originating in New York City, be offering such a gigantic prize? But the announcer went on to explain, as if answering my question, that the prize money had been put up by the station and its many nationwide affiliates to celebrate the twenty-fifth anniversary of the station's success. This was to be a highly publicized one-shot deal that would put the station's call letters on everyone's lips.

As I rummaged around in my desk to find a postcard, I laughed at myself, but I thought, why not? It wasn't any sillier than buying a lottery ticket, something I'd been meaning to do for quite a while. Sometimes life itself presented one with a deus ex machina worthy of a bad movie. With the aid of a magnifying glass, I was able to complete the task, and I dressed and made my way to the corner mailbox as soon as I'd finished breakfast. It was silly indeed, but it was something to do. On my way back to the apartment I half-saw what I thought might be a little dog on the lawn of one of the neighboring houses. Without even thinking I said to myself, "If that doggie comes up to greet me, I will win the contest." The doggie did. We had a fine little minute or two of petting, jumping, licking, and general goodwill between the species. I walked on.

⁓⤳⟋◌⟍⤳⁓

On the Monday morning of what was to become one of my last days in the employ of NSU, the WKRD station manager called me. He told me we were "on the air"—I guess to warn me not to say anything uncouth—and congratulated me on being the winner of the contest's grand prize. Not only did I not say anything uncouth, I did not say anything at all for nearly a full minute. The poor man must have thought I'd fainted; he kept saying, "Mr. MacLeod, are you there? Are you there?" Finally able to complete the conversation and hang up the phone with some modicum of normalcy, I went into the living room and lay down on the couch. My head was literally pounding, as if a great, pulsing, angry beast were trying to be born out of it. I opened my eyes, but could see nothing, and considered that I had gone totally blind at last. I don't know how long I lay there, but I must have fallen asleep rather quickly and mercifully.

When I awoke it was dark outside, the pain had miraculously abated, and my eyesight was no worse than it had been earlier in the day. My first thought, of course, was that it had all been a dream, a ridiculous method of solving the unsolvable created by my unconscious to mitigate the problems of my dismal existence, but I soon realized it was not. I had won an enormous amount of money. The station was sending over a man with a certified check tomorrow; he would be accompanied by a notary and a representative from the IRS. The tax man! Well, fine, I thought, he's welcome to his due. I wouldn't have to worry about money for a while. I thought fifty thousand dollars unspendable: little did I know that by the time I died, having made out a will I thought would bring my prime beneficiary a valuable bequest, almost all of what remained of my precious prize would be promised to very real creditors.

I thought I ought to celebrate somehow. I called my Lizzie and Don but could not reach either of them. Unable to postpone my desire to celebrate, I called a fancy French restaurant several towns away and had a sumptuous meal delivered, complete with champagne. It might have been the first take-out order they'd ever filled: it was no easy chore to convince them to humor me). I tipped the delivery boy lavishly and invited him in for a glass of bubbly, telling him I was celebrating a momentous personal victory over skepticism. I'm sure he thought me a nutcase, but I was clearly not dangerous, and he was kind enough to join me. As I sat there across the kitchen table from that rather silently cheerful young man, sipping my own glass of champagne, I thought to myself how wonderful life was, how mysterious, and how sad. If the boy had been Eliza, I would have been endlessly happy.

25. Hail, Full of Grace

Strangely enough, it was Grace Rinkette who broke the news to me about Sarah and Mussel. Some weeks after the little scene in my office when Sarah lowered the boom on my unsuspecting head, I was shopping for shirts in a local department store. I had put this task off so long I was beginning to look like a frayed old scarecrow. Since Sarah's terrible words, I had been speaking and moving mechanically and forgetting each day almost as soon as it was over. I was surviving, but barely. I'd nearly stopped speaking to Frances altogether, but I think that was all right with her. I acted pretty well around the boys and at school, but that was all it was: acting. Don Rath was the only one I talked to about Sarah, and I hadn't told him much. He was mystified, sympathetic, and friend enough not to press me for details—not that I had many. What broke both our hearts, I think, was that we were so close to having Mussel where we wanted him, and now, though defrocking Mussel for any reason would be a joy in itself, the urgency had mysteriously evaporated, and we both felt its loss acutely. We would take up the banner of our crusade again one day, but we came to a halt for a while, stunned by the injustice of it all.

So there I was in Harwood's, the big department store near school, cruising the menswear department like a sleepwalking mannequin escaped from one of the displays. I stopped in front of a huge stack of white shirts and stood there fingering the cuffs. I'd been aimlessly walking around for so long I felt the salesperson had probably pegged me as a shoplifter. Everything looked so white, so clean, so unreal. After stroking the collars of several shirts, I picked up a couple I thought were my size, though I wasn't certain I remembered what that was.

Frances had been picking out my shirts for centuries; now I was on my own. One of the shirts I'd chosen was white, and one was a clear pastel green—a beautiful color. I felt I had to buy it, though I was fairly sure I'd never wear such a thing. I wondered if this was how a compulsive shopper felt, and if I were turning into one.

I was just about to purchase both shirts when I felt a little tug at my shoulder, accompanied by a whiff of lavender water. I looked down. There was Grace Rinkette, cuter than ever. I realized I had never seen her out of her chair in that baroque study of hers and was amused at her height; she appeared to be a bit less than five feet tall. She was smiling radiantly out of a lacy architecture of scarves and stickpins that would have made Queen Victoria proud.

"Miss Rinkette," I said, beaming at her, "How lovely to see you again."

"And you, Dr. MacLeod," she said. "I haven't seen you in quite a while. You really ought to come by and visit my gardens sometime soon: they're beautiful in every season, you know."

"Thank you, I'd love to. And how have you been feeling?"

"Well," she said, obviously delighted to tell her story, "I don't think I've ever felt quite so well since I was a girl!" Her pink, chubby little face was alight with mischief, and the sight of her lifted me instantly out of my gloom. It was the first truly beautiful, truly glowing human face I'd seen in a very long time.

"That's wonderful news," I said. "You're not suffering from the arthritis now, I take it?"

She pulled me aside to a less congested area and, keeping one hand on my arm, flipped open her tiny handbag and produced a little pamphlet. Her movements, quick and sure, were certainly not those of a woman in pain. I remembered how she used to labor to do so much as lift a teacup. I took the pamphlet from her. On the front was a rather lurid drawing of a dark, elderly, loin-cloth-clad man sitting cross-legged on a vast, glowing cloud. One of his hands was lifted in a gesture of peace, and the other lay across his knee in the frozen yet graceful manner of religious statues. Below him, and encircling the cloud, stood a host of people with their arms lifted in praise, or perhaps prayer. I gave Grace a puzzled look, and she giggled.

"I know what you must be thinking, Doctor," she said, "But I really haven't completely lost my marbles—just a few of them. I've been dabbling in what some people call 'alternative medicine.'"

"My goodness," was all I could muster.

"This man," she said, pointing to the figure on the flyer, "is Rama Bamakresh, an Indian healer—or maybe not Indian, I'm not sure . . ." She paused and gave me a deadly serious look. Her eyes twinkled.

She delighted me so. I felt a genuine smile race across my face and thought, so that's what it feels like—oh yes, I remember that now. "And he's healed you?" I asked her.

"Yes—well, indirectly. I got tired of all my potions and salves. I was beginning to fear I'd get addicted to all those pills. I started to hate my doctor, to miss appointments for no good reason. And my garden was suffering too; I could hardly move to care for it anymore, and hiring a gardener just took all the joy out of it. So one day I said to myself, 'Grace, you'll just have to stop being so stuffy and old-fashioned and try out some of these new cures you've been reading about.' Oh, don't worry, Doctor, I'm old, but I've never been gullible. I wasn't about to start buying copper bracelets or magical Mexican jumping beans or anything like that."

She stopped a moment to allow me to finish laughing. I stashed the shirts I was carrying in a nearby pile of sweaters, put my arm around her, and steered her toward the door.

"Forgive me. It's just been a while since I've heard such a good story, so well told," I said. "I'm dying to hear all about it. Can I offer you lunch?"

"Oh dear," she said, plucking a little cameo-covered watch-pendant from amidst her ruffles, and making an impatient face, "I'm afraid I'm already on my way to an engagement, but thank you so much."

Reminded of her appointment, she began walking briskly away from the store; it wasn't easy to keep up with her. Her feet were so tiny and her legs moved so quickly she looked like nothing so much as an animated hedgehog from some wonderful Disneyesque movie.

"Then, please," I begged her, "do finish your story."

"Oh yes. Well, anyway, I started researching the subject in earnest. I was looking for someone local, and someone who'd had a good deal of success. Finally, I discovered this healer's people through an article in one of those health magazines, and I gave them a call."

"They helped you, I can see that. But how?"

She laughed happily. "I'm just not sure how," she said, "but they certainly did help. They changed my diet all around:

that was the big thing. They suggested I get some acupuncture. They taught me to meditate. And," she continued, still racing along the street like a twenty-year-old, "they gave me these." She pulled a little plastic packet out of her bag and handed it to me. It contained some tiny, grainy-looking pellets that looked like rabbit food.

"What's this?" I asked.

"Herbs!" she announced proudly. "I forget their names, I'm sorry to say, but I have the whole list at home: nothing harmful, but it's supposed to be the delicate combining of them that does the trick . . . and it certainly did the trick for me!" She glowed in my direction, stuffing the pills back into her purse.

A momentary concern for her well-being, a lifelong habit of skepticism, flitted across my mind for a second or two, but then I looked again at Grace and dismissed it. "You look wonderful," I told her. "I'm really very happy for you. Did all of this happen quickly?"

"Oh no," she said. "It took a couple of months, but I noticed some improvement almost immediately: that's what kept me going. And now I'm a total convert. Oh I know it sounds unbelievable, Doctor MacLeod, but at my age why should I care? I hardly have any pain anymore, I can get around all I like, and, best of all, I can garden to my heart's content. I can hardly wait until next spring when I'll reap the rewards of all the new varieties of iris I've planted."

I suddenly realized we were getting quite far away from where I'd parked my car, and that I'd have to be getting back to the campus soon. I decided to ask what I'd feared to ask all along.

"And Sarah must be so pleased with your recovery," I ventured. Grace gave me a soft, wise glance, and sighed a little.

She stopped walking, took one of my hands in both her tiny ones, and patted it.

"I'm sorry, my boy," she said. "I know you cared for her a great deal. I tried not to be too nosey, and Sarah never told me too much, but I could tell that you and she were very close."

She let my hand go and looked off into the distance. "In fact," she went on, "I know it must be painful for you to talk about her, but I have to tell you that I always hoped it would be you she married instead of Dr. Mussel." She stopped, abashed. "But who can fathom the human heart?"

She was wringing her tiny hands and examining my face with the greatest concern. "I really mustn't talk like this. I'm sorry. I'm just a foolish old woman."

I could not believe my ears, but I did not question her further. I made some kind of excuse and beat what I hope was not too rude a retreat. I went directly to a phone booth and called Don Rath. No one answered, either in his office or at home. I knew I had heard Grace correctly. I guess I thought, if I repeated it to Don, he would tell me it wasn't true. If only, I thought, I could take some little pills like Grace's and wake up tomorrow knowing all of this hadn't really happened. A terrible vision of Mussel's greasy face reared up before me as I got into my car. I had to sit there a few minutes before the apparition would go away. People lusting after my parking space honked at me, but I ignored them. I was drowning in unshed tears. The severity of my headache was frightening, but at the time I thought of it only as the result of the shocking news I'd just heard.

I sat there I don't know how long, sweating, and lost in a daydream of incredible clarity. I imagined myself dancing with Sarah through Grace Rinkette's iris gardens. Grace sat on a little velvet tuffet, wearing a yellow and lavender dress and looking like a wonderful, fuzzy old iris herself. The moon was amazingly high in the sky, like the Star of Bethlehem on a Christmas card. There was no music, but we waltzed effortlessly, with exquisite precision. Sarah felt light as a leaf in my arms. She threw her head back and I twirled her around breathlessly.

The more detailed this daydream became, the more I realized its unreality, and the more I clung to it desperately, afraid to cease creating it and return to the real afternoon. The moon in my dream was silver and golden, all at the same time, and the breezes cool and lightly scented by far-off oceans. I wore a tuxedo and had combed-back hair. Sarah wore diamonds. She wore a wedding dress.

26. Making a Date with Don

It was around that time that I first got to know Eliza. I didn't pay much attention to her at first; she was just one of a number of well-scrubbed, long-haired upperclassmen in my advanced psychology course. But after the Patchen episode, we began to run into each other more and more, and at first I could not determine if this were somehow planned by Eliza or if it were only an accident of fate. Eventually, of course, I came to realize that Eliza and I were simply swimming in the same psychic stream and were bound to encounter each other at frequent intervals.

It was also around this time that some of my symptoms really began to haunt me: headaches, vision problems, periods of imbalance, sudden and heavy bouts of depression. But they were all easily and rationally explained away by the trauma around Sarah. My reaction was to ignore them or, when that failed, to try to beat them down, and I worked harder at my classes than I ever had before, becoming the quintessential workaholic and a member of the Great Unaware. I was oblivious to almost everything, centering my whole existence on a foundation of ritual and exhaustion. Somehow it seemed to hold me together.

Each morning I would perform for myself a tightly choreographed dance of punctuality that led me to my office at an unreasonably early hour. One time, forgetting how early it was, I called Don Rath to seek his advice on a technical question relating to some research in an article I was reading. He was forgiving when I awakened him (though Denny, who answered the phone, was noticeably less so), and laughed along with me at my compulsive new habits. Then he asked me quite seriously if I didn't think maybe I ought to slow down. He said I was beginning to worry him, and I said I appreciated his concern and would certainly take stock of my behavior.

I decided that while I couldn't seem to control my vast need for perpetual intellectual stimulation (which mercifully allowed me no time to dwell on Sarah or my pain) I could switch my attentions to less work-related projects, thereby, I hoped, taking some of the strain off my system. I took up, in a manner I had not practiced since I was quite young, the enriching habit of reading strictly for pleasure. It wasn't easy at first. I would find myself taking copious notes or planning critical articles I could write on the subject at hand—but with deliberate effort I calmed myself down a little and began simply to enjoy. I began with an eclectic selection: old favorites like *Jude the Obscure* and *The Bell Jar*, rediscovering with gratitude all the fulfillment well-loved great literature could supply. I concentrated simply on what I liked, not on what I thought I should be reading. It was heavenly. I delved into Patchen again, and thought briefly of my student Eliza Harder, and how happy I was to have found a kindred spirit who loved his work as much as I did.

And I took up memorizing books again as well, though I mentioned this to no one. Thinking back, it was almost as if, somewhere deep inside myself, I knew I had to store up valuable goods for the challenging times to come. Again, I concentrated solely on what pleased me. This memorization, into which I would delve late at night when distractions were least likely to disturb me, occasioned myriad memories of my boyhood as well, and sometimes I would cease my happy labors to meditate on some long-forgotten scene and weave the magic and the lessons of the past into my busy but forlorn present.

And so, because of this process of renewal, I was in slightly better mental shape when Don Rath approached me in my office one day with unusual news. I remember his face so clearly that day: there were specks of grey in his natty beard that I hadn't previously noticed, and a network of airbrushed lines around the periphery of his eyelids that, instead of showing his age, served to draw all one's attention to the remarkable life-light shining from his eyes. He looked like a man on fire from within, and I wondered what on earth he had to tell me.

He came into the room quietly, closing the door behind him, and pulled one of the chairs around from the front of my desk to the side, so that we were sitting face to face without the obstruction of furniture and papers.

"Mac," he said. "I need to tell you what I've done."

I just said okay; I could tell he didn't want any snappy backtalk.

"Remember," he asked, "your plan for checking up on Mussel's degrees?" It was the first time since Sarah's departure that either of us had mentioned the subject. I did not know if he was aware of her marriage, but I assumed so. I sighed.

"I know, I know," he said. "Maybe I should have dropped it. I didn't know if you'd be interested in it any more after Sarah—"

I stopped him. "There's more than just her leaving me, you know."

"Yes," he said. "Precisely. And that is exactly why I felt we must go ahead with this." He stood up suddenly and banged his hand on my desk about six inches in front of my chin. I jumped. "Damn it, Mac!" he continued, his voice grappling with what I could tell was a tornado of emotion. "I know how much this all sucks. For you more than anyone. But, damn it all, don't you see? So what if she's married the bastard? That doesn't mean she's dead—or that you are either. I'm not suggesting that anything we discover or disclose would break them up, but is it any less important now that we try to oust him? I don't know how many people even know about the marriage—they tried to keep it very, very quiet—I only found out by accident—but Christ, Mac, I don't know about you, but I'm still mad! And I'll bet you are too—madder than hell if you'd admit it—if you'd get your nose out of those six million books you've been reading and face the fact that you're hiding. Use your famous brain, man. Jesus Christ."

I knew he was right. I looked at him coldly; I didn't have any reserves of kindness to call upon. "I'm enjoying my reading very much, thank you."

He placed each of his hands on each of mine. It was a peculiar gesture, like something a mother might do, and the very oddity of it made me start and shudder a bit. I hoped he wouldn't take it as a recoil, for in truth his touch had gone straight to my heart and wakened it from its troubled sleep. "What have you done?" I asked him.

He smiled and sat down again. "Well," he said, "I couldn't wait for you to take any action. I knew you were in no shape to do anything right away—so I took it upon myself to write to those schools as you'd suggested, asking for copies of Mussel's diplomas." He laugh-coughed, and smiled widely. I had to smile back.

"I assume this ninety-six-tooth grin means that you got the expected result?"

"Bingo!"

I felt a strange bolt of energy rise from my mid-section and travel along my spine to my shoulders; it was as if a whole flotilla of little hogtied muscles were suddenly released from their bindings and loosed upon an ocean of pure delight. Had someone described to me the magnitude of the unfettering I would experience upon hearing such news, I would have denied the possibility. I allowed myself what I hoped would be a rousing whoop of happiness, but in my weakened state all that erupted from my throat was a pitiful little bleat of joy. This sent Don into a fit of choking giggles, and I offered him my cup of coffee. He pushed it away. When he'd finally composed himself, wiping some tears from his eyes, he said. "Yep. You got it. The old boy's a complete imposter: no Harvard, no Columbia, no Yale . . . no NOTHING!"

I took off my jacket and loosened my tie. A headache was building, but I put it down to excitement. "So what do we do now?" I asked.

"I don't know. But let's not wait too long to decide. I want to do something while the fire's still raging within me—and you, I hope. Maybe we should both think it over and plan to come together and map out a plan later this week. You look like you need a little time to pull yourself together, Mac, if you'll forgive my saying so. What do you say?"

"Fine," I told him. "That's a good idea. Let's have dinner Friday and devise a plan. My treat. You deserve a reward for all your sleuthing. Where do you want to go?"

I could tell this gesture pleased him immensely; I think I sometimes gave Don less friendly feedback than he deserved—and he was such an excellent friend. His eyes sparked up and he said to me, "Let's do it up right. Do you want to go into the city?"

It did seem like a wonderful idea. "Absolutely, "I said. "You pick a place and surprise me. I haven't been into New York in so long I can't think of anywhere to go. Call me Thursday, and we'll figure out where to meet and all that. And Don . . . thanks." I reached for his hand to shake it but changed my mind and got up and embraced him as hard as I could. He felt surprisingly slight inside his clothes: fragile, slender, like one of my sons. "I can't tell you . . ." I started, but he moved away from me. He was smiling, but there was a small, strange shadow of awkwardness in his eyes as well, and he lowered them as if to keep me from seeing it.

"Don't get all sappy," he said, moving toward the door. "You don't have to say a thing. And you don't have to worry so fucking much either, you know. 'Physician, heal thyself!' You're starting to look like a mushroom. Get out in. the sunshine, why don't you, MacLeod, and put a little color in that bald spot, okay?" He grinned and rolled his eyes in mock despair.

"Thank you, Doctor," I answered. "I think I might just take your advice—this once."

"Till Friday, then. And wear a different tie? Those things with the little whales on them went out with the Kingston Trio."

"Black tie."

"Are you kidding?" It almost hurt me to see the happiness on his face.

"No, no, I'm not. We're going to live it up, kid. Two wild academic dudes on the town. I'm going to spend a bundle. Pick out someplace classy and expensive, okay? Someplace where we might run into a movie star or two."

He pulled at his beard. "Right-o," he said. "And don't you dare back down. I'll make the reservations, and I'll pick you up around seven." He moved quickly out the door, as if he were afraid I'd change my mind. But there wasn't any question of that. The idea of having some fun for a change really tickled me. I wondered if I were getting better.

27. It Really *Is* a Dress Rehearsal

I never felt that Eliza had treated me unkindly, even when she finally vanished from my life. I know now, however, that she did not hold the same opinion herself, and that she suffered from sometimes overpowering feelings of guilt.

I've explained how I'd seen Eliza and Miles DiGrazia, and how it surprised me to learn that I was not her only love interest at the time. At the time, in fact, I was unable even to conceive of such a thing—not because of my vanity, but simply because of my unusual and overwhelming personal situation. In my mind, Eliza and I existed on a secondary level of purity and virtual isolation: the primary level of existence was inhabited only by myself, my disease (or dis-ease, as I tried to think of it), and my impending death. We seemed, Eliza and I, pretty fairly abstract—in the sense that, since our physical affair was doomed to perpetual imperfection, it was our souls, for want of a better word, that met and conversed and held each other so tightly, making us dissimilar to other lovers—maybe even more elevated. Perhaps that is another reason why I never dwelt on the subject of Eliza's "other life."

She was entitled to one, after all: I could never really fulfill her, and although Eliza's eventual fading from my own life was very painful, it was certainly not unexpected.

I think I had always known, somewhere deep in my mind, that it would happen the way it did, and that it was necessary, and even good, that it should happen. I knew that we could not stay together, that I could not marry her, that even as much as I needed her I could never allow her to be with me in the final days of my illness or allow her even to witness the brutal beginnings of my last decline. I could not leave her a widow, physical or spiritual. Having gotten to know her character so deeply and so easily, I imagined with great clarity the million tiny daggers the last stages of my illness would drive into her heart and the veil of grief that would descend over her clear, unflinching eyes when she felt them.

I began, at some point, and in very small ways at first, to pull away from her. She knew what I was doing. She ignored it. Once, I did not call her for seventeen days; she let me be silent. When I finally called, she did not reproach me. I abruptly stopped petting her so continually, telling her that any even vaguely sexual effort made my head hurt; she said then of course we should avoid it. When I could bear it no more, using all my waning energies to pull her passionately to the couch and make love to her three seconds after she'd come in the door, bringing her to pleasure in every way I could think of (something, by the way, she would not often allow me to do), she simply said, "I've missed you, Jack." I despaired of ever gathering the courage to leave her.

And so of course, on some level, she must have known she had to be the one to leave. She did not want to, of that I am certain, but her healthy instincts were true, and therefore cruel. Life is that way. Who is lucky enough never to have had to make a choice for the best that tore one apart, that hurt someone else grievously, that made "the best" seem a lame thing indeed? Sometimes lives must be taken that lives may be saved. We don't inhabit the best of possible worlds.

Eliza and I had a short but memorable conversation that day I made love to her what seemed like a thousand times. Exhausted, we lay each in the other's arms like weary children. It always amazed me how sex unsexed one, how immediately after the act of love men and women often return, for a short time at least, to a pure state of innocence that allows them to experience an unrestricted relaxation of the ordinary rules of gender. Eliza and I were like that that day, armored by what we had shared against the influence of our pitiless reality. After a while she got up to fix our tea, remembering, as she always did, to use the tall mugs I loved and to sweeten the drink heavily, the way I liked it. By the time she came back to the couch with the tray, I had, unfortunately, returned somewhat to the world. I took her in my arms again and we sat there, sipping our tea and talking.

"I'm glad you let me do that," I told her. "I loved it. And I'm sorry I've been so absent lately."

"That was wonderful," she said. Her voice shook a little. I knew she was feeling sad that I couldn't have the same kind of physical release she did, and I wanted to stop her before everything was spoiled.

"Eliza," I whispered into her hair, taking both our mugs and moving them to the table, "It couldn't have been better for me. I mean that. Forgive me if any of this sounds crude, but I have to tell you this. I've made love a great many times in my life; it does hurt me a little still that I can't complete the act with you in the usual way, but it's not as important as it was at first. At first, quite naturally, I wanted to impress you; I wanted you to think of me the way you might think of any other man—but that's just not the way things are. We have something different; we've made it something splendid. I don't want you to feel guilty that you can enjoy your body so much; I want you to rejoice in it, Eliza, and to rejoice that such pleasure comes to you with love from me. I don't feel physically frustrated anymore—it's not like that, do you understand? I'm not missing anything, and when I can make you feel so good, even for those few moments, it makes me feel just as much your lover as if everything were going the usual way; I hope you can believe that. It's not hard for me to talk about my impotence anymore. I think I've gone beyond it—or maybe I just worry about different things now."

She smiled; I felt her face loosen where it lay against my shoulder. She made a move as if to speak, but I stopped her.

"Wait a minute. Just one more thing. You made me feel so alive this afternoon, Eliza, that's all; you're the only one who can do that now. Sex is whatever people want it to be, you must know that." I felt her move her head to look at me, and I wiggled my eyebrows and made what I hoped was a comically leering face. She giggled.

"You mean," she asked, "that if we really get good at this 'sex-is-what-you-say-it-is' stuff, we'll be able to make love just by tapping our toes together or something?"

I said, "Exactly." She laughed some more. My head was killing me, though I did not tell her that.

She said, "I want to get so good at this that I can just give you a little signal in a restaurant or something and you'll . . ." She giggled again, this time embarrassed, unable to complete her sentence.

I put on my loftiest, most precisely enunciating professorial voice for her. I pretended to be flustered, like her beloved ancient Professor Pettigrew in the English department. "Good heavens," I said.

She collapsed against me, laughing uncontrollably. Then she said, dreamily, "Yeah. I bet we could do it."

There was something in her tone of voice just then that plunged me suddenly into grief once more. It was the voice of a young, vibrant, playful, sexy woman, and I knew she should have been saying what she'd just said to some man equally as alive. She immediately sensed the change in me, and, I think, what had caused it. She suddenly kissed me, hard, on the lips, occasioning a bolt of pain that shot through my head like a fireworks rocket.

"Stop it!" she said. "Don't get into that again. You'll give yourself a headache, and you'll give me one too. Okay? Will you stop it?"

I said I would, and I tried to. But I had to say one last thing. "A few days ago, I heard someone say that life is not a dress rehearsal, and it made me think of you, sweetheart. You ought to be out there living, not here in the semi-darkness with me just attempting to keep a hand in."

She shifted position, nestling her head into my lap. "If this is 'keeping a hand in' life, then I don't mind a bit," she told me. "And I don't believe that dress-rehearsal stuff either. I think maybe life really *is* a dress rehearsal, you know, Jack? There's something else out there. You and I aren't wasting time; I feel like we're preparing for something. I don't know. I guess that sounds crazy. But I'm not willing to take some silly, glib saying like that at face value, and I don't believe you really are either."

Eliza often made perfect uncommon sense. I had no real idea then what she was talking about—no idea I could have articulated—but of course I know now she was right. Maybe my currently dead state is a dress rehearsal too, who knows? And maybe there is no main act, just an endless series of smaller ones. Anyway, what she said that day comforted me more than any of the hours and hours of tortuous thinking I'd done on the subject. I made love to her one more time that afternoon, and when it was over, I held her face and touched it to my aching, bewildered head in what was certainly a sacramental connection. She did not tremble; she did not cry. She made sure before she left the next morning that I would not do so either.

28. A Funeral, Frances,

and a Moment of Clarity

fter a few days, I knew I would never see Eliza again.
The realization came upon me gradually, and I accepted
it the same way, working diligently to make my peace with
each individual aspect of my feelings until I felt I was able to
face the whole of it. There were no signs; I simply knew. I
tried to be grateful that our last hours together had been such
close ones, and that we had not tortured ourselves with any
kind of goodbyes. Indeed, although I grieved, I did not really
feel that any true break had occurred; although I was certain
we would not ever actually meet again, in some sense I knew
we were still together.

Nevertheless, I was all but overcome. It was worse than
losing Sarah because, for one thing, there was no one else I
could blame, nowhere to direct my anger. I fought despair as
long as I could, but then a time came when I could do nothing
for a week or more but sigh intermittently and think about
Eliza. It was then that my mother died. When the telephone
rang late at night, I was still awake, nursing a headache. I knew

in my heart it could not be Eliza, and yet a faint hope rose. It was my Uncle Perry: Mother had died in her sleep, he said; I was needed at home.

I sat there on the couch until morning; I think I hardly moved. I tried to will myself to die right then, and I think the fact that my body was truly paralyzed with fatigue and sorrow was the only thing that kept me from seriously considering suicide. When I heard some school children chattering on their way to the bus stop, I was pulled back to the world. I got up and took a blistering shower. I called Frances and asked her to inform the boys of their Nonny's death, and asked her whether she thought I should take them to the funeral. She was, thank heavens, very kind. She said she would take them herself and offered to call Perry to get all the details—of course I had not thought of anything so practical as that. She called me back in an hour or so and filled me in; I was to meet her, Mark, and Harry at Perry's house later that afternoon. Perry's enormous house would have room enough for all of us to stay a few days, and, she said, in anticipation of my question, of course he knew we needed to have separate rooms.

Naturally I could not drive, but I did not ask Frances to take me. I called my student chauffeur, who was happy to oblige; when he learned why I was going to Connecticut, he insisted on making the trip for free. I promised myself I would find some way to repay him; I regret I never did.

Harry and Mark had seen me often since I'd moved out, and so I suppose they were used to the way I looked, and accustomed to the thickness of my glasses and my strange new half-blind habits, but I'd been able to avoid meeting Frances for many months. When she saw me get out of the passenger side of the Caddy, she was obviously appalled. She came up to me and took my arm in a painful grip.

"Jack," she said. "What the hell is wrong? I mean I know you loved your mother—and God, Jack, you know I did too—and I expected you might look a little under the weather, but this is ridiculous. What's going on with you? You've lost almost all your hair! How did that happen so fast? You're white as flour. You're positively skin and bones. And those glasses! My God, I've never seen anything like them!"

"Thank you, Frances. It's good to see you too." I unhinged her from my arm. Then, in a quieter, menacing tone, I said to her, "Don't ask so many questions, okay? I'll talk to you later, alone. I'll fill you in. Please just keep your mouth shut for a while."

I guess that scared her, as had been my intention. "All right, Jack," she said and marched off in front of me to shepherd the two boys towards their father. After the three of us had hugged and Harry was heading back to Perry's house with my overnight bag, I heard Frances ask him why he'd never told her Dad looked so poorly.

"He doesn't," I heard Harry say. "He just looks a little different, that's all." Love almost choked me.

People were kind to me that day, probably chalking up my unnerving appearance to my mother's death and my constant "overworking." So many people, in fact, referred to this overworking of mine, that I soon deduced that Frances was spreading a story about me to cover up what she must have begun to suspect to be a terrible truth. I did not love her anymore, but she was not stupid or unkind; in her way, she was trying to spare me any more stress on this horrible day. And, except for the boys, she was the only one there I really knew anymore. I decided it wouldn't be so bad to talk to her.

After dinner, she drove us to a lounge she'd seen from the highway. It was so dim inside I couldn't see a thing and was forced to take Frances's arm and be guided to our table. Once seated, I was able to make out the glow of a candle in the centerpiece, and, thinking it would be encased in one of those bumpy little globes, I reached out both hands to cup them around its warmth. But there was no globe; I got all candle and burned the fingertips of one hand painfully. Frances called the waiter and demanded a bowl of ice. She plunged my hand into it and held it there, hard, with her own.

"Now," she said her voice low and calm. "What's going on?" I could hear naked fear in her voice under the toughness. I felt sorry for her, sorrier for the boys. I realized she was the first person since Eliza that I'd had to tell about my illness. I hadn't had enough practice.

"Brain tumor," I said curtly, cruelly. Then for some reason I couldn't say more. I think I smiled a little.

She pressed my wounded hand so viciously into the freezing bowl that an ice cube cracked. She jumped back at the sound. I wondered if it had been a finger breaking—my hand was so cold I couldn't feel it at all. She said, finally, sounding stupefied, "What?"

"Frances, I have a brain tumor. Not malignant, but slowly growing, and inoperable. My vision is slowly getting worse. I'm sorry to break it to you like this, but there just hasn't seemed like a good time to tell you. The boys don't know. I don't see any reason to make them suffer until the end is near. That's what I want to talk to you about, Mark and Harry. It will be rough on them, Frances, but I'm glad they'll have you. You're a good mother. Don't worry about me; I'm all right. I've known about this for a long time, and I'm learning, as they say, to live with it." I paused, removed my frozen hand from the bowl, and dried it on a napkin.

"How long?" she said.

"No one knows," I told her. "Probably quite a while yet. It seems that the type of tumor I have can wax and wane a bit and even move around some at times."

"No," she exclaimed, impatiently. "I mean how long have you known about this?"

Her agitation was palpable. I felt the air around us heat up with the effort she was making not to scream or shake me or overturn the table. But there was no way around it.

"Before I moved out, if that's what you mean."

The waiter came and took our orders. Frances was sweet to him, even a little coquettish, I thought. I wondered how we looked together to this man, what he thought about us. When he left, she let out a huge sigh and drank a whole glass of water.

"I'm sorry, Jack," she said. "I just can't believe it. I can't believe you knew before you left home either." Her voice was shaky. "You could have stayed, you know. I'm not that bad, am I? Did you think I'd turn you out when you were ill?" She'd begun to cry. It made me angry, but I tried to be nice to her.

"It wasn't that," I said. "I just had to be alone. I didn't want pity, and I don't want it now. What I want to talk to you about is the boys. I know this is a shock to you and that I probably should have told you sooner. I just couldn't, that's all. Frances, there have been a lot of complications in my life since I left you, not just the sickness. I'm pretty well exhausted, body and soul."

"Okay," she said. "I hear you." We had a drink (orange juice for me) and talked about Mark and Harry. We mapped out a strategy for informing them of their father's serious illness. We went back to Perry's friendlier than we'd been in a long time. In the car, I could smell the familiar scent of her favorite perfume, and it made me nostalgic.

"Frances," I asked her, "can I ask you something?"

"Ask away."

"I know this will seem bizarre to you, but please don't make fun of me, and don't ask me any questions. When we were really in love, you and I, did you ever rate me as a lover— in your mind, I mean?"

She laughed, but not callously. "I get it," she said. "I wonder who she is. I guess you're not going to tell me?"

"I told you not to ask any questions. If you don't want to answer mine, just say so, and that will be that."

"No, I don't mind. Let's see. On a scale of one to ten I'd say—in your salad days, mind you—you were about a thirteen." She laughed again. "Sorry. I guess that's an unlucky number."

"Thanks," I said, in an exaggerated way, to cover my embarrassment. "I needed that."

∾∾◦◦◦◦◦◦◦∾

The funeral was sweet and dignified and, of course, emotionally draining. I had loved my mother well, and I would miss her. Somewhat consoling was the thought that she did not live beyond me, did not live to experience the crippling pain of witnessing her own child's death. And, as far as she had known, I had always been a success: perhaps I had brought her some comfort, though at the time it was difficult to imagine myself ever having comforted anyone. I spent the rest of the day after mother's burial with the boys, strolling through the pleasant acres surrounding Perry's house and reminiscing with them about Nonny. They did not seem to mind leading me about by the hand; perhaps it was not odd to them anymore, or perhaps the peculiarities of the funeral-day had obliterated all normal reactions. My many recent sorrows had blended into one overpowering cloud. I fairly sleepwalked, feeling little. I did not even have a headache that day. I did not even feel exhausted, although I must have been.

Everything was suspended. It seemed as if all I did was breathe now and then. That feeling of suspension stayed with me for several days, but eventually my loss of Eliza surfaced. I felt I had to call her one last time, just to hear her voice. I had no intention of trying to see her, or even of letting her know that it all was over. She would come to that knowledge herself sooner or later, if she had not already. I knew it was wrong of me to call, but I thought it might save my life. Getting over Sarah had been hard, but I was whole then. My mother's death had been hard too, but that was natural. Eliza had been my lifeline for so long. I needed help with this one.

It had been perhaps three weeks since our last encounter. I called her mother's house, where I knew she was likely to be spending the weekend, hoping against hope that Eliza would answer the phone. She did. She sounded vague and far away, and it seemed to take her a few seconds to identify my voice. Then she sounded frightened.

"Oh, Jack," she said. "I was just dreaming about you."

"You were? In the middle of the afternoon?" I was so taken aback by her opening statement that I'd forgotten why I called.

She sounded terribly excited and spoke in a rush of words. "I know it's afternoon—I can't explain it. My mother went out to do some errands, and I thought I'd help her out and vacuum a little and things like that, but all of a sudden, I got so sleepy, Jack, I could hardly stand up. I lay down on the couch for a minute, and I must have fallen instantly asleep. For a while, I didn't realize I was dreaming; I thought I was just here in this very room and thinking of you and how long it's been since I've seen you, and then I heard a car drive up in front of the house. I looked out the window and there was a long black Cadillac—the same year as yours, but much longer, like a limousine—and you got out of the back seat and started walking up the driveway. You were walking the way you used to walk, so quickly and with such purpose, and I guess that's when I realized it was a dream. You were different. You knocked on the door, and when I opened it, you looked at me as if you'd never seen me before.

"You were so distant, and I was frightened. Then I realized it was a funeral car—not a hearse—I mean it didn't have anything to do with your dying, Jack—but the kind of car people ride in when they're being taken to a cemetery to attend a burial service. Jack, I'm sorry this all sounds so crazy, but please tell me you're all right. It really scared me. Then the phone rang, and it was you." She was starting to sound panicked. "Oh God," she said, "Jack, this is really strange."

I wished I could put my arms around her. "Eliza, listen, sweetheart, it's all right. I'm okay, really. I'm sorry I haven't called you. My mother died last Friday; I just got back from Connecticut. I had to deal with Frances and the boys and a whole bunch of other relatives and when I got back, I just had to be alone for a while, that's all; I've been very tired."

"Your mother? Oh, Jack, I'm sorry. I'm really sorry." Then she stopped and I heard a little intake of breath. "That must have been the car in the dream," she said.

I was stunned. Of course, she was right. Instead of feeling spooked, for some reason I just felt loved, but I didn't know what to say to her. She was right; it was very strange indeed.

I said, "It does seem that way."

"Amazing," she said.

"Not really so amazing. It seems like we communicate even when we don't try. I like that. I hope it doesn't frighten you."

"No, I'm not frightened. I'm just a little shocked. This time it was so obvious. But anyway, I'm glad to hear your voice. Will I see you soon, or are you still tired?"

So she didn't know yet. I would have to be careful. I wanted to say, Eliza, you've already left me, and I know you've done the right thing. But all I said was, "I really am, love. I think I just need to be alone for a while longer. I was just calling to hear your voice."

"I understand," she said. "Shall I call you Saturday? That way you'll have the whole week. Would that be okay?"

"Saturday would be perfect, "I said, trying to sound normal. "Until Saturday then."

"I love you, Jack. Are you sure you're all right?"

"I'm sure. I love you too."

"Bye."

"Eliza?"

"Yes?"

"Never mind. It'll keep. Take care, love."

"You too," she said.

Saturday came and went. On earth, I never heard her voice again.

<hr/>

But that very same day an odd miracle did occur. At twilight, my worst time of day for seeing, I ventured out for a little walk on the grass. There was a park of sorts behind the apartment complex with a couple of benches and some greenery and such. I thought I should get out of the apartment for a while. I was as sure as I could be that Eliza would not call, so I wasn't worried about leaving the telephone. I walked slowly along the little fence to one of the benches and sat down, thinking of Eliza, my head bent backwards towards the sky. I imagined I saw her face among some stars, but it was purely imaginary, since I could not really see the stars either. Suddenly I began to feel cold, then just as suddenly warm. I wondered if I were having some kind of attack connected to my illness, but then I felt a curious sensation of expectation. It reminded me of something I'd read once about certain psychics who experience an "aura" before some other-worldly occurrence. I told myself that that was absurd, that I was probably just getting sicker.

Then I heard a roaring noise—internally, somewhere inside my head, but more distant and detached than that—and what sounded like trees falling. For some reason I looked down at my feet. Some dried brown oak leaves were swirling there in a little eddy of wind, but the sounds were magnified enormously. The leaves were beautiful: they crackled and scraped along the ground in a graceful wind-dance; their edges were delicately curled, and their stems still lined with traces of jade and acid green. I was *seeing* them. I felt a rush of joy that almost knocked me off the bench. Not only could I see them, but I could see them better than I had ever seen anything before: everything was perfectly clear, perfectly beautiful, perfectly outlined in shadow and light like a photographic masterpiece—a stirring, wind-roaring film of astonishing grandeur.

But as soon as I realized I could see, I could not; in fact, my vision, by contrast, seemed even a little worse. The leaves were still there, dancing. I could feel and hear them. But my moment of clarity and brightness was gone. A last gift, perhaps. Whatever it was, it had happened. It was over. I made my way back to the apartment and got into bed, still wondering about it. I had no one to tell now. I wanted to call Eliza, but I did not let myself. I fell asleep quite bitter. If this one last chance to see had been a gift from the gods, why could it not have been Eliza's face in front of me, and not a bunch of leaves?

29. A Twirling Nosedive

Don and I arranged to dine at a small but elegant seafood restaurant in the Village. We'd both reached the conclusion that the black-tie idea was really a bit much and decided we'd be happier celebrating in a more comfortable way. Driving into the city, I wondered why I had a headache again and decided I was probably just hungry and overtired. Don seemed tired too; in fact, he looked rather sad. This is great, I thought: some celebration. I've got a whopping pain in the head, and Rath looks like his cat just died. But as we neared the restaurant, his face brightened considerably.

"I think this will be just what we both need," he said.

We were given a very good table, secluded behind some bamboo plants and near a thinly curtained window, so that the city lights were softened for us. Don ordered a double Campari with lime, and I followed suit. I loosened my tie; I began to feel better. We both ordered trout and asparagus. When our cocktails arrived, I downed mine speedily and sat back to listen to Don rattle on about some student confrontation he'd had that day. I was in no hurry; I knew we'd work up to the Mussel stuff in due time.

The waiter brought our salads, and then the trout. I looked down at the grilled fish, split down the middle and spread-eagled on the plate like a Picasso print, and felt suddenly very ill. The waiter was asking me something, but I couldn't make it out. I decided to make a dash for the men's room and put out my hand to steady myself on the table, but then everything began to go black and sparkly. I remember thinking, so this is what fainting is like, and then the next thing I knew I was waking up on a leather sofa in somebody's office with Don's face looming over me and his hand on my wrist. He seemed to be taking my pulse, which I thought very odd. When I opened my eyes, he started.

"Oh, thank God. Mac, are you all right? No, no, never mind. You don't have to say anything. You fainted, I think. Very bizarre. Should I call a doctor? I told them not to call 911, but maybe that was wrong. Maybe you're getting the flu or something. Anyway, I—"

"Where am I? Isn't that what one says under these conditions?"

"Well, if you can still be witty, I guess you're going to live. This, my dear fellow, is the manager's office. And this," he said, plucking the sleeve of what I suddenly realized was not my own garment, "this is the manager's shirt. Obliging man, I must say. He said you could keep it. You more or less drowned your own shirt in trout juices on your way to the floor. Very untidy. Lucky thing you'd taken off that nice jacket already. The tie is ruined, however. No great loss."

"On my way to the floor?"

"Oh yes. You made a sort of twirling nose-dive. For a split second I almost laughed, you looked so fucking funny. But then of course I realized you were ill. Do you feel any better?"

I sat up slowly. I still had a small headache, but I usually did in those days. Otherwise, I felt fine. "Yes," I told him. "Much.

No doctor, please. Maybe it was the Campari, I don't know. I did guzzle it down kind of fast. God. I can't believe I keeled over like that. Sorry to spoil dinner."

Don began to bustle around, picking up our belongings and straightening up the couch and cushions. "Don't mention it. And now I think I'd better thank the nice manager, pay up, and get you out of here."

I stood up. I felt pretty good. "Great," I said, "thank you. Did I throw up?"

Don laughed. "No, nothing but a nice genteel yet dramatic fainting spell. Don't worry about it." And he was off, returning quickly with my jacket and bundling me off into the night.

On the way home I stretched out on the back seat of his car, at his suggestion. I felt tired and disappointed. We hadn't even had a chance to form a plan regarding Mussel, and I'd spoiled Don's dinner as well.

I must have fallen asleep, because it seemed like only an instant had passed when I heard Don say, "Here we are, Professor. Beddy-bye time for you." I thanked him again and walked up the steps to my front door carefully, holding on to the wrought iron railing. There was a light on in Frances's room, but the place was perfectly quiet. I went straight to bed, not even bothering to brush my teeth. Just before I abandoned consciousness for the third time that evening, I thought I heard Mussel's voice say "darling." It was a depressing auditory hallucination, and I thought, I certainly hope this sort of thing isn't going to continue. It didn't. But it was no hallucination.

30. Turning Out the Patio Lights

Don Rath and I got together again soon after our aborted dinner date to talk over what was to be done with the information Don had uncovered. I was all for blowing the cover off Mussel's little scam immediately; Don was more circumspect. He convinced me that timing was crucial, that only by letting the gruesome cat out of the bag at the perfect moment could we be assured of the effect we wanted: Mussel's immediate dismissal. I was afraid for Sarah, naturally, but although Don agreed that the scandal would be hard on her, he was sure that the inevitable outcome would be that Sarah would waken from her nightmare, realize her dreadful mistake in marrying the man, and leave him. It might take time, Don said, but it was certain to happen just that way. I wanted to believe him.

But in truth I was out for blood. It was becoming gradually very clear to me that my affair with Sarah had amplified my awareness of my deep hatred for Mussel and all he stood for. Although I didn't really share Don's opinion that Sarah could still be saved (and I certainly didn't think she'd ever again be a part of my own life—I didn't even want her to be), I desperately wanted Mussel out of the picture. Cynically, I figured he would eventually scrape off any tar and feathers we might be able to slather upon him and set himself up in another comfortable position elsewhere, but I did not care. I wanted him to suffer, at least for the moment.

Maybe a little part of me wanted Sarah to suffer too, but it was an unworthy part of myself and I pushed it away. I considered only that she had been duped, assaulted, and forced to lose touch with herself, and that any pain we might cause her through Mussel's departmental defrocking would eventually prove to be for her own good.

It was Don's opinion that the yearly departmental budget meeting would be the beginning of Mussel's end. Don knew, through his friendly association with the weirdly Mussel-fixated Dottie, that her boss was about to recommend that all faculty salary increases be stalled for the second year running, and that he was also planning to reject several important requests for research funding and sorely needed lab and classroom materials. He would use the money saved on these essentials to spiff up his enormous office and allow himself travel to conferences in exotic places. Don felt that the faculty would be so incensed over these blatantly self-serving frugalities that members would be easy to approach with any anti-Mussel propaganda. Once we had a few of the more powerful professors on our side, we would go to the dean with our story. I thought that would probably be as far as we needed to go, but Don felt it highly possible that there were people on the lofty end of the totem pole who, for various corrupt reasons, would try to uphold Mussel's reputation and position. If that proved true, Don said, we had to be prepared to go to the press. We were.

The weeks dragged by and the big meeting approached. Don kept Dottie on constant alert for news: he'd become paranoid that Mussel might try, in his inimitable way, to have someone else do the dirty work for him at the meeting. But when there was less than a week to go, I ran into Dr. M. himself in the men's room. He greeted me in his usual insincere way, and we had one of our usual meaningless conversations, but I was able to ascertain that he did indeed intend to favor us all with his presence at the meeting.

My headaches had been getting worse all this time, and my eyes were starting to bother me more as well, but I told no one. I was already beginning to form an idea of my probable diagnosis, but there was so much happening that I could not stop to think about it long. I was afraid, but I was preoccupied. I'd also discovered that a stiff drink and four extra-strength Tylenol made me feel quite a bit better, and one night, just a few days before the department meeting, I went off with Don to a local hideaway to soothe my head and spirit. After listening to a couple of his hilarious stories and discreetly downing my pills with two bourbons, I felt almost human. We stayed on rather late, each of us seemingly unwilling to leave the comfort of the other's presence: the encumbrance of our secret had bound us together in a strange brotherhood.

All the lights were out when I got home. I looked in on the boys, something I rarely did any more. Harry was lying on top of his still made-up bed in his gym shorts; I covered him with a quilt. He was tall and had Frances's beautiful hair. Mark had left the radio on, and when I turned it off, he twitched a little, as if I had pulled something out of his hand. The radio had been tuned to a classical station, which surprised and pleased me. I wished I knew more about my sons.

As I went into the bathroom, I thought I heard some muffled noises in the kitchen, and then the familiar click of the patio screen door as it closed. Since I had just seen both boys asleep, and since I assumed Frances to be sleeping as well, the noises worried me a little. A prowler was not something I felt up to dealing with, but of course I had to see about the noise.

It was only Frances. She was sipping a glass of wine at the kitchen table and wearing a bizarre outfit unlike anything I'd seen her (or anyone) wearing before: a sort of cheap-looking, satiny, bright pink negligee with marabou trim—like an ensemble from one of those cheesy boutiques that advertise in the backs of magazines. Her hair was combed out long, but was encased in, of all things, a lacy snood of sorts, with little flowery specks all over it, and on her feet were feathery high-heeled slippers that matched the negligee. My first impulse was to laugh. She jumped up from her chair when she heard me, then gave me a frightened, hateful glare. It made her look all the more outlandish, but it stopped my laughing. I felt, in fact, a little scared.

"You have no right to spy on me like that, Jack," she said, sitting back down. "I didn't think anyone was up."

"I wasn't spying on you, Frances, for God's sake. I heard some noise down here, that's all. Did you go out on the porch just now? I thought I heard the door."

"What if I did?" she said, drilling her eyes through me.

I went to the refrigerator and got some milk, pouring it into a big tumbler. I had to find out what was going on and I knew she wouldn't come right out and tell me. I sat down opposite her with my glass and a package of Oreos. I knew she hated to watch anyone dunk them, so I started right in dipping. She turned away from me, but, curiously, said nothing, and made no move to go upstairs.

"So, Frances," I said. "I see you've made some adjustments to your wardrobe."

"I make enough money. I can buy what I like."

"No question about that. Is this what the modern-day

corporate lawyer lady wears to lounge about in of an evening? Or," and I couldn't stop my giggles from coming back, "were you expecting a late-night visit from Bela Lugosi?"

I knew I shouldn't have said that, but I didn't expect her to throw her wine glass at me, which is exactly what she did. Fortunately, I ducked, and the thing shattered harmlessly against the wall over the sink. Frances began to cry. I got up and began picking pieces of glass out of the sink and putting them into the garbage.

"I seem to have upset you," I said.

She went to the cabinet, withdrew a glass, and poured herself another drink. "You shit," she said. Frances hardly ever swore.

"Come on, Frances. Either you want to talk about tonight's strangeness, or you don't. If you don't, please leave me alone. I've got a headache, and I'm tired. If you do, fine, let's talk. But I'm not interested in your histrionics. Frankly, coupled with your tasteful outfit, they're a little hard to take seriously."

That set her off. "Take seriously!" she shouted. "When was the last time you took me seriously? You don't take anyone seriously who hasn't got at least a one-sixty IQ, and you know it. You're a horrible person. You're more interested in a brilliant underachiever than a person like me who has done very well with a slightly less than certifiably amazing intellect. I haven't had your full attention in years, Professor Big Shot." She paused and took a huge gulp of her pinot grigio.

"You don't like the way I look?" she went on. "Who cares! Maybe I'm not dressing for you, did you ever think of that? Maybe not every professor is a goddamned head-in-the-clouds weirdo like you, did that ever occur to you? Maybe—"

I stopped her. "At least keep your voice down, Frances. You can be as hateful as you like at a lower volume. I don't want the boys down here."

She stared at me. "The boys," she said, only a little more softly. "What the hell do you know about the boys? When was the last time you took them anywhere, or even had a talk with them?"

"Guilty. I've been very distracted lately. I'm going to do something about that. But I don't think that's really the topic tonight, is it? Let's get to the point."

"The point is that I'm sick of you always creeping around here after dark. I'm sick of living with someone I don't even know anymore, sick of tiptoeing around my loathing of you, Jack. That's it; that's the topic, if you must know."

"And you want a divorce." It might have been the bravest—or most cowardly—thing I'd ever said.

"I want . . . I don't know . . ." She began crying again. She looked so ridiculous in her Frederick's of Hollywood outfit that it made her quite pitiful. I went up behind her and put my hands on her shoulders. "Frances," I said. "I don't know what to do for you."

She shook off my hands, sprang up out of the chair, and faced me. She ripped the flowered kerchiefy thing from her hair and tossed her head back in a deliberate, seductive movement that was perfectly shocking. For a strange split second, I thought she was about to kiss me. Then, in a low and menacing voice, she said, "I've got a lover, Jack. And so do you, I know. I couldn't care less. One of your little geniuses, probably. I just don't care. You want to know why I'm dressed like this? Because it turns my lover on, that's why. So what if it's not sophisticated!"

I was glued to the spot. She went on, "You think every man on earth is as stuffy and intellectual as you are? You've been walking around like a zombie with your nose in your books for so many years that I'm surprised you even noticed what I'm wearing. And I'm glad you don't like it! That thrills me, Jack! Anything you don't like is okay with me. Wally likes—" She stopped, clapped a hand over her mouth, and stared at me, her eyes wild. She sat back down.

I went to the sink and ran the cold water, but I couldn't seem to remember where to find a glass. I was sure I was going to be sick, but somehow I controlled my stomach. My head was another matter: the pain seemed to pitch it from side to side like a loose barrel on a ship's deck. I put my wrists under the stream of icy water, not even taking off my watch. Frances said nothing.

Finally, I turned off the water and dried my hands. I thought if I could make it to the bedroom, I would never leave there. I would try to will myself to die, but if I couldn't, I would simply stay there forever, holding on to my aching head and watching the shadows change on the walls from morning to night to morning. I couldn't even look at Frances as I walked past her.

But then I remembered the noises I'd heard. It occurred to me that Mussel had probably left the back door unlocked when he went out. I went and locked it, then turned out the patio lights. I went slowly upstairs. I fell asleep quickly, mercifully. When I woke the next day, I realized I'd missed both my morning classes.

31. Don in a Pith Helmet

At some point I began to grow my thinning hair long, according to the latest fashion, though it probably didn't suit me, and I began to see more of Eliza. Mostly we would just meet in my office in the early evenings and talk for an hour or two. She was funny and charming and a little troubled by her inability to fit in with college life. Eliza never wanted to join a sorority or anything like that—she had no desire to mainstream to that degree—but she did find her classmates considerably more frivolous than herself, and therefore felt a bit the odd woman out at times. I helped her relax about that, telling her it was a natural consequence of her advanced maturity and intelligence, and that things would quickly even out for her in the coming years. Being with me calmed her; being with her gave me some kind of reason to go on living. She knew nothing about my life outside of school and she never asked; her respect for my privacy, her high regard for my advice, and her obvious pleasure in simply sharing my company did much to knit together the frayed fabric of my peace of mind.

Frances began divorce proceedings, and I did nothing to stop her. Except for matters regarding the boys, I was relieved. I tried not to think about my physical problems too much; I knew there would be time enough for that later. My most immediate problem was Don Rath.

At first, I could not bring myself to tell him what I'd discovered about Frances and Mussel. Two days before the faculty meeting, I called him into my office and told him I wanted to drop the Mussel thing. It was one of the hardest sentences I ever had to say to anyone. I did not give him any reasons.

"I don't believe you," he said.

"I'm sorry, Don, I'm really sorry. I have to back out. Of course, if you want to carry this through on your own, I won't try to stop you. I just can't support you, that's all. In fact, if that's what you decide to do, I don't even want to know about it. I can't handle it right now, and I'm not in a position to explain why. I hope you'll forgive me, but I'll understand if you can't."

He left my office abruptly, without saying a word, then returned a minute or two later, looking red-faced and drained, as if he'd been punching something. I was still sitting at my desk. He sat down opposite me and grabbed the edge of the desk as if it were a mountain ledge and he was holding on for dear life.

"Jack," he said. "Please! Please, tell me what the trouble is. You can't have had a change of heart so suddenly unless something terrible has happened. You've got to tell me—there's no question of forgiving you or not forgiving you—that's silly. But I think you owe me some kind of explanation. I can't handle it otherwise, Jack; I'm sorry. I just don't understand."

He was right, of course; I don't know what made me think he would just accept my decision and go away quietly: how

could he? He was my friend; he deserved to know. Ever since
that awful night in the kitchen with Frances, my most overwhelming emotions had been anger and sadness. Being with
Eliza now and then had taken the edge off those. But I realized now, just before I filled Don in on the whole situation,
that what was really torturing me was humiliation. I felt so
powerless, so unmanned: two women with whom I'd been
intimately involved had chosen Mussel over me. It stuck in
my throat like a rubbery fishbone—not dangerous enough to
kill me, but uncomfortable enough to make every swallow
an ordeal.

I had some coffee in a thermos, and I poured a cup for
each of us. "I'm sorry," I told him. "You're right. I'll tell you.
But then you've got to accept my decision, okay? Don't try
to convince me to go ahead with this thing. Promise?"

"Sure, Jack, if that's what you want. I promise." He looked
young and solemn, like an altar boy just before the consecra-
tion of the host.

"I found out something last week that set me on my butt,
and hard. Mussel isn't being faithful to Sarah."

"That doesn't surprise me. But what's it got to do with
anything?"

I drained my cup of coffee. I put my head in my hands
and spoke directly into the desk blotter. "He's having an affair
with Frances," I said.

Don was silent; I thought he hadn't heard me, I lifted my
head and said it again, with robot-like precision. "Frances—my
wife, Frances—and Mussel are having an affair," I repeated.
Then, oddly, I added, "In my house."

Don got up and went over to the window. "Oh. Shit," he
said. "Jesus fucking Christ. Worse and worse. But, my God,"
he said suddenly catching himself and turning back toward

me, "I'm so sorry, Jack, I really am. If I feel this way about it,
I can only imagine how you must feel. Or I guess I can't. It's
horrible. I'm sorry."

Now that he knew, I felt a little better. "It's not that I'm
in love with Frances, as you know. It's just . . ."

"Yeah. I get it."

"The two of them, Don. Sarah and Frances. What's the
matter with me? Is this some kind of evil karma? I'm just
about willing to believe anything now." I put my head back
in my hands.

"That's all ridiculous and you know it," he said, his voice
nearly shaking. "There's nothing wrong with you, nothing.
You're fabulous, you're great, any woman in her right mind
would realize that and value you." He paused. "Fuck it, Jack,
let's face it: that's how I feel about you myself. I'm sure that
comes as no surprise to you, and I'm not ashamed to admit it
either. I know you know; and you know I know you know—
but it hasn't changed anything between us, and it won't now.
You're great." He was pacing around now, breathing in little
quick puffs.

"All that's beside the point," he went on. You've had a
spate of unbelievable bad luck, that's all. Come on, Jack; it
won't last forever. I'm a shrink and so are you: we both know
there's nothing 'wrong' with you. I hate to hear you say things
like that. Don't start getting really depressed, or I'll have to
really psychoanalyze you—and I'm sure you don't want that
to happen. If anything will make you nuts, it's having me for
a therapist."

He tried to give me his charming grin, but it came out
sad and lopsided. It unlocked my heart, and my voice. I'd
known he was in love with me for a long time; he was right—it
hadn't changed anything between us, and it wouldn't now, but

hearing him say it was a relief. It meant I could trust him completely. There wasn't any reason to hide anything from him.

"There's something else," I said. "You might as well know it."

"What?" He sighed a little. I knew he was strong, but I also knew he had no reason to expect what was coming."

"I'm dying."

He just stared at me. "No," he finally said. "Come on."

"Yes," I answered. "I'm afraid so. It's true; I'm going to die. Not soon, I don't think. All these headaches, you know? And my vision's been poor too. I went to a friend of mine in New York, a specialist, and he said—"

"Inoperable?"

"Yeah. But it's not malignant, at least."

He went pale, and sat back in the chair, still looking at me with disbelief.

"Don, I'm sorry to have to lay all this on you," I said. "It seems like ever since I've known you all I've done is tell you my troubles. Don't worry about me. I should be able to go on for some time in a relatively normal way. I've got enough pain medication to anesthetize an army, if I need it. I'll make whatever adjustments are necessary. Needless to say, this has got to be our secret. I can't afford to be fired, for any reason. And oh," I added, as an afterthought, "Frances has filed for divorce."

The way I had tacked that on made him explode into one of his laugh-coughs. I chuckled too. "All's well that ends well," I said.

When we'd stopped laughing, Don said, "Oh, brother."

I said, "I'm sorry about the Mussel thing."

He waved his hand. "Doesn't matter. It was becoming too much of an obsession with me anyhow. Someday he'll get his, you can be sure of that. Maybe someday I'll even take

it up again, if he makes me mad enough. Maybe I'll just let
him know what we discovered—wouldn't that be fun? But
for now, I'll be glad to let it go. The important thing is what
happens to you. When are you leaving your house? Where are
you going to move to?"

I hadn't thought about that; I guess on some level I knew
I was supposed to move out of my unhappy home, but it
seemed so unreal to me that I hadn't made a single plan. "I
don't know," I said. "Any ideas?"

"Of course. I know just the place for a wild old bachelor like
you. A new building in a development called Mapleview. We'll
go look at it next week, okay? Or would sooner be better?"

"Next week is fine. That'll be great. I guess I do need a
little help on the practical end."

He smiled. "That's what I'm here for. Denny always says I
should have been one of those old-time personal secretaries—
you know: capable, discreet, ready to handle any detail at the
drop of a hat." He grinned. "Guess I missed my calling."

I got up to walk him to the door. I put my arm around
him. "Thanks," I said. "For everything you said. I don't know
what I'd do—would have done—without you."

"Everything? It didn't make you squirm?"

"No. I feel honored you trusted me enough to tell me.
Also, I'm flattered."

"Thank God," he said, laughing. "I was afraid you'd be
terrified."

"Idiot," I said. "I'll call you tomorrow."

When Don was gone, I looked out the window. I'd thought
he'd be going back to his office, but apparently our conversation had taken too much out of him. He headed out across the
lawn toward the parking lot, briefcase in hand. I saw him get
into his car and sit there quite a while, not moving. Then he

got out again, went around to the trunk, opened it, and took out, of all things, a pith helmet—a relic, I knew, from a student drama production he'd been involved with. He put it on and drove away, looking like he was going into town searching for giraffes. I wished I were gay. I wished I were ten years younger. I wished I didn't know I was going to die.

32. Happy Talk and

the Water Cure

Funny I've waited so long to mention my talk show: it was such an important, though relatively brief, phase of my career. At first when I was forced to leave NSU (more on that later), I had no clear idea of what I was going to do. I moved in a hurry, to a quaint little three-bedroom with a yard in a western Massachusetts town I'd always loved. The rent was about half of what I'd been paying at Mapleview. I'd managed to secure some part-time teaching at a state college nearby, but I knew if I didn't keep busier than that I'd go crazy in no time at all. One of my students got me interested in the talk show idea by bringing up something he'd heard on the radio in a class discussion. The concept was new to me, though I was told the phenomenon had been a popular one for some years, and I began to listen to a New York station late at night when the reception was clear. The host was a woman psychologist whose personality and voice intrigued me no end; I think I developed a little crush on her in fact.

I decided to try and contact her—not just to find out about the mechanics of such a program, but just to have someone to talk to—and the logical place to start was to call during the show. One night I phoned in, and it was the beginning of a long friendship. The lady's name was Dr. Susan Green. After my first call, during which we'd discussed (in a names-changed-to-protect-the-guilty sort of way) a bit of the Sarah-Frances-Mussel scenario (which, although it took a lot to shock Dr. Green, was obviously quite an unusual type of problem for her to handle), she went to a commercial break, kept me on the line, and asked if I'd like to talk some more the next evening. I said yes; it was the first time in ages that I'd felt the dual luxuries of anonymity and compassion. Soon I was a weekly regular on her show. It was great fun. Dr. Green had of course quickly elicited my profession, and she drew me out about my illness and exile gracefully and surefootedly. Sometimes, after the program, we would talk off the air, and although she invited me to visit her any time I happened to be in the New York area, I knew I would probably never meet her in person. I'm sure she knew that too, but she was kind enough to ask.

And then the day came when Dr. Green called me and said she had decided to take a long overdue vacation and would be away from the program for three weeks. Usually, the station played tapes of old programs when she was absent, but in this case, since the hiatus would be more than a few days, they were looking for a stand-in. I had become a popular part of the program, she said, and since I was so eminently qualified, would I consider "subbing" for her? She immediately mentioned a tempting sum of money, but I didn't need much encouragement. She'd thought of all the practical details too: they would hook up a "remote" to my place in the hills and do the shows live from New York with the assistance of a young tech expert who would visit me while the show was in progress. I accepted at once. And, after a couple of nights of feeling rather tentative and insecure, I had the time of my life. The whole experience was extraordinarily freeing and fulfilling. I could be myself, but no one could see me. I could feel people's respect again—something that hadn't come my way in a long, long time. I could actually help people again as well, which gave my confidence a great boost. My visual handicap was no handicap at all; if anything, it allowed me to concentrate more fully on the voices of the callers so that I was able to determine a great deal just from the way they spoke and the words they chose. I felt very close to the people who called, and I felt a warmth coming back from that audience that was reminiscent of my first days of teaching.

When Dr. Green returned, she called me and exclaimed, "A star is born!" I laughed and told her what a good time I'd had. She replied that even before she'd gotten back to her office her assistant had called to tell her how successful the fill-in shows had been, and how callers were already demanding to know when "Dr. Mac" would be back and even when I'd have my own show. I couldn't believe I'd been such a hit, but I was delighted with my success. It was the first success of any kind I'd had in what felt like centuries.

So, with Susan Green's gracious assistance, I was put in touch with a local station that just happened to be looking for a late-night program that would bring their rural listeners up to date with current radio trends. They agreed to try me out for a month, but by the second week they had offered me a contract, and I was on my way. It was wonderful; my disease had threatened to make a real hermit of me, but I had been delivered by a miracle of the electronic age. Every weekday evening around eight o'clock, two young men arrived on my doorstep to set things up for the show, and to help me however I needed them. The three of us became fast friends; they called me "Doc," and saw me through some rough moments.

Tactful and efficient, they treated my near blindness as if it didn't exist, which was exactly what I needed. I came to think of them as Harry and Mark grown up, for I missed my boys sorely in those days. I reveled in this nightly public contact for three months, and then my head started to give me serious trouble.

I surmised, when I could manage to surmise anything, that the end was very near. My symptoms increased suddenly in intensity, and I was shocked. The headaches were overpowering at times, and no amount of medication or self-hypnosis could put a dent in them. My vision was poor, and I became bothered by memory lapses and a terrifying though intermittent weakness in the left side of my body. I stopped teaching. I also had to stop the radio work and the station manager was kind enough, as he put it, "to place things on hold." My intention was to sit back and die, but I could not stick it out, and one night, wracked by physical agony and a sickening fear, I called Don Rath.

I hadn't heard his voice since I'd moved—by my own choice. I'd asked him if he wouldn't allow me a little time to adjust to things on my own, and, although I could tell he was worried, he assented with his usual understanding. The morning I called (it was really very early; I'd been up most of the night with my pain), Denny answered. He put Don on right away.

He'd been fast asleep, but when he heard my voice, he perked up instantly. "Mac," he said gently. Then, without waiting for me to utter a word, "How bad is it?"

"The worst," I said. "Suddenly I'm immobilized. I don't know what I want, Don, or even what I need." I began, unexpectedly, to cry; up until that time I'd been curiously numb emotionally. He let me ramble on a while, then he said, "I've been getting dressed as you were speaking. Don't do anything till I get there, okay? I should be able to make the drive in about five hours. Will you be all right till then? If not, I can call someone for you. Don't take any more pills. Have you got any music?"

"Music?"

"Any kind of music. Any records or tapes or anything— you've got a radio, right?"

"I've got lots of music," I said. "But I'm not much in the mood for a concert."

"Never mind that." His voice reminded me of my father's all of a sudden: that blend of concern and authority that would brook nothing but obedience and respect. "Just please do as I say. You must be exhausted. Do you have, by any chance, a portable tape-deck?"

As luck would have it, I did.

"That's very good. Bring it into the bathroom. Put it somewhere across the room from the tub for safety. Run a very warm bath—put in a lot of salt. Have you got salt?"

"I think so."

"Put in a whole box. Gather up all the Vivaldi and Bach tapes you've got—have you got any?"

"Sure, yes, of course, lots."

"Pick out the longest one and set the player on a loop if you can. No pop music, okay? Nothing with lyrics. No words. Get in the tub. Stretch out. Roll up a hot, wet towel and put it behind your neck. Put a hot washcloth on your forehead. Then dive into the music. Each note. Let yourself float away. Wait a minute . . ."

His voice was beautiful, deliberate, calming. I heard the sound of the phone being placed on a table, a short pause, then he came back. "Sorry. Had to find some shoes. Just dive into every note. Don't think. Don't think about your body or anything else. Just relax. Concentrate on the music. Have you got that?"

"Yeah. Sounds dreamy," I said, thinking it was a sweet idea, but somewhat naïve—I didn't think anything was going to help me at this point.

"Right-o. That's what I'm hoping. Stay in the tub until you shrivel up, then go to bed. Leave your door unlocked—is that okay? I mean, it's safe enough to do that up there in the wilderness, isn't it?"

"Perfectly safe," I said. "Except for the bears."

"Yeah, well, animals like you, right? Go draw your bath. I'll be there as soon as I can, you know."

"Okay," I said. "But Don, you don't know where I live."

"Of course I do. I've had the route mapped out since you left. Someday I'll fill you in on my detective work."

Then I heard him say, off to the side, "Denny, what time is it?' and then, "Good grief."

To me he said, "See you before dinner. Are you sure you're okay for a few hours?"

"Yes. Don, I don't want to put you out—it would be enough just to talk to you, I think. I—"

"Get in the tub, please. I've got to go. If anything weird happens—anything at all—call Denny. He'll be here all day, and he doesn't mind. I'll stop and call him along the way to see if he's heard from you. Now, are you going to follow my directions, Mac?"

"Yes. I will. Thank you, I—" But he'd hung up quickly.

I followed all his suggestions, and they worked like a charm. Although my head still hurt, the pain was manageable, and before the tape was over, I was ready to try to sleep. The music had worked its magic on my panicked mind, and the hot, salty water had rendered my body limp and compliant. I remember girding myself in a towel, sloshing into the bedroom half-wet, and falling on top of the covers like a thirsting man into an oasis. I dreamed every dream on the books that morning, I think. It was more like a fever-sleep than anything else, but I needed it sorely. When I finally awoke, I lay there for a while, then reached over to a chair for my robe. Don handed it to me. He must have been sitting there for hours.

∽∽∽◇◇∽◇∽◇∽◇◇∽

The very next day he drove me two hours to a doctor in Boston. He stayed over. The day after that, armed with some stopgap, super strength painkillers and tranquilizers, we drove to New York to see my friend Gerry.

I actually enjoyed the drive; Don was quieter than usual, but whenever I was awake, he kept me occupied listening to his wonderful, funny stories. I heard a lot about his life that day, although I didn't do much talking myself.

Gerry didn't keep us waiting. He seemed very glad to see me and scolded me for staying away so long. I wished I could clearly see the expression on his face, which I knew would tell me a lot about how he thought I looked, but all I could do was run his voice through my now very sensitive ears. I thought he sounded extremely worried. The three of us talked for a few minutes, and then he sent Don out to the waiting room and started my examination. It didn't take long. I've noticed that the more serious one's complaint, the less time one spends with one's clothes off in the doctor's office. In my case, there were a lot more tests to be done, but they had to be done in the hospital, and Gerry arranged for Don to accompany me there that very afternoon. Before we left, Gerry and I had a little talk: a little talk I'd been dreading.

"Gerry," I said straight off, "if it's as bad as I think, I don't want to waste a lot of time getting tortured and prodded by your finest colleagues. The only reason I'm here is because things deteriorated so suddenly. I've been prepared to go out slowly for a long time, but I got really scared when things went sour so fast. Have you been able to form any opinion today, or do I really have to go through with the testing?"

"I think you should," he said, looking at me over the top of his bifocals. "I have a suspicion I want checked out. The tests I've ordered are fairly simple, and you should be able to go home again tonight, if that's what you want. Or you could stay in the city and come see me again tomorrow afternoon when I'll have all your results. Is your friend free to stay with you? If not, I'm sure I can arrange for you to stay here."

"I'll ask him. He can probably stay. The poor guy drove all the way up to get me the night before last, then drove me down here this morning; I don't think he's expecting to get home for dinner."

"I'm glad you have someone to help you out. How are Frances and the boys?"

Poor Gerry. I always felt sorry for people who blundered into quicksand because the map was defective: I'd given Gerry no clue. I sighed. "Frances is divorcing me. That's why—well, that's partly why—I've been living up north. The boys are fine, I think, but I miss them."

"Good lord, Jack. I'm sorry to hear that. On top of everything else, it must be really rough."

The phrase "on top of everything else" struck me as rather funny; the man didn't know how much suffering those few words embraced. But I didn't want him to start feeling sorrier for me than he already did.

"Yeah," I said, "but up until a few days ago I was plugging along. Sorry I didn't keep in touch, but it just wasn't possible. You understand. Nothing personal, Gerry; you know that."

He said he did, of course, and we arranged to meet again just before dinner the next day. Then Don whisked me off to another part of the hospital for my tests. It really wasn't too bad, and they even gave me a shot for my newest headache as a kind of special treat, I guess. It was an experimental drug (I had to sign about twenty papers before they'd try it on me, and they made it clear that this was a one-time deal) for what they called "discomfort management."

The injection was so effective that by seven o'clock I was actually lusting for food. Don couldn't believe it. I talked him into taking me to that same restaurant where I'd fainted. We ordered the trout again, both of us behaving like starving men. Then we got a big room in a nearby hotel. The two double beds were hard and the pillows big and fluffy, just the way I liked things. I fell asleep very quickly. My last memory that night, before the wild dreams started, was seeing Don propped up on his bed reading a book that looked like it weighed sixty pounds. I wondered what it could be, and if he always carried such things around with him. All I could see was a silhouette of him there, but it soothed me unimaginably. I guess I was never really meant to be alone.

33. An Elevator Dream

I said "before the wild dreams started"—and what dreams they were. I've always been a champion dreamer, and for years, when I was young, I kept big fat journals detailing everything I could recall about them. It seemed, and still does, like another life altogether: a brilliant, curious, superbly active life that took place only after I'd closed my eyes and given over mind, soul, and body to a purely magical state. Eliza and I used to spend a lot of time talking about dreams, engaging in a delightful kind of one-upmanship that would leave us fascinated, awed, and hungry for more.

My most remarkable dream that night in the hotel was a variation on a recurring dream I'd had for as long as I could remember. I called it my elevator dream. This event was often terrifying, and usually accompanied periods of great transition or unrest in my life. Always, there was a huge, many-floored building of some sort, with labyrinthine halls and scores of closed or half-closed doors that gave me the feeling there were people behind them listening to me and watching my every move. I was always in a hurry to get to another floor in the building, always on the run, always searching for a stairwell, but I never could find one and there were elevators everywhere. I would get into an elevator with a feeling of relief that I would reach my destination at last, and then somehow the elevator would get loose. It would begin to spin and lurch and sail out into space like some devilish amusement-park ride gone berserk. Sometimes the walls would disappear, or would become rubbery or slimy or transparent, or would flap in and out in a fashion that seemed designed to hurl me out into the void. This terror would continue until I couldn't take it anymore, and I would awaken in a sweat, weakened and shaken.

But that night there was a distinct change in the script of the dream. I was being pushed through the endless corridors in a wheelchair, and though I could not see who was doing the pushing, I had a feeling of safety that surprised me. In fact, I was cognizant that the dream was progressing in an unusual way and felt curious to see what would next transpire. At last, I saw the elevator door, and when it opened, I was wheeled inside. Everything appeared to be normal: the elevator did not differ in size or shape from any normal elevator. There were several other people aboard, everyday-type folk who paid me no special attention. The elevator went up a few floors and some of the people got off; a few floors later, the rest of them disembarked. There remained only myself and my mysterious wheelchair driver. I turned my head as far as I could but still could not see who it was, and he or she never said a word or gave any identifying clue whatsoever. I even looked down at the floor to see if I could catch sight of some shoes, but, curiously, there seemed to be nothing behind me.

All this time the elevator had continued to climb. A small portion of the old terror began to surface in my heart, and I longed for the thing to stop moving. I wanted to ask my wheelchair driver to push one of the buttons on the wall, but found I could not speak, nor could I seem to control my arms to move the chair myself. I was not exactly paralyzed, but simply immobile. It was as if I couldn't recall how to move. Just when I thought I could stand it no longer, and was indeed beginning to will myself to wake, the elevator stopped with a little shudder and the doors opened. My chair was pushed out and the doors closed behind me. I knew I was alone, that my attendant had left me there and would not return.

I found I could move again and got out of the chair gingerly. I felt in my back pocket and was relieved to find my wallet still there; then I felt my shirt pocket and took out a pair of glasses. When I put them on, I could see perfectly. I was standing in a normal-sized living room furnished in a comfortable, old-fashioned manner. A canary sat on a limb of a little orange tree by a window, singing its heart out. It made me happy that the bird was not caged, and I went over and stood quite near it. The notes that issued from its throat were thrillingly beautiful, and I thought to myself they were a little like a Vivaldi piece for flute. There was a noise behind me, and I turned. Eliza was there, and she smiled. I tried to speak to her, to go to her, but I was again immobilized. She stayed in the doorway, her arms folded gracefully across her breasts like a Madonna on a holy card. She looked at me lovingly. She said, "I'll grow up now." And then she vanished, leaving behind a kind of shadow of herself for a moment—a smile and a movement in the air. The canary had gone on singing the whole time.

When I related the dream to Don the next morning as he was shaving, he smiled and said, "That's a great one. I love it. You're a talented dreamer, you know? Some people are better at it than others, I think, or maybe just better at remembering.

Don't you feel that way when you listen to patients? A dream can pack in a lot of meaning and helpful information and still be pretty dull. But that one isn't. Do you want me to analyze it, kiddo?" I could just imagine the mischievous look on his face.

I laughed out loud. "No, I certainly don't. There's nothing worse than two shrinks in a hotel room analyzing each other's dreams! Disgusting. I just wanted you to appreciate the esthetic value, which you have, and I thank you."

I heard him rinse his razor, brush his teeth, gargle, and turn on the water in the stall. While he showered, he whistled Vivaldi like a bird. It cracked me up.

34. A Red Velvet Kneeler

Frances must have set in motion one of the speediest divorce proceedings in the history of our state. Even while Don Rath and I were securing another place for me to live, the thing was nearing its grim conclusion. By the time I was actually ensconced in my new, inferior housing, the deed was done. I'd managed to sandwich in some time with the boys and had talked seriously with them about what was happening to all of our lives, but they seemed to take the news pretty philosophically. "It's better, Dad," Harry said at one point. "You and Mom were really getting on our nerves." I was still terrifically upset about not living with them and felt guilty whenever I thought about them.

I was also consumed with what was going on at work. Don and I began to notice a certain atmosphere of doom in the psychology department at NSU. We had divulged our findings about Wally Mussel to no one; indeed, we hardly even mentioned the subject in our private conversations. And yet, inevitably I suppose, other faculty members began to mumble secretly about their dissatisfaction with our fearless leader. It was obvious that most people wanted him out: his absentee leadership, his repulsive personality, his total disregard for the needs of the instructors and students, his rampant misogyny, his other blatant bigotries, and his seeming ignorance regarding all academic matters had finally combined to tip the scales against him. What our colleagues lacked, of course, and what Don and I had in our possession, was the key to Mussel's certain dismissal, and we thought long and hard about whether we should repeal our vow of silence on the matter and make our valuable knowledge public.

I was not sure at that time whether Frances and Mussel were still carrying on their affair, but I had gleaned enough little clues from things that Harry and Mark had said, to know that Frances was certainly carrying on with someone. I don't think even the boys knew who it was, and I never felt as though I should cross-examine them on the subject. As for Sarah, she was a complete mystery. She did not teach anymore, and no one ever saw her in town. I knew she still lived with Mussel because one night, on a whim, I called his house and she answered. I hung up at once, having found out what I wanted to know.

Mussel somehow caught wind of the faculty mood—I was sure he must have had at least one spy—and decided to take defensive action. When I realized the action he was taking was initially directed against me, I was certain he was still seeing my ex-wife. The manner in which I became aware of his vendetta was a curious one.

Late one afternoon, after my last class, one of my students asked to have a word with me, and of course I assented. We stood, this young man and I, leaning against the door outside one of the classrooms, and I was immediately aware of his nervousness. I thought perhaps he wanted to consult with me about some affair of the heart; now and then a student would seek me out for nonacademic counseling.

"What is it, Frank?" I asked. "Something personal? Or have my lectures been causing people to fall asleep in class again?"

He laughed. "No, Dr. MacLeod," he said, "I don't think anyone could sleep during your classes. They're too interesting."

"Thank you, and you get an 'A.' What did you want to talk to me about?"

He put his books down on the floor and struggled hastily to open his jacket, as if he'd suddenly become very warm. "Well, it's kind of hard to explain," he said, "but did you know Dr. Mussel's been asking questions about you?"

As calmly as I could, I said, "What do you mean?"

"I didn't know whether to tell you or not, but I thought I ought to. I don't even know Dr. Mussel—I mean, I know who he is, I know he's the department chairman, but I've never spoken to him before—and I like you, so I thought I'd tell you. Even though he told me not to. He's kind of a creepy guy, Dr. MacLeod."

"Can you tell me what happened?"

"He called me at home the other night—which was weird enough, you know—and asked me to stop by his office the next morning. I thought it was possibly about my grades or something, but I couldn't figure out what. I'm a pretty good student, and I didn't think I'd done anything wrong on campus or anything. But when I went to see him, he didn't want to talk about me at all; he started right in asking a lot of questions about you. He wanted to know if you stuck to the subject in class, if you were ever late, if you tried to force your opinions on us, stuff like that. He asked me if there was anything 'strange' about you lately, too, and that really got me mad. I told him there was nothing strange about you at all and that you were a great teacher and that I wanted to know what all the questions were about. He said it was nothing, just routine faculty evaluation stuff, and ushered me out of there pretty quickly. He said I should keep it all confidential. But it gave me the creeps, it really did."

I couldn't help letting a little sigh escape me. "Thank you for telling me, Frank," I said. "I appreciate that. Don't worry about it anymore, okay? You know there are a lot of silly political things that go on with college faculties, don't you? This is probably just Dr. Mussel's way of checking up on a few of us, that's all."

"Yeah, that's what I thought at first. But then I mentioned it to a couple of other people in the class, and it had happened to them too. Maria Colippi said Dr. Mussel seemed to be trying to get her to say that you'd been harassing the female students. Maria was furious. She said she told him that you'd never do such a thing, and that it was a stupid question, and that Dr. Mussel got really mad at her, and she wanted to come to you about it right away, but she was too embarrassed. I told her I'd tell you what she said, and she said that was fine with her."

I wanted to run into the men's room or someplace and be alone, but I had to deal with Frank. Suddenly I thought how fortunate it was that Eliza had already graduated; all Mussel needed was to catch wind of our relationship and he'd be off and running with my head. I told Frank I valued his loyalty and thanked him for his information. I think he was relieved when he left, though of course he was still puzzled. Who wouldn't be? It was maddening to think that Mussel would involve the students in his sickening little games. As soon as I got home, I called Don Rath and told him what Frank had said.

220 My Famous Brain

"Well, that's it, then," he said, as soon as I'd finished speaking. "We're going to have to lower the boom on that bastard now, don't you think? Maybe we should go straight to the president and not mess around with the faculty at all. What do you think, Mac? I'm ready when you are; just say the word."

"I don't know, Don," I said. "I'm just not up to it. I'm too weak, and I'm too tired, and I don't know how much longer I can go on teaching anyhow. Maybe it would be best in the long run if I just disappeared. And you know what else? I'm not so sure about the faculty. I've suspected for some time that Mussel's got spies—or one spy at least. We could run into some real trouble."

There was silence on the line. I knew Don was angry. I knew he wanted our battle to be fought—that he'd always wanted that—and that he wanted to defend my honor and critically wound Mussel all at the same time. There was also the matter of his own persecution at Mussel's hands. As close as we were, there was really no way Don could fully understand my situation, my feelings, my deep weariness. I didn't really care about Mussel anymore; I just wanted to be free of the whole thing so that I could get on with whatever was left of my life. Finally, Don spoke.

"I know what you mean about a spy," he said. "And I think I know who it is."

I was flabbergasted. "Really?"

"It's Dottie," he said. "I've thought so for a long time, so I've been telling her little lies to see if they end up with Mussel. They *always* do. She tells him *everything*, and because she's such a quiet old thing with ingratiating manners, people tell her all sorts of stuff. She's in love with Mussel, Mac. I'm sure of it."

I don't think my mouth was hanging open, but it might as well have been. "No," was all I could muster. "I can't believe it."

"It's true. I asked some of the staff in other departments in our building who have been here as long as she has, and they told me all about her. She and Mussel worked together before he came here, and it was one of those things where the new department chair got to hire his own secretary. He brought her here. There's never been anything romantic between them that anyone can prove, but Dottie is insanely devoted to Mussel. She lives and breathes Mussel, and she'd do anything for him. She's never had any man in her life other than that horrible creep, even though she only gets the crumbs, and only at work. I don't think she even has any friends. It's so pathetic. I've met a few women like her. You want to rattle their bones until they come to their senses, but they never do; they just live to breathe the air around their obsession. But anyhow, I'm sure Dottie is feeding Mussel all sorts of crap, and he's gobbling it up."

"Dottie." I couldn't get my head around it.

Don started laughing. "I didn't think this would hit you so hard, old boy," he said. "Listen. This is worse than that stuff you hear about guys who have a 'work wife.' This is pathological. One time I was with them in a car going to some kind of luncheon, and it was a very warm day and Mussel took his tie off and handed it to Dottie, who folded it up carefully like it was a precious sacramental garment and tucked it in her purse. Then when we all got to the restaurant—Indian—he asked her what he liked, and she told him what he wanted to order. Totally creepsville."

"So you think she's told him—"

"God knows what. It's frightening. And she masquerades as such a wimpy old lace-hanky type."

"God almighty," I said, thinking back to all the conversations I'd had with Dottie over the years. "I never guessed."

"I'm not sure why I did, except that I'm a paranoid type, I guess. But I want you to think long and hard about all this, Mac," he told me. "I know you'll probably decide against doing anything, and I might feel the same way in your shoes, but just think some more about it, okay? I know I promised you a long time ago not to try to change your mind, and I'll stick to that. But, whatever you decide, if Mussel tries to smear your reputation, don't expect me to stand along the sidelines and say nothing. That part of it's *my* decision, you know?"

"He'll drag you into it, Don. Just let it go. There's more than just my reputation at stake here."

"Did that bother you when it was a question of defending Sarah's honor? Never mind. Forget it for now. We'll talk again. How are you feeling—physically I mean? Need any milk-shakes or anything?" He'd noticed my growing enthusiasm for life's little comforts.

"No," I laughed. "I just had one this morning, as a matter of fact. I'm doing okay. I'm just really, really tired. Even when my head doesn't hurt it just takes me so goddamn long to do everything now."

He breathed out heavily, and I was sorry I'd complained. "I know. Don't try to do it all yourself. Give me a call whenever, will you?"

I said I would. My brain was swimming with all he'd said—all of it.

⌒⌒∞⌒∞⌒⌒

And then I was fired. Or, as the academic bullshit-speak put it—my contract was not renewed. I'd stuck to my guns about keeping Mussel's past a secret, and I don't completely understand that to this day. Partly, as I'd explained to Don, I was just so incredibly tired. Partly, I knew that if I put up a fight, or if Don put one up on my behalf, the gossipmongers would inevitably get hold of Mussel's affair with Frances. I didn't care a pin about that anymore (except, I suppose, that it would have hurt what was left of my pride), but I didn't want the boys to be involved. And partly, I thought, there was the chance that the whole world would find out about me and Sarah too, but I doubted that: Mussel wouldn't want that part of the past dug up at all.

Sarah. Did I really care that she, as Mussel's wife, would share his shame? Not really. Was I afraid that I still wanted to hurt her? No, I wasn't. I actually didn't care. Too much had happened since she'd been part of my life. Somewhere within me I felt she was suffering dreadfully already. I thought the whole thing might tear her apart—finish her off, so to speak, so that she'd never have the chance to be whole again. From my wiser vantage point now, of course, I know I was way off base. Sarah was basically finished before she started; there wasn't really any hope for her, but I couldn't see it then.

I received a note from Mussel one afternoon asking me to stop by his office at my earliest opportunity. I waited three days before I went—not because I was trying to put off the inevitable, which was of course entirely out of my control, but just because the phrase "at your earliest opportunity" tickled me so.

When poor, pathetic, crazy Dottie, looking flustered, sad, and shy, and little suspecting what Don and I had discussed about her, ushered me into the pig-man's den, I realized with a funny little shock that I had never been in his office before. In all the time I'd been teaching in that department, I'd never once entered the holy of holies. Not only was Mussel loath to subscribe to an "open-door policy," he treated his office like a private boudoir. He was on the phone when I came in, so I took a good look around.

My first impression was an olfactory one. The air in the room was stale, musty, slightly sour, with a pervasive odor of something like liniment overlaying the surface of all the other smells like a waxy film. I wondered which part of his grotesque anatomy had been rubbed with what soothing concoction—and by whom. Gagging a little, I made my way to the chair farthest from Mussel's desk: an ancient, heavy, leather recliner that would have been more suited to the basement playroom of a taxidermist. It was comfortable enough, actually, but when I ran my hands over its wide arms, I was amazed to find them grimy to the touch. I knew the building's janitorial crew personally and knew them to be some of the most fastidious, thorough creatures ever to wield a feather duster or mop, so Mussel must have made his office off limits even to them. I stifled a smile when I thought of how delighted the old bastard would have been to find Don Rath rifling through his desk that time: ah, what a jolly little scene that would have been.

I looked around the room but could see nothing of interest until my poor eyes fell upon what appeared to be an antique prayer bench that must have been uprooted from some ancient cathedral. Obviously pricey, and gleamingly polished, it seemed to be the one item that Mussel considered worthy of being kept clean. Its blood-red, velvet-covered kneeler looked as if its cushions had been recently reupholstered. My Freudian instincts began to play delightedly with this apparition, and I wondered whether Wally would invite me to kneel down while he bestowed upon me his evil benediction. But I did not have much time to ruminate.

His phone call over, Mussel came out from behind his

desk and approached me, hand outstretched for a shake. I
barely touched it with mine.

"Dr. MacLeod," he said, in his wheezy whine. "Thank
you for stopping by. Would you care for some coffee?"

Fat chance, I thought. He'd probably serve it in unwashed
cups.

"Thank you, no," I said, and nothing more. I was going
to make this little execution as much work for him as possible.
Several hundred scenarios had played themselves out in my
head during the three days and nights since I'd received Mussel's
note. I didn't really know which one of them I'd set into motion
until I got there; all I did know was that I would be in complete
control. Devious and cruel as Mussel might be, I knew we were
not a match intellectually. His wits were slug-slow. I also knew
he wasn't at all aware that I could best him; he and I had never
had more than a cursory conversation, and it was probable that
he simply considered me a poor, befuddled chump, someone
of whom he need take little notice. After all, hadn't he been
screwing my wife for quite some time right under my nose? I
didn't know then whether he was aware of my affair with Sarah,
but I was just getting into embellishing my imaginings when
he finally spoke. "I'm sorry to tell you, Jack—may I call you
Jack? —that I have some rather bad news for you," he began.

I put up one hand and stopped him immediately. "Please
don't call me Jack," I said evenly, "if you're going to fuck me
over. I come by my title honestly, so I'd like you to use it." He
made a small, low-pitched gasping sound. It was like being in
a stuffy room with a tiny, near-to-erupting volcano. I actually
thought I felt an increase in air temperature.

"Listen here, MacLeod," he burbled, "I'll call you any
damn thing I please. If you don't want to conduct this meeting
in a civilized way, that's all right with me, but—"

"Is there anything civilized," I asked, "about your skulking around behind my back questioning my students and making indirect assaults on my personal and academic standards?"

"I'm sure I don't know what you mean," he sputtered. "You are certainly mistaken."

"Am I? Of course I'm not. Let's not waste a lot of time here, okay, Mister Mussel?" I laid a lot of emphasis on the Mister. "It's perfectly obvious that you're going to get rid of me. If I don't go quietly, you'll see to it that I go out with a bang—but go out I will. I don't doubt your ability to carry off your plan. And I don't much care; I'll go, you'll be relieved to know, quite willingly. I've had enough. I've had enough of you and your ignorant, criminal, bullying ways. I only came here today so you could have the pleasure of telling me in person. Now, please go on with your happy task. I'm all ears."

Mussel had clasped his hands in front of him, as if he were going to say something very intimate. "You surprise me, MacLeod. I have to admit, you surprise me. You've got more guts than I thought you had, but then that's probably part and parcel of your superior attitude. You came here with your famous brain and expected special treatment. Well, that's not what's happening. Since you already know why you're here, let me tell you a few things you don't know. It's not as bad as it might be, you see. I could have just booted you out; I have the means; I have the power . . ." There was a whinny in his voice when he said the word power.

"But I've decided simply to fail to renew your contract. You don't even have to bother to resign; you can just fade out, tell everyone you've decided to let things go, to move on elsewhere. I won't put anything in your way. You may have the same letter of recommendation we send out for any departing faculty."

"That's very generous of you," I said. He didn't catch the tone of my voice.

"Yes, it is, considering that you could easily be terminated for various infractions of the rules, not to mention your obvious personal deterioration. I think you may be completely unfit to teach, but that is not my concern any longer. I don't know what your problems are, physical or otherwise, and I'm frankly not interested. You can take your problems to some other institution. Do you have any questions?"

"How's your wife?" I said.

He was off balance. "I beg your pardon?"

"How's Sarah?" I repeated. "How is it we don't have her on our esteemed faculty since your marriage?"

"My wife is very well, not that it's any of your concern. Whether or not she chooses to teach here is none of your affair either. I meant, do you have any questions about your contract not being renewed?"

"I know what you meant." I got up from the chair and went over to lean across Mussel's desk. I could smell his foul breath from four feet away, but I still leaned forward. I knew a bully could be intimidated by the physical threat of even such a weakling as I had become.

"Please sit down," he said. "Or better yet, leave. I think you've become completely unhinged. Don't forget, MacLeod, all I have to do to summon help is to call out for Dottie. I should think a man in your situation would want to preserve some semblance of dignity."

I pushed his Rolodex aside and sat on a corner of his desk. "Don't call for Dottie just yet," I said. "You can tell her all about this later, the poor besotted woman. I'm not going to hit you; I wouldn't want to soil my hands. I just want to have a little chat. About old times. Friendly-like. About me and you

and Sarah and Frances. About your college days, old sport.
Stuff like that. Won't that be fun?"

He pushed his chair back as far as it would go. "You're going
too far," he said. "I want you out of here. You're crazy. Get out."

"In a minute," I told him. "I have some more questions.
About *your* contract, as a matter of fact. I wonder how well
your fat old contract would hold up if anyone knew that you
never even graduated from college. I really think it would be
very interesting to find that out, you know, Wally? May I call
you Wally?"

I was having a ball.

He stood up and backed up against the window ledge. "I'm
going to give you ten seconds to get out of my office," he said.

"Now calm down, Wally. I told you I'll be going soon. If
you call Dottie, I'll just have to tell her what we were arguing
about, and goodness only knows who she'd tell. You know how
gossip spreads around here, right? Or maybe you don't; I don't
suppose anyone but Dottie ever tells you anything, do they?"
He was breathing in quick little snorts, like a bull; I wondered
if he'd have a heart attack before I'd finished. "For example,"
I went on gleefully, "did anyone ever tell you that just before
your romantic elopement with the delightful Dr. Bowe, that she
and I were—how shall I put this delicately? Courting?"

He didn't say a word. He shifted his ample rump upwards
and put his entire weight on the windowsill; it occurred to me
how easy it would be to lunge at him from my perch on his
desk (the angle was perfect) and push him through the glass to
his everlasting reward. Then I remembered we were only on
the second floor. Just as well. I went on with what was turning
into my monologue.

"You didn't know that? I'm shocked. I guess Dottie didn't
know it either, or she would have told you. But it's true, you

see. You don't know much about me, but I know all about you. I don't, I admit, understand why Sarah married you, but that's beside the point right now. No doubt you forced her to it, just as you forced her to submit to your sick desires for years before that."

"Wait a minute, MacLeod." His voice had changed to the noise a balloon makes when you force the air out through a pinched valve. "Why are you doing this? What do you want? Your job, is that it? We can talk about it, we can—"

"No, no, no, Wally. I already told you I don't want to work here anymore. I'm not even trying to make you feel bad—because I don't believe you're really capable of doing that. But you are capable of fear, of paranoia. I just wanted you to know, from here on out, that there's somebody out there who knows your whole story. That's kind of a comforting thought, you know? Everyone wants to be understood. And I understand you, Wally."

"You can't get away with threatening me," he said, struggling to regain control of his whine. "You can forget about that letter of recommendation, for one thing, and—"

I thought I'd die laughing. I howled and hooted. Dottie knocked timidly, opened the door, and asked if everything was all right.

"Fine, Dottie, fine" I panted. "This clever boss of yours was just telling me one of the jokes he's planning to use in his next speech. Have you heard it? The one about the department chairman and the spy who loved him?" She giggled and said no, he hadn't, and withdrew quietly, closing the door. Abysmally stupid, tragic woman. I got off Mussel's desk and went back to the chair, settling back and crossing my legs as if I intended to stay quite a while.

"You really are very funny," I told him. He must have been sweating all the way through his crappy suit; I could smell it. "Who the hell cares about your letter? There's nothing at all you can hold over me. In fact, for reasons of which you are entirely unaware, I am perfectly indestructible."

He snorted. "No one is that," he said.

"You'll see," I replied. "But there is one little topic we've yet to mention: good old Frances. Now it's really of no concern to me what Frances chooses to do with her time and her body, demented as I might feel her choices are. But I am concerned about my boys. I don't want you near them; I don't want you even in the same universe they inhabit. So I'm telling you right now that from this moment on you'll be having nothing further to do with my ex-wife. Is that clear, *Mister* Mussel?"

"You can't tell me what to do," he sputtered.

"Oh, but I can. Because if I find out—and believe me, I find out everything, even without a slave like Dottie reporting to me—that you are still seeing Frances, or if I find out that you've divulged any part of this conversation to Sarah, or that you've taken any action whatsoever against her, or that you abuse her in any way, ever, you will be quick to discover your tawdry little story has mysteriously become the talk of the university—and beyond. Newspapers just love stories like yours. I don't think I need to explain to you what effect something like that might have on your distinguished career."

"Get out."

"Okay," I said, affably, shrugging my shoulders. I approached him with my hand outstretched, just as he'd approached me a few long minutes earlier. He did not take it. I had a hilarious vision that he might go over and fling himself upon his kneeler.

"Very well," I said, "if you wish to be rude. Just to wrap things up: the semester ends next week. I'll be out of my office by Friday afternoon. Thank you for your time, Mister Mussel."

I bestowed a gracious smile on Dottie as I passed her desk and sauntered out into the hallway like David Niven. I deserved an Oscar. I doubted if anyone could tell that my head felt like a blazing kettledrum hammered upon by a madman. Once safely behind my own office door, I locked it and took out a little flask of brandy that had been hidden in my bottom drawer for years. I took a long swig with two of my pain pills and put my head down on my desk. I trembled violently and wept for a long time. Though my performance had nearly felled me, I felt wonderful. I thought about how wonderful I'd feel later on when I called Don Rath and told him what I'd done. I slept for a few minutes with my head on my notebooks. Nobody came to look for me: no devils, no angels, no students or colleagues. I was truly gone from the place; I knew it would take me no time at all to pack.

35. Don't Worry About a Thing

When Don and I arrived at Dr. Gerald Hamilton's office the day after my tests, he had some very interesting news to tell me.

"It's as I suspected, Jack," he said, and my heart did a little loop-de-loop, expecting to hear I had five days to live. But Gerry's verdict was somewhat to the contrary.

"The tumor has grown quite a bit since I first saw you. There's no way to really tell, since I haven't been able to follow you closely, but I have a feeling that it was more or less dormant for a long time, then started a growth spurt not too long ago. The sudden increase in symptom severity that you noticed recently is probably due to the fact that the lower half of the mass is now pressing heavily against the side of your skull. I can show you the pictures later if you want to see them. That's bad news, I know, but it's good news as well because I think we can get at it now, at least a good portion of it. Are you willing to give it a go?"

For a moment I had no idea what he was saying. Give what a go? Then I realized he meant surgery. Gerry was saying that given the new size and position of the tumor, a surgeon might just be able to saw off a part of my head and go in and get the thing out—or part of the thing, anyway. The question was, is that what I wanted? A million philosophical dilemmas galloped through my brain, but I put them aside. I needed more practical information from Gerry.

"You mean surgery. You think it could succeed?"

"If I didn't think so, I wouldn't suggest it, Jack. That doesn't mean there aren't some big risks; I'm sure you realize that. And an operation won't cure you, not completely, or at least the odds are against it. It will, however, buy you some time."

"How much?"

"I can't say exactly, of course. But with a little luck, if they're able to remove a good portion of the tumor, we could be talking a couple of years."

"Jesus. You mean good years, not vegetable years?"

Gerry ran his hands through his hair and smiled at me. "I can only give you my best educated guess, but yes, I think they could be pretty good years. You'd still have problems, and they would gradually become worse again, just as they have now. But they'd let up for a while at least. I can't promise anything about your sight, though. That's just too iffy; we'd have to wait and see. The headaches would definitely diminish, and I think your balance problems and left-side weakness would disappear entirely for a while."

It certainly wasn't perfection, but it was better than the current state of affairs. I was surprised how happy this little bit of hope was making me. For so long I'd gone on without any hope at all.

"I want it," I said.

Gerry held up his hand in a stop-sign. "Hold on, there, my friend. Not so fast. Don't you have other questions?"

234 My Famous Brain

"Yeah," I said, smiling. "You're right. What about the risks? I could die on the table, I suppose, but that's not such a big deal to me now, Gerry, believe it or not. What else? I could become a turnip?"

"You're already a turnip, Jack," Gerry said. "I'm glad to see you've still got that weird sense of humor. But yes, you could be worse off. Brain surgery, needless to say, is pretty delicate stuff. The absolute worst scenario would be complete paralysis; another possibility is total and immediate blindness. There are other 'ifs' too—a lot of them. I'm not trying to scare you, Jack, but you've got to consider the worst."

"I will. But what are my chances? If you were a betting man, Gerry, would you bet on me?"

"You'll have to have a conference with your surgeon, Jack, to get a handle on the odds and all the details. But yes, I think I'd bet on your coming out of it on the plus side. You're relatively young and your body's still fairly strong, though I'm sure you don't think of it that way now. Go home. I want you to wait a few days and see if you have other questions. Call me as soon as they come up. You can call me at home if you need to, okay? This isn't something to be entered into lightly. Nor is it the answer to all your prayers. It's a crack of light under the door, that's all. No guarantees, you see. I wish there were."

"What about recovery time," I asked. "How long would I be in the hospital? Would I need nurses at home or something? Where would I have it done, in the city? Have you got a surgeon in mind?"

"See?" Gerry smiled. "The questions are starting already. That's good. Yes, you'd have it done here, and yes, I have a man in mind—the best in the country, and he's here in New York. If all went well, you'd probably be functioning again in a month or so. I don't think you'd need a nurse very long. As for time in the hospital, that question would best be directed to your surgeon." He got up and came around the desk and took hold of my shoulders, half-lifting me out of the chair.

"Jack," he said. "I'm not kidding when I say I want you to think long and carefully about this. It could be a very good thing if it works out the way I hope it will, but no matter what happens, it won't be any picnic. Talk to someone about it, okay? Maybe your friend Don? Someone. Don't brood on it alone; you need input from others. Be sure to call me; don't worry about being a pest. And now I think you'd better go home. How are you feeling today? Is there anything you need before you go back to the hills?"

"I feel great," I said. "All I need is a crystal ball. Gosh, Gerry, I wish I were a religious man: I'd go into a corner and pray myself into understanding all this."

"You'll pray in your own way," he said wisely, his arm around my shoulders as I walked to the door. "Call me soon."

Gerry's news had sapped me of all energy. I could barely speak when I got in the car with Don. I told him we could go back to my place, that I had some interesting news from Gerry, and asked him if I might take a little nap before we got into a big discussion. He asked only if the news were good, and when I said "not bad" he sighed happily and set me up with a pillow in the back seat. "Sleep on," he said. "Don't worry about a thing. I'll just put the radio on, and I'll wake you when we get to heaven."

It was an odd, endearing thing to say—or maybe I misheard him. As I drifted off to sleep, lulled by the hypnotic automotive noises and snatches of songs from Don's radio, I tried to analyze the second chance I seemed to be getting. Better to wait and see if anything really panned out. But in my heart, I felt there was really no question that I would go ahead with the operation.

36. A Perfect Patient

That night, after Don had tucked me up on the couch with some Ovaltine and a thousand pillows (some of them taken from his car: he was certainly a traveler prepared for any eventuality), I told him what Gerry Hamilton had said. He was elated. He tried to be sensible, but he couldn't stop his happiness from shining through. Before we turned in that night, he had made me promise that I would enlist his aid in getting back and forth to see the surgeon, and that he should be in charge of any recovery plans I needed to make. He could take a short leave of absence if need be, he said, and come to Massachusetts to stay with me a while; or I could come and stay with him and Denny until I could be on my own once more. He said there was plenty of room, and that Denny, even though he'd never met me, could be relied upon to react favorably to such a scheme. I wasn't so sure about any of it, but I said nothing to dampen his good will. I knew Don was offering too much, but after a lot more discussion, I assented. I could always insist on adjustments later if I felt I was becoming a burden to him. Don came back again a couple of weeks later to ferry me to my surgeon's appointment. I was in sorry shape; all of my symptoms were sending me toward oblivion at a dizzying rate. My one fear was that the doctor would feel I was not a good surgical risk, and refuse to take my case, but, as it happened, luck was once again with me.

My soon-to-be favorite surgeon, Dr. Logan Bitterby, was one cool customer. He spent so much time looking me over that I began to sweat and tremble, but he seemed to take no notice of my fear. He listened to my heart so long I began to think he had fallen asleep at the stethoscope, and he performed a lengthy, wordless examination of every bodily surface and orifice until I wanted to writhe and scream. He flashed his little red and white lights—each one brighter than the one before—in front of my eyes for what seemed like months, peering into them endlessly and breathing his hot, cinnamon-scented breath into my face like a dragon. I was terrified of him. His bedside manner was like that of an undertaker—someone who did not expect his clients to have any need or desire for communication.

But finally I was dressed again and sitting across from him in his office. He let me sit there, still sweating, for another six years while he read over my file. Then he looked me full in the face and smiled broadly; even with my poor vision I could make out the brilliance of his teeth. I became more terrified still.

"Well, Dr. MacLeod," he said jovially, "my examination is complete—except for the blood tests, and we will have those results tomorrow. I don't expect any surprises." He closed my folder and sat back in his chair, as if that were the end of it. I wondered if I were supposed to leave.

But I found some courage somewhere. "And?" I said. My voice sounded like it was coming from some room down the hall.

"And," he repeated, "I am willing to perform your surgery if you are willing to have me. I will do my utmost for you, and

I expect you to do the same for me. I only allow myself perfect patients—by that I mean those who strive to cooperate, who work very hard to achieve results, and who desire the only result acceptable to me. That result is life. If there is any part of you, Dr. MacLeod, that is not prepared to walk on the coals of hell and still cling to life, you must tell me now. There are many other doctors." He paused. I knew I was supposed to pledge my fealty. This is crazy, I thought, but I was hooked on his voice. It sounded the way I'd imagined as a boy that Merlin's voice had sounded to the young Arthur.

"I want to live," I said, delivering the line as if I were in a lurid soap opera. "And I want you to do the surgery." Maybe, I thought, an archangel would appear above us, wielding a glowing sword—or scalpel.

He clapped his hands together soundlessly, then reached across the desk and shook mine.

"Splendid," he boomed. "We will succeed together. Now we will discuss the particulars. I am sure you have many questions. No question is stupid or too small, remember that."

And then he became as open and communicative as anyone could wish. We discussed every angle of the operation, from beginning to end. Since I had a better-than-average knowledge of medicine, he went into exquisite detail; since I was a psychologist, he explored with me some of the emotional difficulties I might encounter. He was a fascinating man, and I could see why he had such a fine reputation. Gerry Hamilton had told me that my luck in getting such a quick appointment with Dr. Bitterby was the equivalent of stopping by unannounced for tea with the queen at Buckingham Palace. I was impressed.

A date two weeks away was set for my hospital stay.

37. I Don't Really
Think She Forgot

A few years after I left NSU, Eliza wrote to me; unfortunately, I had recently died. She mailed the letter, which I reproduce for you here, to my last address, and it was soon returned to her by the Post Office marked "Forwarding Order Expired," so although Eliza thereby learned I had moved (and was puzzled by the fact), she had no idea I was no longer among the living. I believe the Post Office also has a little rubber stamp that says "Deceased," but thank God they did not use it that time. She learned of my death a few weeks after the letter came back to her, from my lawyer, as I have told you. Not long ago—and I use that phrase with caution, since time has no meaning to me as I am now—this letter was revealed to me in one of my "visions," and you will perhaps be able to imagine the effect it had upon me.

Dear Jack,

I'm sending you what is probably the six-hundredth draft of this letter, not counting all the attempts I've made mentally over the years to compose some kind of note to you. It's been a long time since we've seen each other, but I feel in some ways that I never left your side—or perhaps, more correctly, that you've never left mine. I don't know what your life is like now: I can only pray (and I do, daily) that you are happy, and that you are not alone. I am not alone; I am married, but I am not writing to tell you details about my life.

It's my heart I want to discuss, and, especially after all this time, perhaps you will think that I have no right to do so. Nevertheless, I will trust to your sweet nature and go on. I blame myself for losing touch with you, Jack, at a time when you needed my support very badly. I have suffered this guilt as well as the loss of you every day, and I do not say that to assume some kind of dramatic pose, or to try to "get you back." Both efforts would be inappropriate to say the least. I just don't know how it happened, Jack—do you? One day we were together, and then somehow we were not. Nothing was really stopping me from calling you, writing you, going to see you, but I felt as if it would have been wrong—that something undefinable had constructed a mountain range between us, and that I was powerless to change it, although my heart was breaking, and although I hungered for news of you every day, and especially every night.

I've gone on with my life of course (one has very little choice), but the need to contact you has grown so strong over the past few months that I did not think I could go on another day without making a serious attempt to do so. It became an emergency I could not ignore.

Why now? Again, I don't know. It's just become overwhelmingly urgent. It's true that I've wondered why you never made an attempt to contact me again either, and that was painful, but I am sure there are many good reasons for it, and, again, I trust to your wisdom and intuition.

You may not wish to respond to this letter, and I will understand if you don't, believe me. I know you will not think me a fool if I tell you I've spoken to you in my dreams, and you have spoken to me. I did not always understand what you said, but I am always trying, and I hope we may speak that way again and again. Let me repeat my wish for your happiness and freedom from pain: you suffered too much, Jack. That was always something I could not understand, no matter how you tried to convince me we would both someday understand it.

And I hope this letter will cause you no moment of pain or unease; I realize you may be having someone read it to you, so I will not go on any further. I hope what I've already said will not embarrass you in any way. But if it helps to know that someone out there has never forgotten you, and never will, then I have, at least, at last, done something to repay you in small part for the invaluable gift of your presence in my life. If there is anything, ever, that I can do for you, I will: that's love, is it not? Consider it a timeless offer.
Still yours,
Eliza

No matter what Eliza said about my so-called wisdom, I have no doubt that had I received that letter while I was alive, I would have done everything humanly possible to find her. I would have sent Don Rath rushing to the ends of the earth with the admonition not to return to me without her. I know he would have succeeded: he always did. And perhaps, had we been reunited, Eliza and I, a great many things would have turned out differently. Who knows? At least I could have soothed her silly guilt, could have made her understand that we parted indeed because of a "mountain range," and not because of any failure of hers. It's true I've tried to instill that knowledge in her through dreams and other kinds of messages, and perhaps her own development and the sense of her soul has brought her some measure of that truth as well, but I have still not evolved to a high enough state to say that it was just as well that the letter was mailed too late. It was not—is not— "just as well."

What vexed me the most was the realization that Eliza's mother had never told her about my one last phone call to her daughter. I guess I'd always imagined that she would. Maybe she had her reasons, or maybe she just forgot.

But I really don't think she forgot.

Small things can do so much damage.

38. Meeep

I'll spare you the details of my surgery and recovery. Let me just say the experience was, as I had been warned, no picnic. I was in the hospital for weeks, but fortunately I suffered only minor complications. My doctors (there seemed to be scores of them besides Drs. Hamilton and Bitterby, many of them interns and residents who were eager to learn from my case) appeared to be pleased. At first, I noticed no change in my condition whatsoever and began to rue the day I'd agreed to the operation, but gradually, as the trauma of the surgery itself began to wear off, I started to feel quite a bit more cheerful. Occasionally I would have headaches, but they were remarkable in that they had a definable ending: they did not hang on forever and blend into each other the way the old headaches had.

My vision had not improved, but neither had it deteriorated, and Dr. Bitterby felt that it would probably remain stable for quite some time. That cheered me. Don Rath burst into happy tears when I grabbed him by the goatee one day, so genuinely tickled was he to be "seen" by me. By the third week, I was allowed to sit on the side of my bed, and I noticed no problems of balance or space perception. I began to wonder if all this extra suffering were going to pay off after all.

But more than anything else I wondered how I was supposed to get along at home. There was no question but that I would need a medically skilled companion until the literal hole in my head was fully healed. The hospital sent me a kindly social-worker lady who arranged with various interstate agencies to provide me with male nurses who would live with me until such time as I could make do with daytime visits alone. I had specified—no, demanded—male nurses because I could not bear the idea of having some starchy female sleeping in my spare room and fussing over me as if I were an invalid child. It's also true that, knowing the weakened condition of my emotional fortitude, I greatly feared forming some terrible libidinal-umbilical attachment to an angel in white. I was informed that male nurses, who were few and far between even in the city, would cost far more than my insurance was willing to pay, but I agreed to take on the extra financial burden.

Little did I know, however, that other arrangements were being made—not by an angel in white, but by a guardian angel: Don. He'd been to visit me ten times at least during my hospitalization, and he was there the day of my release. I had hired a car and driver to take me home. Don and I joked around while he packed my things and got me settled in a wheelchair for a last promenade down the cream-and-green hospital corridors. He wheeled me through the front doors and out to the sidewalk. I could make out the shape of a car waiting there. But just as I was being gentled into the back seat, I realized there was no hired driver, nor was this a hired car: it was Don's own. I remembered the very smell of it: waxy and bookish and tinged with a pricey cologne, just like its owner.

"Wait a minute. What's this?" I asked, but Don pushed me gently into the seat. The many pillows were still there, and he arranged me among them like a prize pineapple in a fruit basket, swirling a plaid blanket down over my knees. He closed the door quickly, ran around the car to the driver's side, and hopped in breathlessly, as if he feared I'd make a run for it. I laughed at him.

"I can't believe you're going to make this drive again," I said. "Don't you have anything better to do, kid? Not that I don't appreciate it, really, but you're starting to make me feel guilty for taking up all your spare—and un-spare—time."

He cough-laughed. "Don't think about it; I just wanted to do it, that's all. I have to satisfy myself that you're properly settled at home. As for feeling guilty, you know what you can do with that."

I had to admit I was happy to have him there; I hadn't looked forward to a long drive with a stranger. "Okay, Doc," I said. "but someday I'm going to be strong enough to fight you off, you know."

"I'm looking forward to it," he said. I immediately went to sleep. Everything exhausted me, even happiness.

∞◦◦◦◦◦◦∞

When we arrived back at my little home in the hills, Don did indeed "settle me in properly"; in fact, I found he'd already made some preliminary arrangements. The kitchen was supremely stocked, there were cut flowers in several vases around the living room, and, wonder of wonders, my old bed had magically been replaced with an automatic one. It wasn't exactly a hospital bed, but it had lots of bells and whistles. I joked about the bed a great deal, but after a day or two I was devoted to it: such comfort, and such sweetness on Don's part.

But that was not the last—or best—of the improvements Don had made to my domicile. We'd arrived back rather late in the day, and after a quick snack and an inspection of the premises, we'd both gone quickly and gladly to our rooms, so I did not notice Don's fabulous present until the next morning. I woke and turned on the radio, which announced that it was after ten o'clock, and I lay there a few minutes with my eyes closed, half-dozing and thoroughly enjoying the experience of being home again. Then I noticed a peculiar sensation in my left foot, which seemed to be moving involuntarily, and there was an intermittent "pinching" sensation in the big toe. Oh no, I thought, the beginning of a new symptom: would my legs become numb now, and then paralyzed? My heart sank. The strange feeling began creeping up the leg, which lay half-uncovered. It felt as if a huge spider with fuzzy feet were doing the cha-cha there. Experimentally, I moved the leg: success. I could still control it. The weird sensation stopped. But then in a moment it began again, this time closer to my groin.

Spider or no spider, I had to find out what was going on. I opened my eyes and looked down, and much to my amazement I spied a small dark shape near the top of my left thigh. My heart was beating fearfully, but I was delighted to realize that something outside myself had been causing my symptoms. I could not, however, make out what the thing was. I put my hand down cautiously, and it hopped away. I sat up. The thing had moved to knee-region.

I reached for the control panel on the side of my magic bed and sent the lower portion of the mattress into action; as my knees rose, the little dark shape rolled suddenly into my lap.

"*Meeep,*" it said.

I picked it up—cradling it in both hands, it was so small—and held it very close to my face. It placed a tiny paw gently on each of my cheeks and bit my nose. I laughed and yelled for Don, who arrived so quickly that I knew he must have been watching the whole scene from the hallway. "What," I said, holding my catch out to him, "is this?"

"This is a Tillie," he said, taking the little package from me and addressing it solemnly. "Tillie, I'd like you to meet Dr. MacLeod, who will be living here with us. He's a little cranky in the mornings, so you'll have to take care not to munch on his toes." He paused, handing Tillie back to me. "And Mac," he went on, "This is Tillie. She's the lady of the house now, so I'm afraid there will have to be a few changes made to your bachelor routines. How do you like her?"

While he was speaking, Tillie had fallen instantly asleep against my chest in that hilarious manner of kittens, who can drop off in the middle of the craziest antics—or even their dinners. She weighed next to nothing and was as soft as air itself. I stroked her fur, which was slightly longer than that of the average house cat, and looked down at her curiously. She was calico technically, I guess, but sported an unusual color scheme: very dark orangey-brown, with a darker face and ears, and a white-tipped tail. Don filled me in.

"I don't know if you can make out her feet the way she's curled up now," he said, "but they're black. Her eyes are green, but I don't know if they'll stay that way. She's box-trained of course, and she's already shown a great talent for dancing. She seems to have taken to you."

I felt a sudden twitching of the heartstrings as he described the little cat. "My God," I said, suddenly identifying the chord that had been struck within me. "She looks like Cybèle!" I'd told Don the Cybèle story while I was in the hospital and was comforted by the sympathy he'd shown me. It was often difficult to gauge just how people would react to stories about animals, but Don had obviously felt the terrible injustice of Cybèle's death just as I had. And now this.

"Where on earth did you find such a treasure?" I was nearly overcome. The little package on my chest was now kneading my pajama top in a lazy, contented motion. "She's gorgeous."

"I ordered her from Sears," he said smugly. "Never mind. You don't need to know where she came from. She's just here." He paused, then in a little-boy voice, said, "So, Dad … can we keep her?"

I guffawed, the movement of my chest sending poor Tillie into a literal tailspin. She whirled and twirled and got herself all tangled up in the bedclothes, until Don and I were reeling with laughter. We played with Tillie for another ten minutes or so, until she fell asleep again on top of one of my hands. I felt a fan of tiny whiskers move as she breathed, like the silky undulations of a fingerprint brush. Then something Don had said returned to my mind.

"Don," I said, as he fiddled about the room picking up slippers and such, "Did you say, 'can *we* keep her'? Was that a figure of speech?"

"Yes, I did say that," he answered, sitting down on the clothes hamper, "and no, it was not a figure of speech."

Good God, I thought, how should I handle this? It had been in the back of my mind all along. During the drive home the night before, I'd questioned Don about what sort of nurses I'd be having, when they would arrive, etc. He'd skirted my questions skillfully, and I was too groggy to pursue the answers. I remembered thinking, briefly, that it was absurd to imagine that Don was thinking of staying on with me himself. He had a full life elsewhere: a live-in lover, a decent job, a host of friends. I'd put the idea out of my mind, but there it was again. He really was planning to stay, and I had to stop him. But I couldn't hurt him. I didn't know what to say.

"Listen, Mac," he began, coming over to sit on the bed and holding my foot awkwardly, as if it were my hand. "I know you think you ought to argue with me, but why bother? You know I'm going to win in the end." He emitted his laugh-cough and went on. "I've had it all planned out since you went in for surgery, and you're in no position to argue. It's all arranged. I've taken a little leave of absence from school, that's all—it's no big deal. In fact, I can really use a change of scene. There's no problem with Denny either; we've worked it out, and he'll come up to visit once in a while—if that's all right with you, of course. You need more than a nurse now, you need a friend, and as for the actual nursing part of it, don't forget my medical training—like you, I almost became an MD."

I just looked at him.

"So what's the problem? There isn't any. This is the perfect solution. I'll stay around a while until you don't need me any-more, then I'll move on. Can you honestly tell me you'd rather have a stranger living here? And can you honestly say, if the tables were turned, you wouldn't do the same for me? If you accept it now, old boy, you can save us both a lot of drama."

Tears betrayed me. Don was right, the whole idea of living for months at the mercy of strangers—however kind—had been making me quite miserable, though I had mentioned this misery to no one. In my deepest heart, I wanted him to stay. Was that so terrible? True, it would be the biggest gift I had ever accepted from anyone, but if Don were telling me the truth, if his staying on for a while really wouldn't disrupt his life irreparably, and if he honestly wanted to do it (which I did not doubt) shouldn't I be humble enough to accept it? I'd been willing once to throw a large part of my burden onto Eliza's shoulders, and it would have been a far greater sacrifice for her than the one Don was making would be for him. I reached out a hand to him. I could say nothing. He took my hand for just a second.

"Right-o, then, that's settled," he said briskly. "I must say you handled that rather well. I was prepared to beat you senseless, but that would have been difficult to explain to the good Dr. Bitterby. Now for some lunch." He made for the doorway.

"Lunch?" I said. "I just got up, didn't I?"

"Yes, you lazy bastard, you did. But I, and Tillie the little powderpuff there, have been up for hours. We'll have lunch. You'll have bruncheon. Come on, Tillie-girl," he said, scooping up the now yawning kitten from the bed, "let's let old Dr. Mac get all primped for his appearance in the kitchen. I'll whip up some nice fat little shrimpies for you or something, okay?"

"You'll spoil her," I called after him.

"That's what I'm here for," he sang out happily. "Dr. Don Rath the Spoiling Machine. I spoil fox-faced cats, bandage-headed shrinks, and other freaks of nature. Call our 800-number for the juicy details." In a minute I heard the blender buzzing in the kitchen.

39. As Long as You Live, or Longer

There was a long period in my present existence (I think it was long, though I really can't tell you how long it was) when I did not "see" Eliza at all; it seemed for quite a while that my visions centered mainly on my early youth, and while they were very interesting and instructive for me, they would probably only bore you. I must admit, however, that even while I was absorbed in these meditations, I often hungered for another glimpse of Eliza, at any time in her life. It didn't have to be about me; I just wanted to learn all I could about her. At last, I was rewarded, and rewarded grandly.

Without the usual dreamy sense of introduction that generally preceded these sightings, I was suddenly watching Eliza sunning herself on a lovely beach. It appeared to be New England, probably Cape Cod, if memory serves: the height of the dunes, the scrub-pine crawling along their rims, and the texture and color of the sand looked familiar to me, for I had spent some time there as a boy and had loved every inch

251

of the place. At any rate, it was a sunny, windy day, and there was Eliza.

She was sleeping, or appeared to be, lying on her back near the water's edge on a brightly striped beach towel, and she was wearing a modest black bathing suit that, on closer look, was so old it was turning a shiny, darkish green. Her hair was tied up in a scarf, and she was wearing huge sunglasses, but it was unmistakably Eliza. I could even see the odd birthmark on the instep of her foot that had so appealed to me: a little constellation of many-sized freckles and pigmented streaks all pooled together crazily in what she called "my Jackson Pollock." I remembered the first time I'd seen it, when she wore her sandals to class one warm afternoon, and how many times I'd kissed that constellation. Scattered about her on the sand were various objects that made it obvious she had not come to the beach alone, chief among them a sand-chair and a beach umbrella. I knew that Eliza would never have brought along such encumbrances on a solo trip to the ocean.

I did not have to wait long to see her companion. A young woman, taller than Eliza, very blond, and wearing a bright tropical suit, emerged from the waves and approached Eliza's towel. Dripping, she shook some water over Eliza's sleeping form. Eliza sat up quickly and smiled.

"Mmmmm," she said, yawning. "That felt good. I'm baking out here! How long have I been asleep? I'd better get out of this sun. How's the water? Is it lunch time? God, I'm so hungry. Do you want to go in again?"

No one I'd ever known could go from sleeping to waking as rapidly as Eliza. She could fall asleep anywhere, at any time, and go directly into the deepest of dreams, but she would wake up perfectly clear, and usually talking a blue streak. Her friend, now toweling herself off, laughed at her. "Slow down, will you?" she said. "I can't keep up. One, you've only been asleep about a half hour. Two, the water is pretty damned cold, as you might have guessed. Three, it's not even close to lunch time, but there's a lot of fruit in the cooler if you're hungry. And four, no, I'm not going back into that ice-cube tray again right now. Any more questions?"

Eliza laughed too, and took off her glasses and scarf. She moved the sand-chair under the umbrella and began brushing her hair. I could see now that she was no longer twenty-three or -four, but I knew I'd have to wait for other clues to fix her actual age at the time of this sighting; as I've told you before, I always had trouble with her age. The other woman, though, looked to be in her late twenties or early thirties, so I assumed that Eliza was too. That would mean it was near or just after the time of my death. I knew it was conceited to think that way, but I couldn't help interjecting my own interests into the scene on the beach.

For a while the two young women just chatted about little things—making observations about other sunbathers, commenting on a film they'd recently seen—and it was clear to me that they were very fond of each other indeed. They were perfectly comfortable with one another, and I was glad Eliza had enjoyed such a friendship.

But then the conversation lapsed into a long silence as they watched the breakers taper off closer and closer to their feet. Eliza's friend suggested they move back up the beach a little, but Eliza just sighed.

"What's the matter, Eliza? You've been a little off for days."

Eliza sighed again. "Oh, I'm sorry, Charlotte. I hope I'm not spoiling anything for you. I am a little down, but it's nothing so terrible." She gave her friend a bright smile. "Let's move our stuff back a little, before we get wet."

She folded up the umbrella and began gathering their belongings together. In a minute the two of them had moved everything back a good thirty feet. Eliza spread her towel out again and lay down on it, face skyward. Charlotte did the same.

"You're not spoiling anything for me," Charlotte said. "I'm having a lovely time; I'm so glad you thought of our corning here for a few days. But I was a little worried about you, that's all."

Eliza said nothing for a while; Charlotte turned over on her stomach. Then Eliza began speaking. "Char," she said, "do you remember I told you the story once about that psychology professor I knew in college?"

Charlotte said she thought she remembered.

"It was a long time ago—that I told you, I mean. It seems like only yesterday that I knew him."

"I have to admit, I forget some of the details. Wasn't he sick or something?"

Eliza sighed a third time. Without getting up, she reached into her bag and took out her sunglasses and scarf, tying the latter loosely across her brow and putting on the glasses. "Yes," she answered. "He was very, very ill. In fact," she paused, then went on slowly, "I found out recently that he died last month."

Charlotte sat up and looked down at Eliza, who did not move. "God," she said, "that's really awful. How did you find out?"

"A lawyer called me," Eliza said. "It was really strange. Jack's lawyer—that was his name, Jack MacLeod, and said I'd been named chief beneficiary in Jack's will. He asked if I could come to his office to discuss the details." Eliza got up and moved to the chair under the umbrella. She poured a cup of something from a glass jug, and offered it to Charlotte, who shook her head. After taking a long drink, Eliza continued.

"So I went there, last Thursday. As it turned out, there was no money left to speak of, but I'm to receive some of

Jack's papers and all his books. I'm still stunned. I can't believe any of it happened. I've been walking around in a daze, not understanding anything. That's why I wanted to come up here this weekend, and with you. For the first time in my life, I really felt afraid to be alone." She sat up, removed her glasses, covered her eyes with her hands, and turned her head toward Charlotte, who came over and hugged her.

"You poor thing," Charlotte said, gently. "I can't believe it's taken you this long to spill the beans. Keep talking; I think you've got to talk, okay?"

Eliza blew her nose and smiled. "Okay. Yeah. But I don't know where to start."

"Anywhere," Charlotte said. "For example, what did he die of? How old was he? Had you kept in touch over the years?"

"Now you sound like me," Eliza said, laughing a little. "All those questions! That's good, that's okay; it'll get me going." She paused and took a long breath.

"He had a brain tumor," she said, finally, "and I guess that's what he eventually died of, though I didn't ask the lawyer any details. I should have, and the lawyer seemed like a nice man, but I was so shocked I could hardly speak to him at all. I think Jack would have been forty-something when he died; I can't quite figure it out exactly. But young. God, Char, he was so young. And so brilliant and funny and kind. It's so unfair, I can't tell you how angry it makes me."

She was sniffling again, and Charlotte handed her tissues. "Go on," she said. "You're doing fine."

"He had really blue eyes," my Lizzie said. My soul sang. Then she went on. "Well," she said, "those are the only facts I have, really. The rest of it is really all in my head. How much of what I told you about Jack do you remember? I don't want to bore you with some long story you've already heard."

Charlotte patted her hand. "Don't worry about that. You know my memory is like a sieve. And anyway, you should just tell it the way you want to—whatever way feels good. I'll prompt you if you get stuck."

"I'm stuck already," Eliza said. "Char, I'm really all screwed up about this—it's really gotten to me. Ever since that lawyer called me, I've done nothing but think about Jack. I always thought about him a lot anyway, but now it's more like an obsession, and it frightens me a little. I think if I still feel this way when we get back to town, I'll have to look for someone to straighten me out, you know?"

"That's a good idea, honey," Charlotte told her, "I know just the person to recommend: that shrink Bob saw last summer. But I wouldn't worry; if I know you, you'll snap out of it. You've just been alone with it too long."

"I hope you're right."

"I'm sure I am. So get back to your story. When was the last time you saw him?"

Then Eliza began to tell her friend the long story of our relationship, starting backwards, at the point of what I call her fade-away from my life. She told her friend just about everything, including the dreams and all our blessed coincidences, and Charlotte listened intently, interjecting little questions and comments here and there to fill in the blanks. I was pleased to observe that Eliza's version of our story differed very little from my own. She wept quietly on and off, and Charlotte kept feeding her tissues, and when it seemed that Eliza was finished speaking, Charlotte said the most remarkable things. I understood then just why they were such good friends.

"Eliza, baby," Charlotte said, playfully heaping sand over Eliza's feet and patting it down around them. "I think this Jack may have been a kind of supernatural soulmate for you."

Eliza looked amused. "What do you mean?"

"What I mean is this: some people have one person in their life who takes on an importance that goes beyond love, beyond sex, beyond the ordinary boundaries of life as we know it. This phenomenon doesn't necessarily have anything to do with the person you marry—or with anyone else you love. It's a different thing altogether. Personally, I think everybody's got such a person, but not everybody recognizes it. You did. Sounds like so did he. You're not obsessed with your Jack, you're just in absolutely perfect tune with him—always were. Do you know what I mean? Or am I making perfect nonsense here?"

Eliza wiggled her toes out of the sand pile. "Go on," she said. "I want to hear this."

"Well, look," said Charlotte. "You had a special affinity for this man when you first met him, didn't you? Maybe that's what people sometimes mistake for love at first sight. You and he had a special way of communicating that had nothing to do with Ma Bell, right? That communication has gone on over many years, even though you haven't spoken to one another. And what's most important is that this communication went on and on, even though you didn't know he was dead. How common is that? It doesn't make any 'common' sense at all, that's what's so beautiful about it."

"Char," said Eliza, "you're a genius. You've pinpointed the very things I've always felt. And best of all, you don't seem to think I'm crazy."

Charlotte laughed as she packed Eliza's feet back up in sand. "Oh, I know you're crazy," she said, "but who cares?"

"But there's still one thing that bothers me more than anything else," Eliza said. "And that's my guilt. Why did I just let go of him like that? And why, in all these years, didn't I try to look him up, to find out how he was at least? That's what tortures me, really. I'll always wonder if I could have helped him, made things easier for him when he was so ill. I thought about him so much, but I never did a thing to try to find him. Maybe he died lonely and miserable; maybe I could have done some little thing for him; maybe . . ." The sentence trailed off and she began to cry again, this time in earnest, wiping her eyes on the ends of her headscarf.

"Maybe you should go a little easier on yourself," Charlotte said. "After all, he didn't try to look for you either, did he? And you know why I think that was? Not because he didn't care about you. Because he did care. Because he cared enough and was wise enough to know that the two of you weren't meant to be in touch that way. You had—you still have—another channel for your togetherness. It's a weird one, I admit, but what of it? Don't you see, Eliza, you're torturing yourself for nothing. Doesn't the fact that he mentioned you so exclusively in his will tell you anything? He never forgot you; you never forgot him. It's fucking beautiful, you idiot, if you'd just stop bawling long enough to see it. Eliza, it's out of this world! And it's not over, that's the best part. It will be with you as long as you live, and maybe longer for all we know. Imagine the joy of that. You can't relive the past; you can't make him live again. All you can do is be your own wonderful self. I never knew this Jack, but from what you tell me about him, I'll bet that's what he'd say to you this minute if he were here."

Eliza stopped crying and looked at her friend. "You're right," she said. "Thank you. I'll try. And thank you for listening to me. I feel a lot better. I think I'll go in the water now. Want to come?"

Charlotte said no, thanks, that she'd not yet thawed out from her first little dip. Eliza leaned over and hugged her, then tore off her scarf and sunglasses, bolted from her chair, and ran into the surf. She screamed when the first icy breaker hit her. Charlotte yelled something and waved. The scene was fading from me; I tried to hold on to it. I could see Eliza's head bobbing in the frothy green and white waves and fancied I could taste their salt and feel the exhilaration of the freezing water hitting my neck and face. I imagined I was there with her, lifting her light frame over the waves and holding her against my chest when the big ones hit us. The vision faded. But at last, I'd heard so much of what I'd always needed to hear.

40. Let Her Be Spoiled

With Don around, my recovery was fairly easy. He performed whatever actual nursing chores were necessary with the greatest skill and discretion, pushing me gently but convincingly to do for myself whatever I could handle—sometimes even a little more. He respected my modesty and privacy, ignored my intermittent foul moods, fed me like a king, trucked me back and forth to the hospital for check-ups, kept me entertained with his conversation and Tillie's antics, and executed every household function with impeccable efficiency and style. Moreover, he liked me, he liked caring for me; one could see it was no burden to him at all. This lifted my guilt and soothed my nerves and filled me with an invaluable sense of being wholly befriended. I could not imagine how I'd ever gotten along without him and dreaded the day I knew would have to come: the day of his inevitable departure.

Ironically, because of his skillful care, I was making rapid progress, and it was soon obvious to both of us that Don's ministrations were, in large part, becoming altogether unnecessary. I'm sure it was on his mind as well as on mine, but we never mentioned it. Then there came a day when Don revealed that he'd soon have to go down to New York on business. He broached the subject at breakfast, which I no longer took in my room.

"What time will you leave?" I asked him.

"I'd like to go quite early tomorrow," he said, "so I'll miss some of the traffic through Connecticut." Then he paused. "I was also thinking," he went on, "that if you think you can get along all right, I might spend the evening with Denny and come back the next day. We haven't seen each other since his visit here last month, and I really owe him some time. What do you think? Would you feel comfortable being alone overnight?"

It was the opening I'd been waiting for; there were things I'd have to say for him, doors I'd have to open.

"Of course I will," I told him. "Stay longer if you like. I'm doing really well; you say so yourself every day. There's no earthly reason why you can't take a trip and feel relaxed about it. Not that I won't miss your grubby little beard over coffee tomorrow, but Tillie and I will make do, won't we, Tillie?" The little cat—more of a teenage-type cat now—was asleep on my knee. At the mention of her name, she opened one eye and looked at me, then went back to sleep.

Don was stirring his coffee maniacally. "Good," he said. "Yes, I think you'll be fine. It's not you I'm really worried about." He took a long sip of coffee. "It's Denny."

"Oh no. Are things deteriorating because you've been up here so long?"

"I'm not sure—maybe . . ." he said. "But it goes beyond that. I think my time with Denny is over, Mac. Even before I came up here things were falling apart. We were inching away from one another, and bitching at each other a lot. I thought a little separation would be good for both of us, but nothing's really improved. I don't know if you noticed the tension between us when he was up here, but it really tore me up. I think he wants to be rid of me once and for all but lacks the guts to say so. I think I'll have to help him, and this might be the time. It's shitty—it's always shitty when people break up—but I know in my heart I really don't want to go back and live with him again. So maybe I really will stay down there a couple of days, if you're sure you're okay. I don't know how long all of this will take, and I don't want to rush it. And I'll be in touch with you every day by phone, of course."

"I'm really sorry to hear about you and Denny," I said, "but I'm sure you know what's best. As for your staying in New York, don't give it a second thought. Stay as long as you need to." I poured him another cup of coffee, filling it up halfway with milk the way he liked it. "You know, Don,' I continued, "I really would be all right on my own now—I mean, as much as I love having you here, maybe this is the right time for you to go. Besides the situation with Denny, which may take longer to resolve than you think, there's your job to think about. I worry about that, Donald. You can't keep NSU on hold forever you know; sooner or later they're going to want their favorite professor back."

Don again stirred his coffee and then stirred it some more. He breathed in and out heavily. I hoped I hadn't hurt his feelings. I was only trying to give him the opening he needed, somewhat the way I'd opened things up for Eliza when I knew she'd have to leave me. I wondered briefly why I found myself so often in that role, and if I were prone to jump the gun in such situations—but I knew that wasn't true. Eliza and Don had their own full lives to live. Don cut himself another slice of his homemade bread, toasted it, and smothered it in apple butter. He ate almost the whole thing before he spoke.

"Mac," he began, "there's something I should have told you a few weeks ago. Now that you've brought up NSU, I guess the time is right."

I braced myself. I think I knew what was coming.

"I quit," he said.

"When was that?"

"A few weeks ago. You don't have to feel it had anything to do with you. The closer my little sabbatical came to ending, the clearer it became to me that I could never go back there. Mussel's still there, Mac, and that's one thing. I simply can't stand to be around him, to work for him, even to see his name on a memo. And then there's the fact that I've just been there too long. I felt that if I didn't take this perfect chance to get out, I'd be in danger of stagnating there forever, you know?"

Don looked a little embarrassed, as he always did when he was about to praise me. I think he was afraid that I would think he was being too nice because of the crush he'd once had on me. But I didn't think that. I was certain the crush had matured into a perfectly beautiful friendship. I rarely thought about his homosexuality at all anymore, even when Denny had been visiting, and they had slept together in the bedroom next to mine.

Don went on. "You've always rather inspired me, you know: your intellect, your ethics, your stalwart grip on life. You're one of my heroes, Mac—maybe my biggest one." He looked at me sheepishly.

"Good grief," I said, trying to cover my emotion. "Next you'll be telling me you're authoring a superheroes comic strip in my honor. What are you going to call me, 'The Amazing Balding Man'?"

Don laughed and coughed. I'd noticed that since he'd been living with me this little habit had decreased in frequency quite a bit. He was calmer in general, more peaceful, more centered. "Very funny," he said, "Nevertheless, I meant what I said. I tried to imagine you staying on at NSU in my situation and realized you never would have done it. And anyway, I really wanted to go. So I did. You see before you one middle-aged, unemployed therapist-academic. Oh, did I mention I've decided not to resume my private practice again either?" He gave me a sly look.

"Nope," I said. "Isn't that a rather drastic step? I mean, if I may be so frank, what are you going to use for money? Or do you have something else lined up that you 'forgot to mention' as well? I know you've been living off your savings the whole time you were here. I should have been paying you that salary I mentioned the very first week; you should have accepted. I've a good mind now to force the whole retroactive sum down your stubborn little throat."

"My, my," Don said. "We certainly are feeling our oats today, aren't we?" He laughed. "Don't worry about my finances. I've got tons of money in the bank, really; this little 'vacation' has hardly made a dent in it. After all, a single boy like myself has very few expenses, and I've been working for a very long time. I don't have any prospects at the moment, but I don't think I'm exactly unemployable. Once I decide where to settle, I'll sink my teeth into the job problem pronto."

His last statement shouldn't have surprised me.

"You're not going back to the city?"

"I don't think so. I think once I've worked things out with Denny I'll want to move on. The city is dirty and noisy and full of too many people just like me. I look around on the street sometimes and see myself everywhere: it's depressing. Even driving across the bridge to NSU every day used to be a treat, if you can imagine that."

"Where are you thinking of going?" I asked. But I knew. Don came around the table and picked Tillie off my lap. He held her up in the air, at eye level, and spoke, as if to her.

"Here," he said, "if that's all right with you." Then, with one finger, he gently moved Tillie's little head up and down in assent. He smiled at me. "She says okay," he stated. "What about you?"

I had to admit he had staged it perfectly. What could I say? To say I didn't want him would have been a lie; to say it wouldn't work out would have been ridiculous. There was nothing standing in the way, no reason on earth not to agree with him.

"Don," I said solemnly, "have you really thought this through? Of course it's okay with me—it's more than okay—but do you truly realize you'd be saddling yourself with all my problems? I know, I know—you've done that already, and you've handled everything beautifully, believe me. You must know the depth of the gratitude in my heart. But our situation as it stands now might be misleading. I'm fairly well now, Don, but I'm not going to stay this way forever. Who knows how long it will be before I become totally dependent? What kind of a life will you have here if I—when I—begin to get sicker and sicker again? I don't know, Donald. I have a good mind to kick you out once and for all and be done with it." As I spoke, the things I was saying made me angrier and angrier. They were true. He shouldn't stay. I realized I'd been making a fist around my piece of jam-soaked toast and relaxed my grip. Don handed me a napkin. I wiped off my hand and covered my eyes.

"At best," I said, "you'll be saddled with a partially disabled man. At worst, a vegetable. Think twice, my friend, before you sign on with this army. It's marching into the valley of death for sure."

Don sounded angry too. "You jerk," he said, flatly. "You have to make a big fucking drama out of everything, don't you? Do you think I'm a moron? Don't you think I've considered the big picture? I said I wanted to stay, and I do, but if you're going to be some kind of tortured martyr all the time, I think I will back out. Just remember, Mac: this was my idea. I wanted to come here, and I want to stay. You don't have to take any responsibility for any of it. If you don't want me, just say so, and I'll be gone. I don't want your gratitude; I just thought we lived well together. Who the hell knows what's going to happen to whom? Suppose something happens to *me*. Would you head for the hills? You're so fucking brilliant you can't tell your ass from your elbow, as my father used to say. Your famous brain is letting you down, man. Let me know your royal decision in the morning. I'm going for a walk." He started up from the table, but I grabbed his arm. We were both weeping. The wrist I grabbed was trembling.

"Stay," I said, shakily. "Stay forever if you can stand it. Nothing would make me happier."

"You're sure?"

"Positive," I said. "I won't even thank you."

He sat down again and took a deep breath. "That's more like it," he said. "I think we'll be happy."

"I'm happy already," I told him, and it was true. Tillie scrambled up my pants-leg and vaulted onto the table. She walked right into the middle of Don's breakfast plate and began to nibble on some crumbs.

"She's absolutely spoiled," Don said. "We're going to have to set down some rules around here."

"Why?" I asked. "Who cares? Let her be spoiled. In fact, let her run amok if she wants to!"

Don howled with joy. "Yeah! Let her run amok! We don't have to answer to anybody, do we, Tillie, old girl?" The cat ignored him. I went around the table and embraced his shoulders.

"It's going to be all right," he announced cheerfully. It's going to work out fine."

"I know," I told him. "I think you could be right."

41. Dreaming of *Innocence*

For almost a year and a half, Don Rath and I lived together in harmony. We had fun every day. I had disability payments and also some money from investments I'd made with my radio prize money, and Don was making a passable wage as a part-time therapist at a nearby veteran's hospital. At first, I thought this choice of occupation rather a peculiar one for him, but he seemed to thrive on it. Early every morning he'd trundle off to the hospital, returning at noon or thereabouts (there were occasional emergencies) full of stories, and quite exhilarated by the contact with his patients. Sad as many of their situations were, Don had the gift of discovering value in each of them and giving them hope. There were very few older veterans in that particular hospital; most of the residents were Vietnam vets, and Don seemed to have a special affinity for those "boys" (as he called them) and a special compassion for and insight into their problems. There were difficult and intractable cases of course, as there are in any such facility, but on the whole I think he felt that his success rate was high and that he was learning a great deal from the experience.

Certainly, it was a drastic change from college teaching, and change is what he constantly assured me he was searching for. With two of us paying our very reasonable rent, there was no need for him to work more than he wanted to.

As for me, I eventually went back to my talk show work every weekday evening. I was "Doctor Mac" to my faithful listeners, and I enjoyed the anonymity this afforded me—to those people I was whole and sane and helpful. Doing the show was easy, it was fulfilling, and, for the most part, it was fun. This evening schedule left Don and me the afternoons to be together if we wanted to, and we often did want to—in fact, more often than not. I think my illness had aged me in a funny way: I probably did not look much older than my years, but, having been through so many personal crises in so short a time, I felt like a much older man.

Don, however, seemed to grow younger and younger as the bustle of city living and the pressures of a full-time job fell from his shoulders. He felt like a son to me, and that was a gap that needed filling: I didn't see much of Harry and Mark. They were off on their own for the most part now, and while they did come up and visit every now and then, they never stayed long, and they seemed uneasy around Don. I worried that Frances (or someone else) had filled their young heads with some stupidity about him, but when I questioned the boys, I could tell I was wrong. I guess it was natural for them to be somewhat uncomfortable with a slowly dying father and his caretaker-roommate. It was not any kind of normal situation.

Afternoons with Don came to mean a great deal to me. Without him, I would have been essentially housebound, or at least it would have taken a great deal of organization and effort on my part to get myself out into the world. But with his usual good humor, Don became my guide. My vision, though it remained more or less as it was at the time of my surgery, was undependable and foggy at times. Don would take me shopping, on picnics, on long drives in the hills, or simply on little walking expeditions around the neighborhood. The small but fierce Tillie would accompany us on these journeys, wrapped in a little walking jacket attached to a leash. It had taken some time to get her used to the harness arrangement, but eventually she learned that it meant fun outdoors with her humans. We couldn't risk losing our beloved companion.

Unfortunately for Tillie and Don, my energy level was rather low, so we never went too far, but Don managed to fill these excursions with such a wealth of informative detail that I felt as if I'd gone very far indeed. He knew so much about nature, it astonished me. Our conversations were a delight to me.

But I'm not sure I was too delightful myself. I talked about death a lot, and I worried sometimes that Don would become weary or wary of the subject. He treated it, however, as a philosophical problem, not a clinical or personal one, and so we were able to investigate the topic at our leisure. Once I commented on how funny a picture the two of us must have made: one "elderly" middle-aged man and one youthful middle-aged man, strolling along with a cat on a leash, talking about beetles, phobias, acorns, children's bicycles, Freud, dinner recipes, and death. He laughed. "It's really wonderful, isn't it?" he said. "We're living every dedicated conversationalist's dream."

Not that every day was rosy. There were times when I wanted nothing more than the luxury of being alone with my thoughts, and I don't doubt Don had similar wishes as well. We came to intuit each other's need for privacy, and sometimes Don would take off for a few days, or, by an unspoken mutual agreement, we would simply leave each other alone. I used these times for rest, which I needed more and more: it was gradually becoming awfully difficult for me to keep up with Don's energetic, upbeat approach to living.

I admired him exceedingly, but he sometimes wore me out. He did it on purpose, I know; he was not a Pollyanna by nature, he was trying to keep me alive by means of charm, cheer, and choice. By the latter I mean that he knew that to please him, if for no other reason, I would choose to take on the onerous task of living. But I think even he knew our game could not go on forever.

I used my alone time not only to rest, but also to read. True, I could no longer make out the words in an ordinary book too easily, but I had obtained some large-print volumes from the nearby university library. Even that print was a little difficult to read, but read it I did, with the aid of a magnifying lamp, plus of course my own thick spectacles. I had to pursue this activity when Don was not around, because it had proven to be the one thing he could not bear to see me do. Once he had come upon me with my nose literally to the grindstone practicing this clumsy art and had been reduced to tears. He told me later that the effort I expended laboring over every syllable seemed to him too great a price to pay even for literature. He offered instead to read to me whenever I asked, if only I would cease torturing myself, and even though I tried to explain to him that being read to wasn't the same as reading, I could tell it was something that made no sense to him at all.

The fact was, my reading was becoming more important to me than anything else. If you'll remember, I promised myself when I first realized I was ill that I would someday memorize one last book, and recite it as well, as a final celebration of life and a testament to my once-impressive powers. It was a prideful exercise, but I needed to indulge in it, and I felt the day had come to begin my task. Although I had no reason to suspect that death was actually on my doorstep, I realized that if I waited too long to try to satisfy this dream, I might not be able to read anything at all. Having Don read to me, or listening to a book on tape, simply would not work: there was some kind of magic inherent in the memorization that had to be activated by my own eyes, imperfect as they had become. And so I labored secretly, to spare my friend the pain of my pain, and to devote myself whenever I could to what I considered my last worldly mission.

At first, the problem of what book to select was a daunting one. The university's inventory of large-print books was limited, and while they did stock most of the classics, there was a dearth of the less-well-known masterpieces and practically no poetry or drama at all. I selected and hauled home a weighty copy of *Moby Dick*, but, respecting and enjoying Melville as I always had, I knew I did not want to memorize that book. I tried it on, but it did not fit. For weeks I was stymied; I wondered if I would have to give the project up. And then, while speaking with the university's librarian, I learned of a wonderful service for the visually handicapped. There was a small company that, for a nominal sum, would create large-print books from any manuscript or volume; the only problem being that it took some time. It took months, in fact: the waiting list was quite long and the production process lengthy. Again, I was frustrated, for I did not know how long I had.

But I reasoned that the more quickly I made my selection, the faster my adventure could begin. For two days I concentrated on that problem alone. I was so preoccupied that Don expressed some concern, but I calmed his fears by telling him I was just working out a personal issue with the boys, and, as always, he graciously allowed me my separateness. So many questions absorbed my attention. Should I choose a book I'd already read and loved, or should I test out an unfamiliar work, hoping that I might discover something new along the way that would add even more meaning to my project? Should it be a short work or long? Fiction, poetry, philosophy, drama? Something in English, or something in a foreign tongue (I could read French, Russian, and German well)? On the evening of my second day of rumination, I fell into bed despairing of ever making a choice. I should have known better than to despair when I could dream.

With perfect clarity I dreamed of the book I wanted. In the dream I was young and healthy, and I reached with ease to the top shelf of my bookcase to remove a well-worn volume. I caressed the cover and read the title and author out loud: *The Age of Innocence*, by Edith Wharton. The perfect choice: I couldn't imagine why I hadn't thought of it before. When I awoke, I knew just what to do.

I had originally been introduced to the book by Eliza. She adored it. When I told her I hadn't read it, she was amazed, and, saying that she could not possibly relate to anyone who had not read one of her all-time favorite books, she'd gone out immediately and bought me a copy.

To my dismay, however, sometime during my move, Eliza's gift had been mislaid. I comforted myself with the fact that it had been one of the few books she had given me that she had not inscribed with some wonderful words of her own, so it was only a book—an object—that was missing. I asked Don to procure another copy for me, which he did readily. I called the friendly librarian and copied down the address of the large-print firm. I sent them the book; I sent them the money. I also sent them a letter in which I humbled myself enough to say that I would more than appreciate any speed with which they could process my order, since I was a dying man who wanted to read the book before he died. The package arrived in less than two weeks. Bless them.

∽∾∾∾∾∾∾∾∾∽

I then began my work in earnest. Not willing quite yet to let Don in on all the details of my plan, I was forced to offer him little white lies in order to gain time alone with my reading. Slow going as it was, it brought me increasing joy, and nightly I would come upon little phrases and scenes that Wharton had drawn with such a fine pen that they sent tiny shocks of recognition and appreciation through mind and soul.

So much of the book reminded me of my connection with Eliza. For example, Wharton wrote: ". . . there had been no farther [sic] communication between them, and he had built up within himself a kind of sanctuary in which she throned among his secret thoughts and longings." And also: "I swear I only want to hear about you, to know what you've been doing. It's a hundred years since we've met—it may be another hundred before we meet again." The book was indeed a treasure that Eliza had known I would recognize.

In order to keep my project from Don, I had devised a workable plan that satisfied his need to be sure I was not over-working my eyes and mind. I told him I needed an hour or so each night after my radio program to take notes on the tape recorder regarding each evening's callers. This seemed to make sense to him, and indeed I suppose it actually would have been a smart thing to do—but I had no time for it.

I was busy with what I'd come to consider, in all senses of the phrase, my life's work. It was coming along famously: since the reading itself was so arduous, the memorization was really a breeze. I was delighted to find that my mind was still working so well, considering what my physical brain itself had to deal with. It took a couple of months, but I finally finished the memorization.

For several days afterwards, I was able to carry on more or less normally, but every now and then I would visit that area of thought where I had carefully placed each sentence of Wharton's masterpiece, lingering over particular phrases that were especially meaningful for me—or just beautiful. I loved, for example, the last part of the last sentence of Chapter Twelve. Young Newland Archer was taking his leave of his true beloved, the Countess Olenska. I could almost see him, almost hear his labored breathing. He "plunged out into the winter night bursting with the belated eloquence of the inarticulate."

I was dying to recite the book for Don.

42. Don's Dilemma

I had my book lodged firmly in my memory, and all that remained was to choose a time to recite it to myself. If that went well, as I was confident it would, I would add a second plan to my "ceremony," this one including Don.

Like a child planning a birthday surprise for his parent, I daydreamed the whole scenario. "Donald," I would say one morning, when the breakfast things had been cleared away. "If you are free this afternoon, I have a little surprise for you," and Don of course would say that indeed he was free and that he looked forward to whatever I had planned. He'd try to tease the secret out of me, but I would have none of it. When, after lunch, we'd made ourselves comfortable in the living room, Don with his brandy and me with my tea, I'd casually ask him if he'd ever read *The Age of Innocence*. No, he would say, he hadn't had the pleasure: could I lend him my copy? And I would reply that no, I had a better idea, and if he cared to hear the book, I'd be happy to recite it for him.

He would be astonished, delighted, intrigued. He'd had no idea of this secret talent of mine. I knew he hardly believed I could do it (or that anyone could, for that matter), but I proceeded to prove him wrong. He was mystified, entranced, and begged me to go on and on, but the clock had reached seven and it was time for me to prepare for my radio program. Also, my voice was wearing out: he wouldn't want me to go hoarse on my audience, would he? Of course not, he said, still sitting on the couch with his brandy snifter in hand and Tillie on his lap, a look of enchantment in his funny grey eyes. But would I go on reciting tomorrow afternoon? Naturally I would, I'd be delighted to do so. He embraced me, he told me how wonderful I was, and he praised the book as well, saying that now he wanted to read everything he'd ever missed, and would I draw up a list for him? That was my daydream; I could hardly wait to make it a reality. The recitation of Wharton's novel would be not only a gift to myself, but perhaps my final gift to Don—something only I could give him, something worthy of him, something fine. But I did not rush into it; I felt I would simply know when the time was right.

With the book securely under my mental belt, I felt armed and reassured, as if I'd set my affairs in order. I did not feel close to death, but I felt prepared for it; the only thing that could go wrong would be if I were to die quite suddenly, and the very nature of my ailment rendered that likelihood remote. During that period, I came as close as I'd ever come to living each day to the fullest, without regrets, without expectations, and with a grateful sense of simply being around. I wished I could have said the same for Don.

I'd noticed his moods becoming increasingly introspective and grim, especially when he returned from the hospital each noontime. When I inquired if he were feeling all right, I was

278 *My Famous Brain*

assured it was nothing physical, and told that he was sorry
to be such a grouch, but that there were a few things at work
that were preying on his mind. No, he didn't really need to
talk about them just yet, but he would probably want to discuss them with me at some future time. Would that be okay?
I assured him it would, and I wondered about his formality,
which seemed to me to suggest he was even more upset than
I'd thought at first.

Not long after that conversation, he broke down. Tillie
and I were setting up for lunch one day when we heard his car
on the gravel outside. The sound of it always sent Tillie into
a little pirouette of joy, after which she would run to the side
door to be picked up and petted by Donald, who doted on her.
(It was odd, but the more she grew to resemble Cybèle, the
closer the two of them grew; this pleased me enormously. It
was as if two of my favorite beings were blessing me by their
mutual regard.) That day, however, Don nearly tripped over
Tillie, then looked at her without saying a word, and marched
down the corridor to his room.

I picked Tillie up and consoled her briefly, then followed
him, cat in arms, to try to find out what was wrong. His door
was closed. I knocked. No answer. "Don," I said, "what's
wrong? Can I help you?" After a short silence, he opened the
door and invited us in. He took off his sport coat and immediately lay down on the bed, gesturing towards his favorite
overstuffed armchair, where Tillie and I took a seat. "I'm so
sorry, guys," he said, sighing. "I'm exhausted. I'm depressed.
I've had a really shitty day."

I put Tillie down and she leaped up on the bed beside
Donald, snuggling up next to him as if she knew where she
was needed. He stroked her sleek back and shoulders silently.

"Would you rather be alone?" I asked.

Don sat up and propped himself against the pillows. "No," he said. "I'd rather you'd stay. I want to tell you what happened today and get your opinion. Personally, I'm very confused. Professionally, I'm really stuck. You've had more experience with clients than I have, Mac; I think you can help me."

"I'll try," I told him, "but don't forget how rusty I am. It's been many years since I had a real practice, and my radio people don't really count, you know."

"It's your common sense and intuition I'm interested in," he replied. "But, come to think of it, I'm starving. And I don't want to loll around in here—it makes me feel even worse. Let's talk over lunch."

So we repaired, all three of us, to the kitchen. I set Tillie up with a little dish of goodies and gave Don a sandwich. He just sat there, looking glum; ordinarily he'd be bustling about, unable to allow me free reign in what had become his kitchen. I sat down opposite him and began to eat.

"So?" I said, "Let's have it."

"Okay," he said, wiping his brow with his napkin. "Mac, do you remember my talking about this kid called M. G.? He's not a kid, really; he's one of the Vietnam boys, but he seems like a kid to me. He's a paraplegic who's only recently regained his ability to speak. The physical therapists worked wonders with him, but it's taken a long time. He's bitter and unpredictable. I think I've mentioned him before."

"I think you have. Isn't he the one who just got the motorized wheelchair? You were so happy about that."

"Yeah, that's right. I was happy, and I think he was too, at first. After a couple of days of practice, he was a real whiz on the thing, and used to take long rides through town every afternoon. For a while he'd take a companion, but after a couple of days no one wanted to go with him. The other guys said he was a real pain in the ass, and one went so far as to suggest that M. G. was heading for real trouble. We couldn't get anything more out of him than that, and eventually everyone forgot about it. I was assigned to M. G. shortly thereafter, but it was clear from the first day that we were mismatched. I couldn't even get him to speak to me. He ignored several appointments. Then this morning I was informed by one of the nurses that M. G. was on his way in to see me. In he came. The first thing he said to me was 'Hiya, faggot.'"

I put my sandwich down. "Oh Christ," I said. "What did you do?"

"I was shocked, I admit. It's been a really long time since I've had to take that garbage from anyone—since leaving the city, in fact. As I said, M. G. is miserable, body and soul, and I guess he needed someone to take it out on. So, I said what I always say when someone insults me: 'I beg your pardon?'"

"Good ploy."

"It's not an original trick, but it frequently works. Not this time, though. He repeated his greeting with an even uglier term. I refuse to repeat it. I have to admit, Mac, that as sick as he is, and as conscious as I am of my role as his therapist, I wanted to punch him. But I controlled myself of course; my anger passed in a minute. I asked him why he wanted to hurt me. He told me to go fuck myself. I asked him why he'd said that. He exploded, wheeling around the room and knocking over everything he could. An attendant in the hallway heard the ruckus and came in and took him away."

"I can see why you're so upset. It must have been terrible for you."

"That wasn't the end of it. That interview took place pretty early this morning. After they took M. G. away, I hunted down the guy who'd intimated that he was heading for serious trouble, and finally got him to tell me what had upset him so. It seems that on one of their wheelchair jaunts, M. G. had exposed himself to a group of high-school girls. I was amazed that the police hadn't gotten in on it, but apparently the girls hadn't told. They had run away, fast. The soldier told me he was afraid of M. G., and that's why he hadn't said anything until now.

"Clearly we needed to do something about M. G. immediately. I was going to talk to the head of our department, of course, but I decided to see if I could find M. G. first and talk to him a little. I hated to leave things the way they were. Some of the other boys told me he was in the library.

"I found him there, all right, but he wasn't reading. He'd pulled his chair up to one of the big windows and was just sitting there looking out. I watched him for a minute; he'd knotted up one end of his jacket and was twisting it violently and smacking it again and again against the side of a bookshelf like a cudgel. The strength of his arms and hands was obvious and appalling, and I felt a little afraid, which unnerved me. But I went up to him, carefully approaching from the side instead of the rear so that I wouldn't surprise him.

"He gave me a big, fake smile. 'Hi, Doc,' he said, 'Come to smoke the old peace-pipe, I'll bet.' I said that would be nice. I told him I was sorry we'd gotten off to such a bad start and asked him if he'd come back and see me tomorrow. He kept smiling at me in that awful way, and said, 'Sure, Doc, I'll see you tomorrow. Why the hell not? You and me'll get real buddy-buddy, right? Just the way you like it? Sure, Doc, I'll be there. You can count on it.' And then he zoomed away. I sat there for a while, just stewing. I've got to deal with him tomorrow, and I'm not sure of the best way to begin." Don sighed. "Any ideas?"

What I'd been hearing had worried me of course, but I couldn't make sense of why I felt such intense foreboding.

Hostile patients are common enough, God knows, and some-times disturbed persons have an uncanny way of homing in on a therapist's sore spots. But I knew Don would be skillful enough to handle M. G. once the initial shock of their first day's encoun-ter had worn off. There was something else going on, though; I couldn't put my finger on it, but it made me feel uneasy.

"Well," I finally answered, "Have you thought about having yourself removed from the case?"

Don looked at me quizzically. "Thanks for that vote of confidence," he said.

"No, no, Donald, I didn't mean that you can't handle it," I told him. "I'm sorry if it sounded that way. I know you can handle this young man as well as anyone—probably better than most. But for some reason—intuition or whatever you want to call it—I'm getting a bad feeling about the whole thing. It wouldn't be shameful for you to drop the case, you know. I'm sure no one would think the less of you for doing that."

"That's not the point," Don said. "I could get out of the situation easily enough if I wanted to, but I feel I have to face him. It seems important to me; I want to see how I do. And I want to help M. G. too—I've always liked him. I remember how exciting it was to watch him relearning speech, and how we all stood around and cheered the day he came speeding through the wards in his new wheelchair. There's a lot of good in that kid, Mac. He's just had so many lousy breaks. I've got to figure out some way to get through to him."

"I understand," I said, "I'll help you any way I can. I did have a similar experience once with a very violent-minded youngster in New Jersey named Luther. We made a lot of progress together." We continued to talk about M.G, all through lunch, and after a while Don relaxed. As for me, I still felt nervous. This is silly, I told myself; you've been away from the real world so long that you've really become a wimp. Help Don with this boy, I told myself; be useful. He'll succeed, I told myself, and then we'll celebrate. We'll all be the better for it, I reasoned, and that's what we're here for, isn't it?

43. A Sky Bar

For several weeks Don struggled with M. G.'s case, making little headway. The only comments M. G. would make to him were hostile, taunting ones, and he often refused to show up for scheduled appointments. Don's supervisor was in favor of assigning another therapist but had agreed to give Don until the end of the month to make some kind of meaningful contact with M. G. Don also struggled with his knowledge of M. G.'s sexual transgression: naturally, he considered it very serious and was fearful that it might happen again, but he also feared that any interference from correctional authorities would cause M. G. to reject help altogether—and perhaps even land him in prison. He told me he thought that the mere fact that the boy was speaking to him at all was promising.

I continued to worry. And I was adamantly against Don's keeping the young man's public behavior a secret. I tried to convince Don that he had to think not only of his patient, but of all the women and children who might fall prey to M. G.'s exhibitionism. Don countered that, wheelchair bound as the boy was, there was no chance whatsoever that anyone could be physically harmed, and when I told him flat out that that was an irresponsible position he became very angry with me. It was the first time we'd really been at odds, and it felt terrible. Nevertheless, I had to stand my ground. The rotten thing was, I knew Don agreed with me in his heart. Obviously, M. G. could do real harm without ever leaving his chair. The fact that Don was trying to overlook that was astonishing to me. He had invested so much in this case that it was clouding his professional perceptions drastically.

But gradually, like a married couple in disagreement over some insoluble problem, we returned, at least on the surface, to our normal existence. I knew Don was under pressure, and I tried to allow for his moodiness; in his turn, he tried not to bring up M. G.'s case any more than necessary. He also promised me that, should he be forced to give up the case at the end of the month, he would divulge all he knew to the new therapist. That calmed me somewhat, and I told him I thought that was wise. I think in my deepest heart I was hoping that would happen. It was selfish of me, but besides wanting the best solution to M. G.'s problems, I wanted the old Donald back. I wanted to protect him from what I felt would turn out to be a painful experience. Even if he learned a lot, the cost might be too high.

<hr />

Looking back, I suppose I did everything I could to change Don's mind, but at the time I blamed myself completely for what happened. I should have argued with him more; I should have stifled my fear that our friendship would be damaged and gone right for the throat of the dilemma. Maybe it wouldn't have made any difference, but I couldn't get that thought out of my mind. Don was less experienced than I; he looked up to me. I should have been able to save him.

The telephone rang shortly before eleven one morning as Tillie and I were having a little game of floor hockey with an aluminum foil ball she'd become very fond of. As I spoke into the receiver, I was vaguely conscious of the little cat still skittering about on the linoleum, batting at her silver puck. Suddenly I had a premonition and felt all the blood drain from my head— even though the first words I heard were only "Dr. MacLeod?"

"Speaking."

"This is Dr. Gallieri, at the V.A. hospital—Don's supervisor?"

"Yes, of course. What can I do for you? Donald's not home yet. I think he—"

He stopped me mid-sentence. I already felt sorry for him. I knew he was struggling to give me bad news. "Dr. MacLeod, there's been a terrible accident. I didn't know who else to call. Is there any way you could get down here right away?"

I sat down on the floor with the phone and Tillie ran over my lap, still chasing the silver ball. "Is he alive?" I said.

"Yes, yes, he is, but he's in serious condition. I think it would be a good idea for you to come down here now, and I could fill you in when you arrive."

I told Dr. Gallieri my predicament as far as travel was concerned, and he said he'd send a man out with a car right away. In less than fifteen minutes, the car arrived. The driver offered me no information, and I didn't ask any questions. I was busy trying to hold my guts together. When we arrived at the hospital, Gallieri came out to meet me and guide me to Donald's room. He started to speak about the accident, but I asked him to wait. I wanted to see Don first; I didn't care about the details. Dr. G. said he understood, but to prepare myself for a shock. I was holding on to his arm as he guided me down the long corridors, and I realized I had a death-grip on him. It must have been uncomfortable, but he didn't mention it.

It was one of those rare times when I was glad I couldn't see very well. Don's room was brimming over with figures in white, and the walls were lined with lit-up medical machinery, but when Dr. Gallieri and I appeared, a hush came over the room, and the sea of people around Don's bed parted silently so we could get through. Dr. Gallieri took my hand off his arm and gently placed it on Donald's. I could feel an unnaturally rapid pulse beating through his fingers, as if he were trying with every last ounce of energy to stay alive. I made a noise I couldn't identify. I reached for his face, but someone stopped me. "Be careful of the tubes," a voice said, and I leaned forward as far as I could to try and see Don's face. I still could not tell if he were conscious. One entire side of his head, including his eye, was bandaged—there was fresh, bright, red blood still seeping through. He had tubes in his nose and mouth and an I.V. in his arm. I reached around them and touched the other side of his face.

"Don, it's Mac. Can you hear me?" I was weeping openly.

Dr. Gallieri said, "He's opened his eye. He sees you. He knows you're here."

But that was the only response any of us was to get from Don Rath that morning. He died just after noon. I was with him, and I tried to let him know I was still there, but I was grateful he was not awake to suffer. When it was over, Dr. Gallieri led me to a quiet room with a couch. He brought me a Valium, a pitcher of ice-water, and a blanket. He told me to simply pick up the nearby intercom and ask for anything I might need. He said when I was ready to talk, he'd be ready to see me. And then he left me. He was a kind man.

∽∾∾∾∾∾∾∾

I wept for a while, lying on the couch. I was wholly sad, wholly bereft, but in such shock that I don't think I could have even told anyone why I was crying. After a while, I swallowed the Valium. It put me immediately to sleep. When I awoke, soaked in sweat, I felt as if my head had been removed and then resewn to my body. I could tell it was late afternoon by the way the light played along the thin white curtains. I picked up the intercom and Gallieri answered immediately. "I'll be right in," he said.

Gallieri walked me to his office. Quite a few people lined the hallway; I found out later they were reporters and policemen. Once inside the office, Gallieri closed and locked the door and sat me down on another sofa. He asked me if I were all right, and I said yes: a meaningless question and answer.

He removed some crisp green hospital scrubs from a little cabinet, handed them to me, and ushered me across the room to a private bathroom. "Take a shower if you want," he said. "I'm not in any hurry."

So I did. It woke me up a little. The scrubs made me feel suitably out of this world—nothing seemed real. A huge, pounding headache had started, but I almost welcomed it: at least I knew I was alive. Gallieri had what I thought was lunch sent in and, when I came out of the bathroom, he led me to the sofa again and handed me a tray with a sandwich on it.

"I know you don't feel like eating," he said, "but please try. It's almost six o'clock and you never had lunch. If you'll forgive me, Dr. MacLeod, I know you're not a well man, and you need to keep your strength up." He paused. "I sound ridiculous, I know. I don't know what I'm saying today. Please forgive my awkwardness. But please do eat something. Then we can talk."

I took a bite of the sandwich just to please him. He had a kind voice. He was a very large, silver-haired man, and he smelled of a lemony after-shave, but of course I could not get close enough to him to see any details of his face. It was just as well. His eyes would be so sad. There would be frown lines everywhere. I didn't need to see it.

After a couple of minutes, he began to speak to me. "Dr. MacLeod," he said, "I was very fond of Donald. This is an unspeakable day. As his friend, you must be devastated. To offer you my condolences would be an impertinence." He wiped his hand across his brow.

"What happened?" I said. My voice seemed to be coming from another time and place. It sounded ten years old.

Gallieri sighed. "I assume Don told you about his patient, M. G.?"

"Yes."

"In detail?"

"In detail. Yes."

"Well, things got very much out of hand this morning. I was not aware of what was going on until it was too late—not that I could have done much. From what I understand it all took place in a matter of seconds. There were quite a few witnesses who—"

I could bear it no longer. I stood up, upending the tray of food on my lap, and more-or-less lunged toward Gallieri, stopping just short of touching him. It was really more of a falling forward than a lunge, and he looked as if he were ready to catch me.

"Dr. Gallieri, please!" I said, very loudly, "Please just tell me what happened to Donald." I flopped down again on the couch. Sandwich was everywhere.

"I'm sorry," Gallieri said. "I didn't know how to approach it. It was M. G. He's in police custody now. The brutal truth is that he went into the staff lounge this morning, pulled out a revolver, and shot Donald in the head. It happened very quickly. Nobody knows where he got the gun. Nobody seems to know anything, in fact. M. G. isn't talking. He tried to turn the gun on himself just after he shot Don, but somebody grabbed him." Gallieri paused. I could hear the tears in his voice.

"In all my years, in all the institutions I've worked in, I've never experienced anything like this. I'm so sorry, Dr. MacLeod, so sorry. Don was a wonderful person. Everyone loved him. Perhaps I should have taken him off M. G.'s case at once, but he convinced me he could help the boy, and that a breakthrough was only a matter of time. I was wrong to listen to him, but you know how convincing he could be."

We talked a while longer. Talking helped me to erase the picture of Don's bloody head from my mind. Gallieri seemed to need to talk too; we spent a lot of time assuring each other neither of us was to blame. When I was ready to go, he called a car for me, and escorted me safely past the reporters outside. He made me promise to call him if I needed any help whatsoever. He gave me the blazer Don had been wearing that morning, and a manila envelope containing Don's wallet and other personal possessions. The police, he said, had told him it was all right to do so. It occurred to me that I needed to call Denny.

When I was safely in the back seat of the car, I put Don's jacket on over the scrubs. I buttoned it up and put my hands in the pockets. I found a candy bar in one of them. I'd told him again and again not to eat so much sugar. I'd wanted him to take care of himself. I'd wanted him to live a long and happy life. I ate the candy; it was a Sky Bar, and I savored each one of the four fillings. I think Don had liked the caramel best. I dreaded going home alone. Tillie was not going to understand this.

44. A Mental Bookmark

After Don's funeral, after the long period of semi-celebrity I endured as the roommate of the murdered man; after Denny's weekend visit (during which I discovered why Don had loved him—he was an extraordinarily sensitive person); after the sad business of dispensing with Don's possessions (Don's parents were deceased: he'd left me some money and his car, bequeathing the rest to Denny, various charities, and a few far-off relatives); and after Frances, my sons, and Dr. Gallieri had satisfied themselves that I could get along on my own, at least for a while, I settled down to the enervating business of everyday life. I never asked Gallieri what had become of M. G.: I knew from the news stories that he was in prison, awaiting trial, but I did not want to know more. I think I was afraid of my reaction should he be freed or dealt with leniently by the justice system. I knew M. G. was not sane, but my professional training did not help me with my emotions. I could not fathom how a person like M. G., in a place like that hospital, could have obtained a gun. I guess I was naive. Tillie was still a great comfort to me, and I could not have gotten along without her warm presence, but now she reminded me not only of my lost Cybèle, but of Donald: both of them victims of a cruel and senseless world. Many times, playing with her or caressing her, I would find myself in tears instead of smiles, though I suppose even that was helpful, providing a needed release.

Not that I was sad all the time. I tried to keep busy, and since so many daily tasks were challenging for me, keeping busy was an easy chore. I built up a little army of practical helpers to take the place of Don's tireless assistance. Once again, I hired a young man to chauffeur me, and I also hired a motherly local woman, Mrs. Jennie O'Neill, to shop and keep my domicile civilized. The radio station kindly provided an assistant to help me with the program, which, since the newspapers had unveiled "Doctor Mac" as the bereaved friend of the slain psychologist, had leapt to prominence in its ratings. The telephone lines were jammed every night, mostly with young men who identified somehow with Donald's case: they were either Vietnam veterans with problems of adjustment, or people who had latched onto the somewhat distorted story the media had made of Don's last days. Since no one really knew what had gone on in M. G.'s deranged mind, everyone had a theory. At first, I found it difficult to deal with all of it, and wondered if I should even take such questions, but eventually I relaxed. I tried to do what I felt Don would have wanted me to do. And, in fact, without the program, I might have lost all touch with the outside world.

For the truth was, I was slowly retreating. I had not yet told anyone, but my worst symptoms were returning: the headaches had begun to trouble me severely even some weeks before Don's death. I was taking nothing for them and had not yet informed my doctors of their reappearance. What was the point? A "third chance" was out of the question, I knew.

There was also a frightening and overwhelming weakness that would sometimes flatten me for hours at a time—a kind of non-physical paralysis that I found particularly scary. I knew I was no longer eating properly (my appetite was nil) and tried to counter my dietary imbalances with vitamin supplements for a while, but I lost interest. I began to spend my days in a dreamy never-never-land.

Each day, after feeding Tillie and spending a little time with her, I would try to eat breakfast. Then I would wait for Mrs. O'Neill's cheery visit: she'd bring my groceries and flutter about the place for a half-hour or so until she was satisfied that everything was shipshape. If I had to, I'd make my phone calls then. If necessary, I would call my driver and attend to any errands in town. Then the long afternoon would stretch out before me, the time when I missed Donald—missed life—the most.

I had kept Don's room essentially the same (except for giving away his stylish clothes, mostly to Denny), and there I would go each day after lunch. If I had a headache, I would practice some self-hypnosis, and this procedure eased me so much that I soon began to indulge in it even if my head didn't hurt that much.

Lying back in Don's old armchair, I would give myself over to a living daydream, where memories, ideas, fantasies, and myriad physical sensations would reveal themselves endlessly on a revolving stage. The physical sensations were perhaps the most astounding: with my eyes closed, I could see everything clearly; with my ears "closed" (except to two sounds: Tillie's little cry, if she needed me for anything, and the rude clang of the alarm clock I would set every day for six, in time for me to get myself together for the evening's radio program), I could hear the voices of everyone I'd ever loved. Indeed, I imagined I could even "speak" to them—to Eliza, Don, Mark, and Harry, lost friends from any period in my life—and carry on fascinating conversations with them on topics none of us had ever tackled in real life.

And this is very, very odd, but I must tell it to you: one time, one astonishing time, while thinking about Eliza—about making love to her the way a healthy man might have done—I experienced what felt to me like an actual orgasm. So intense was this feeling that it woke me immediately from my reverie, and while—if you will excuse my bluntness—I could find no physical evidence of this event, nevertheless I was quite sure of what had happened.

I suppose I should have been worried about these strange daily meditative interludes, but I was not. Although I began to feel more and more like a visitor from another world, I didn't notice that anyone else had remarked on any change in my behavior. Except for an occasional questioning from Mrs. O'Neill regarding my eating habits or health in general, no one seemed to notice my gradual withdrawal. This continued for several months.

I felt very spiritual. I also felt very ill. Finally, I made an appointment for what I called a check-up with Gerry Hamilton's office in New York, for the first Friday of the following month. I spoke to Gerry himself when I called, and he agreed to the relatively far-off date because I lied to him that I had noticed no changes in my condition. He was happy to hear from me; he'd called me right after Don was killed (he'd seen it on the news), and had checked in every few weeks ever since, but this was the first time I'd made the first move. I guess he saw it as a sign that I was coming out of mourning and facing up to my daily responsibilities. I let him think so. I suppose, subconsciously, I was already covering my tracks.

Eventually, after a great deal of self-examination, I decided it was time to attempt my final recitation of *The Age of Innocence.*

It saddened me greatly, of course, that Don would no longer be the sole, honored member of my audience, but I felt that I could still dedicate the performance to him, and that, somehow, he would know it.

I chose a Sunday, the Sunday before my appointment with Gerry Hamilton. Mrs. O'Neill did not appear on Sundays, I did not have to do the radio show, and I could pretty much depend on having a completely quiet day to spend on my project, free of interruptions. I knew it would take up the entire day, and a big slice of the night. Then I would rest and continue the following Sunday. Just to be safe, I would turn off the phone.

I planned for this day as if I were planning a grand dinner party: everything had to be perfect. I picked out some loose, comfortable clothes and made sure they were clean and ready. I decided upon a breakfast menu that would be substantial enough to carry me through most of the afternoon. I would force myself to eat it. I laid in a supply of fruit juices, teas, and mineral water that would stand ready to quench my thirst and soothe my throat once the recitation began. Figuring on a late afternoon break, for a nap and a snack, and to feed and play with Tillie (she would become lonely if I left her to herself too long), I set a mental bookmark halfway through the book. I would stop for a while, rest and build myself up, then continue to the end the following Sunday. When my triumph was complete, I would drink a glass or two of champagne, even if it killed me. I could already feel an exhilarating sense of accomplishment; I was very excited. The only thing that could possibly inhibit my plans would be a crippling headache, and I searched all through some old boxes I'd never unpacked until I found an almost full bottle of the old, extra-heavy-duty prescription I used to use for such emergencies. For some reason,

I put the bottle on the dresser in Don's room. I would count on these pills, coupled with my recent expertise in self-hypnosis, to carry me through if the need arose.

I was ready. I had about two weeks to savor my anticipation. It was winter and the world was deeply comforted in white. My eyes seemed slightly worse, but I hardly even noticed. I could see within. I could feel my power.

45. Don's New Robe

$\smile\!\!\!\curvearrowright\!\!\!\curvearrowright\!\!\!\curvearrowleft\!\!\!\smile$

My final recital was a dismal, heartbreaking failure. When the great day came, I woke with the most delectable anticipatory feeling in my heart. I completed all my preparations just as I had planned and set myself up in Donald's room right after breakfast, intending not to leave again until my projected break was due. In my own peculiar way, I invoked Don's spirit, asking him to accept this late but heartfelt gift, and I gave a loving spiritual nod to Eliza as well, thanking her for suggesting the book to me, and blessing her existence, wherever she might be now.

Everything went fine for about five minutes, and then, my voice breaking in despair even before my brain realized what was happening, I began to repeat whole sentences, then paragraphs, then pages. Then I lost track altogether. And when I tried to go back to the beginning, the beginning simply was not there. I tried once more, but that was the end of it.

I was convinced the book had vanished from my mind, as irretrievably as a mislaid dream. I sat in Don's old armchair with my aching head in my hands until Tillie's scratching at the door wakened me from my despondent musings. I understood, for the first time, why many religions consider despair one of the gravest sins. They say it can kill you.

I was broken, but I could not ignore my Tillie. I fed her, tossed a little ball around to her for a while, then decided to go for a walk. I felt blank and ill—so blank in fact that I did not even remember that I could no longer really take a walk alone in safety. I just had to get out of the house: it embarrassed me to stay in a place I had once so loved and had now reviled with failure. My famous brain had never really let me down before. I put on coat, hat, and boots, and, feeling my way along the brick wall that bounded the edge of the property, shuffled slowly towards the tree-lined avenue that led downtown. It occurred to me how easy it would be to just wander out into traffic; then I laughed scornfully at myself. Considering the volume of traffic we had in those hills, it might take days before anyone hit me. Anyway, I didn't have the energy to complete even so uncomplicated a mission, which I soon realized. It was all I could do to find my way back to the house.

By this time, my head seemed to be on fire. I tried to lie down: that made the pain worse, but I was too weak to get up again. I considered calling Hamilton, or even the local ambulance corps, but it all seemed too dramatic. After all, hadn't I been too dramatic altogether of late? The way I had planned the recitation suddenly disgusted me—my hubris, my foolishness—and the more agitated I became, the more my head hurt. At times, the pain was so bad that it lifted me out of myself. I suppose I was semiconscious for much of the afternoon, unable to get myself a drink of water, or look for my medication, or even remove my boots. For some reason, they were bothering me intensely. My feet seemed to be burning up, just like my head, and all I wanted was to plunge them into cold water. The rest of my body seemed to be gone: I wondered if I were dying. The last thing I remember was Tillie jumping up to what I determined to be my chest and stretching out there. It must have been her magic that finally lulled me to sleep.

When I awoke, the pain had abated by about half. I immediately gathered up my tape player and some music, then ran a bath and got into it, hoping Donald's water cure would bring me enough relief so that I could decide what next to do. It worked wonders, as always, and, after drying off and dressing in my old terrycloth robe and some very soft slippers, I was even able to swallow a little soup; I knew I needed nourishment to stay alive—that idea took precedence over all others. Remarkable, I thought: the body's stubborn insistence on survival. I took my soup and crackers out to the living room. I needed to think.

I thought what a pitiful, useless bastard I had become; then suddenly I remembered the radio show. Tomorrow night, unless I made some immediate arrangements for a substitute, I would have to go on the air. That was unthinkable. I called my producer, and, on the pretext of some sudden family business, begged off, for Monday and Tuesday at least. I suppose I must have sounded funny, for the poor man asked me a number of times if there was anything he could do. I told him I was fine, that I just needed a day or two to take care of things, and finally he relented. So genuinely considerate was his voice and manner that something in me almost cried out to him, almost asked for help. Luckily, I caught myself.

Then—for some reason: just to hear a familiar voice, I suppose—I called Mark and Harry, but alas, neither one of them was at home. It's just as well, I thought. It wasn't my regular night for calling them, and, coupled with this rare deviation from routine, something in my voice or manner might have caused them to worry. Having eaten as much as I could, I began to take my tray back into the kitchen, when I suddenly realized that the terrible pain in my head that had begun earlier in the day must have signaled some new deterioration of my vision. While rounding the corner of the kitchen door, I bumped smack into the edge of the counter, dropping the tray and all its contents, and bruising my hip severely. I cursed my clumsiness, then bent down to see the extent of the mess I had made. Shapes were blurrier than ever before, and, now that I was concentrating on my sight, I noticed a funny sort of halo surrounding the larger shapes still visible to me. It occurred to me that I could leave the clean-up for Mrs. O'Neill, but then I remembered Tillie: she would no doubt consider the scene a fine chance to do some mischief, and might injure herself on the broken crockery. So I set about sweeping things together, mopping up the liquid, and disposing of the cracker bits and pieces of soup-dish. It took forever. At last, I was finished (or thought I was: I felt around on the floor and could find nothing more) and I went upstairs to rest. I was wiped out, and I was frightened. I went to my room and lay on the bed, closing the door to Donald's room as I passed along the hallway, not wanting to be reminded of my morning's failure.

I threw myself on my bed, and, when I closed my eyes, I wondered if I were going suddenly insane. I began to see pictures of people—clear, snapshot-like pictures, something akin to what had been happening to me during my daily meditations, but a great deal more immediate and more bizarre. It was as if the pictures were coming not from within me, but from some external source. At first these portraits flashed themselves before me in seemingly random order: people from my youth, people I'd only met once or twice, my parents,

Frances, students, or patients. But then, when my initial fear had worn off, I began to try to control them. Soon I could do so; I could stop the parade of "photographs" at any point and spend as long as I liked with any individual likeness. The longer I examined a picture, the more three-dimensional it seemed to become. After a while (I have no idea how much time was passing, really), I decided to try and call up pictures of certain individuals at will. This was frustratingly unsuccessful at first, but gradually it began to work. I practiced on a picture of Eliza.

The portrait that emerged came directly from my favorite memory of her (the day I'd shown her my Patchen books), and, having tried so many times to call it up in the past (the way one does with long-lost or deceased friends, only to find that after a while it's almost impossible to call up an exact likeness), I was more than delighted to find her. I concentrated on her picture a very long time, until she had attained that near-three-dimensional status I described to you, and when I finally felt I truly "had" her, I tried another experiment. I spoke.

Oh, I didn't really speak out loud, of course, but I spoke in my mind. "Eliza," I said, tentatively at first, and sounding, I thought, more than a little ridiculous, "Are you there? Can you hear me?" And, miracle of miracles, although she did not speak in turn, the photograph-figure turned its head and looked me full in the eye, smiling slightly.

I no longer felt a fool: I was bewitched, and unable to say anything more to her for quite a while. But then I loosened up. I found that Eliza—or her likeness—listened intently to everything I said, and her expression changed with startling rapidity and exquisite gradations of emotion. It was just as easy to understand this face as it would have been to listen to and understand a person speaking—perhaps easier. What did I say to her? Funny, but, although I felt we were climbing together out of a morass of confusion toward a paradise of ineffable harmony, what I said was nothing special. It didn't seem to matter what I said, because this Eliza could obviously read everything between the lines. I did tell her about my failure with the recitation, and I was comforted both by her expression of sympathy and by the understanding she gave me that it really did not matter. My relief was instantaneous, and it was real.

I forced myself to open my eyes; I suppose I felt that I was drifting too far off into this magical world, that I was losing control, that I might not be able to get back to this one. I got up and drank a glass of water, taking more time for that ordinary task than I had ever before taken in my life.

While so occupied, I decided to leave Eliza for a while and try to "speak" with someone else. Oddly, I had no fear of bidding her farewell: so comforting had our contact been that I felt certain I could reach her again if I so chose. After drinking the water and washing my face, I went back to my room, lay down, and continued my exploration. It took a little time to reach the point at which I had left the pictures, but with a little practice I was again able to call likenesses up at will. Taking a deep breath, I proceeded with my plan: like a lawyer calling one of his star witnesses to the stand, I asked for Sarah.

It wasn't as easy to find Sarah as it had been to meet with Eliza or any of the others. I suppose I had buried her memory deeply, and with good reason. But, at last, reasoning that it would be easier to face an early apparition of Sarah than a later one, I called up a likeness of her as she'd been the very first day I'd met her. I was shocked by her beauty, and by the way my heart still pounded at the sight of her. I spoke her name tenderly but received no response; then called it out again, this time angrily demanding an answer. She looked at me.

It was the same picture, true, but the eyes were dead: it was heartbreaking. I suppose I'd thought that this encounter with Sarah would give me the same sense of communion and empathy I'd experienced with Eliza—that within this magical meeting would lie some sweet revelation to bridge the terrible chasm that had opened between us when she married Wally Mussel. But it was not to be. I tried to reason with her, to get her to give me some sense of why things had happened the way they had, hoping against hope, as always, that there had been some secret and compelling motive for her actions in those long-ago days. She did not respond. Her eyes acknowledged me the way one acknowledges a pesky door-to-door salesman: she was too ladylike to be out-and-out rude, but too disdainful to be truly kind. Finally, unable to bear her cruel stare any longer, I awakened myself from my visions and tried to clear my head.

I realized quickly that it was going to take more than an act of will to clear it: a headache almost as debilitating as the one I'd had earlier in the day was starting up again. I thought that while I could still navigate, I would go look for the painkillers I'd laid aside as an emergency measure for my recitation period. I knew they were still safe in Don's room and that I had to go there to retrieve them, but it took all my resolve to do so. I stood a long time in the hallway with my hand on the doorknob, unable to reenter that room. But at last the headache reminded me to hurry, and I went in.

Don was stretched out on his bed, smiling at me. I wasn't really surprised. It had already been such an extraordinary, reality-shattering day that I suppose all my normal disbeliefs had been suspended.

"Donald," I said, choking a little. "This is wonderful." I could see him perfectly; he had a small bandage on the side of his head, but otherwise he looked just fine. He held out his arms to me, and I went and embraced him. He was as warm and real as anyone I'd ever held. Finally, we released each other, and I propped myself up next to him on the pillows. He passed me a handkerchief. He gave his old laugh-cough.

"Here, sport," he said, sniffling a bit himself. "Clean yourself up, will you?"

I blew my nose, and I stared at him. I noticed that he was wearing a robe I'd never seen before.

"New duds?" I asked him.

He pulled at the blue satin lapels. "This old thing? Certainly not, Mac. Maybe you just never looked at it before." He chuckled.

"Very funny," I said.

"Sorry," Don replied, "I actually don't know where this thing came from. Maybe there's a wardrobe angel or something. Listen, Mac, I haven't got much time here, I don't think. I guess we really shouldn't waste it fooling around. Today's been really hard on you, I gather?"

I heaved a great sigh. "To put it mildly," I said. "Do you know all about it?"

"Pretty much. Not everything, though. I wish I could have helped you with the book, or advised you against thinking too much about Sarah, but I can't interfere. I'm only here now, I think, to comfort you a little. Maybe it won't really do any good, but I thought I'd try."

"Are you kidding?" I said, "This is the only decent thing to happen to me all day—well, almost. You know I contacted Eliza?"

"Yes, I'm glad about that. It made you feel better?"

"Very much better. You know I never talked to you all that much about her, but she's never been out of my mind."

"Curious phrase," Don mused. "'Out of my mind.' Do you feel like you're out of your mind now?"

I looked at him. It was so precious to see so clearly. I did notice, though, that when I turned my eyes away from Donald my vision was as poor as ever. "No," I said, "certainly not. But I do know that whatever is happening is, to put it mildly, highly unusual. For one thing, I know that I actually have an abominable headache that I can't feel at the moment. Do you know about that too?"

"Not really," he said, shaking his head. "I don't have a good grasp of physical reality at all anymore. I guess I haven't been dead long enough to know much. A lot of things bewilder me. For example, isn't it kind of funny that I have this Band-Aid on my head, when I don't really even have a head?" He laughed and poked me in the arm.

I laughed too. "Well," I said, "It's a whimsical touch. What are you, anyway, Donald, an angel or something? A ghost? Are we in a movie?"

He continued smiling. "Don't know that either. But it sure is great to be here again. How's Tillie?"

"Tillie's perfect," I told him. "Shall I call her?"

"No, that's okay. I'm glad she's well, and that she was here for you when I . . ." He paused, then went on again slowly. "You know, Mac, you were right about M. G. of course; I never should have gotten so involved with that case. I don't know why I didn't listen to you; I was vain and stupid. I thought I could cure the devil himself, I guess. Have you forgiven me yet?"

I had to be honest with him. "Only recently. For a long time, I had so much anger I thought I would die of it. But I forgave you, and I eventually forgave myself for not trying harder to stop you." I paused. "But Don, you know, I never forgave M. G. Just like I never quite forgave Sarah, you know? It's the sickening truth, but there it is. I'm just not up to it."

Don turned to me and gave me an earthshaking look. His eyes were as deep and bright as a snow-covered chasm: I would have fallen into them and been lost had he not spoken. "Mac," he said, in a tender but commanding voice. "Forgive them. There isn't much time. It's only an act of will, that's all—you don't have to 'feel' it. That comes later. Forget about using that famous brain of yours—don't reason so much. Just do it. For me, okay? It's very important now."

His voice reminded me of the time he'd commanded me to get into the bathtub and listen to Vivaldi to soothe my pain: it could not be challenged. I looked down at my hands, which were just fuzzy forms, then back at his clear and beatific face. An act of will: of course. I'd never thought of it quite that way. I reached out and took his hand.

"Then I forgive them," I said, "for your sake, Donald."

Even as I said the words, he began to fade away. It did not surprise me, nor was I saddened. To the contrary, I felt a bit relieved. All this communicating with living and dead souls was beginning to take its toll on my brain, and it cried out for rest.

At Don's disappearance, my headache came back with an almost audible "boom." I felt along the dresser top until I found the bottle of pills. I put it in my pocket. By this time Tillie had come into the room and was rubbing herself around my legs (she'd probably heard me talking to someone and come to investigate), and I carried her out to the kitchen to give her a snack. I kissed the top of her head and the tip of her tail and told her what an excellent girl she was. Then I called Mrs. O'Neill, told her I was going to New Jersey for a few days to visit my sons, and asked her to drop in on Tillie. She was overjoyed to hear my plans and agreed to care for Tillie for as long as I wanted. I thanked her and told her that in that case perhaps I would prolong my visit by a day or two. She and Tillie were the best of pals, so there was really no reason to worry.

Then, while Tillie was eating, I took the little bottle of pills and a glass of water into Don's room and sat down on the bed again. I closed the door, for Tillie's sake. I was terribly tired, and I could barely sit upright for the pain. I knew that years ago, when my headaches were at their worst just before my operation, it had taken only two of these super strong tablets to numb my aching brain. I made a little indentation in one of the pillows and poured out the pills. There were twenty-six. I swallowed twenty of them one by one, leaving six in the bottle so it wouldn't look suspicious. I took the glass and pill bottle back to the kitchen, put the glass in the sink, and the pill bottle in the cabinet with all my other medications and vitamins. Then, quite happily, I made my way back to Don's room, crawled into his bed, and covered myself with his antique crazy-quilt (a psychologist's pun of a present I'd given him on his last birthday). Strangely, although some time had elapsed since Donald's visit, his side of the bed was still rather warm. I drifted off into dreams of some unfamiliar vivid rural landscapes for a while, and then I guess I died. No brilliantly lit tunnels or sensations of floating along the ceiling looking down at myself or anything. I'm not even sure when the life ebbed out of me. Sorry I can't remember more about it.

∞∞∞∞∞∞∞○∞

Oh, yes, there was one most remarkable thing. Just as I was sliding out into my final slumber, the entire gorgeous text of *The Age of Innocence* came back to me. Although I was too far gone to try to recite it, its appearance, whole and exact, was a gift for which I was truly grateful. Apparently, it had been there all along: my lack of faith had hidden it from me. In that sense, I had failed, but I was delighted to know that, to the very end, my best-loved talent had not really forsaken me. So, as the saying goes, I went out happy.

Mrs. O'Neill, the dear woman, discovered my body the next day, and while I was sorry to have left her that burden, I knew she was strong enough and wise enough to understand that all had happened for the best. My dear little Tillie went to live with her, as I knew she would.

My sons were saddened by my passing, no doubt, but they had known of my illness and were not too surprised. No autopsy was performed, and that pleased me: it would have upset them. I was able to view my funeral not too long ago, and, curiously enough, I had the distinct feeling that among those who attended, only Frances had guessed how I had died. She was there with the boys, looking sad and stylish. I hope she's kept my secret.

I still have not told Eliza about my suicide; perhaps one day I might give her a hint at least—I'm not so sure. I'm a little ashamed of taking my life, I suppose, though there isn't any reason to feel that way. I know I probably would have died in a matter of days anyway, judging by the severity of my last symptoms, and my passing seemed natural to those who knew me. I'd made as much peace with my life as anyone is likely to make, and I'd wanted to die. I didn't want to call anyone or be taken to a hospital. It was my life for the taking.

And it seems it's a life I'm still living somehow. I can't explain it. And I don't know what, if anything, will happen next, but nothing would surprise me.

Epilogue

~e~re~re~

As Clear as the Sky Above the Fog

Eliza liked the ordinary days. She woke up very early, before anyone else, pulled on a thin old army-green sweatshirt and some shorts, slipped her feet into some raggedy sneakers, and crept down to the dock. She untied the small rowboat, climbed in, and rowed out to the middle of the pond. The fog was so thick she had no idea where she was going, but just above her head she could see a faraway clearing. It was going to be a good day. When she arrived at what she thought was the center of the pond, she pulled in the oars, and sat there. It was silent, except for a few trilling frogs. The air was cool and damp and silver. The boat smelled of fish. The boat was rocking slightly. She thought it was perfect.

Out on the lake in the mist and calm, all sorts of things would run through her head. She loved to sit there and sway gently with the boat and let her mind wander. She thought about a strange phrase from the religious school she'd attended as a child: "assumed into heaven." She assumed she knew what "assumed" meant: that one day her body would die, and her soul would fly upwards in a spiral of clouds. Sometime later someone would knock at the door, receive no answer, peer in the window, and see her body lying there. They'd know she had been assumed. But, she said to herself, that sort of thing just never happens.

Then for no reason at all she was suddenly vividly aware of a beautiful sentence from one of her favorite books, *The Age of Innocence.* She didn't even know she'd memorized those lines but there they were, as clear as the sky above the fog: "Seated side by side on a bench of the half-empty boat they found that they had hardly anything to say to each other, or rather that what they had to say communicated itself best in the blessed silence of their release and their isolation."

It was going to be a good day.

End

Acknowledgments

My most affectionate thanks to my early readers: Robert Wald, Ellen Wittlinger, and Donna Reid. And especially to Carey Reid, as always, for his love and unwavering support across the years.

About the Author

Diane Wald's novel *Gillyflower* was published in April 2019 by She Writes Press and won first place in the novella category from the Next Generation Indie Book Awards, first place in the novella category from American Book Fest, first place in Fiction: Novella from International Book Awards, and a bronze medal from Reader's Favorite. You can read more about *Gillyflower* at *www.gillyflowernovel.com*. Diane has also published more than 250 poems in literary magazines since 1966. She the recipient of a two-year fellowship in poetry from the Fine Arts Work Center in Provincetown and has been awarded the Grolier Poetry Prize, The Denny Award, The Open Voice Award, and the Anne Halley Award. She also received a state grant from the Artists Foundation

(Massachusetts Council on the Arts). She has published four print chapbooks (*Target of Roses* from Grande Ronde Press, *My Hat That Was Dreaming* from White Fields Press, *Double Mirror* from Runaway Spoon Press, and *Faustinetta, Gegenschein, Trapunto* from Cervena Barva Press) and won the Green Lake Chapbook Award from Owl Creek Press. An electronic chapbook (*Improvisations on Titles of Works by Jean Dubuffet*) appears on the Mudlark website. Her book *Lucid Suitcase* was published by Red Hen Press in 1999 and her second book, *The Yellow Hotel*, was published by Verse Press in the fall of 2002. *Wonderbender*, her third poetry collection, was published by 1913 Press in 2011. A fourth poetry collection, *The Warhol Pillows*, was published in 2021 by Finishing Line Press.